HEART OF FIRE
Dragon-Mage Book One
by Raina Nightingale

AREAER NOVELS

Return of the Dragonriders
DragonBirth
DragonWing
DragonSword
(Available as omnibus)

Legend of the Singer
Children of the Dryads
Sorceress of the Dryads

Dragon-Mage
Heart of Fire
Scars of Fire
Healing of Fire*

Novellas and Standalones
The Gifts of Faeri
Kindred of the Sea
Gryphon's Escape
Promise of Fire

KAARATHLON NOVELS

EPOCH OF THE PROMISE: Dawn
Unseen
EPOCH OF THE PROMISE:
Vision's Light
EPOCH OF THE PROMISE:
Wings of Healing
EPOCH OF THE PROMISE:
Darkness Bright*

Other Novels

Kingdom of Light

*Not yet available

IIEART OF FIRE
Written by Raina Nightingale

Paperback ISBN: 978-1-952176-23-4
Ebook ISBN: 978-1-952176-22-7

Summary: When the human slave, Camilla, defies her captor's wishes and bonds to a young dragon, she receives magic that has only ever belonged to the dragons – and which may be all that can save her and those she loves from a threat far greater than the elven slave-owners.

Cover art and design by Raina Nightingale.
Map by Raina Nightingale.
Interior Design by Raina Nightingale.
Illustrations, chapter headers, and scenebreaks by Raina Nightingale.

Published by Raina Nightingale
www.enthralledbylove.com

Preface

I first imagined *Dragon-Mage* when I was eight, perhaps nine years old. I knew who Camilla and Radiance were: I saw the moment when their souls recognized and the Fire made them one. Since then, I've tried to write the *Dragon-Mage* series a great many times. This is probably the only time I've consistently re-written a story, without it changing so much in the re-writes as to be unrecognizable, apart perhaps from a few nearly superficial elements, like a similar-looking main character, or some similar names – you get the idea.

But it was never right. It was never the story it was meant to be. Eventually, I got the feel for what that would be, and started abandoning my attempts half-way through book one, or maybe on chapter three. Even when I realized I needed to remove the love interest character, who was there only because that was the "pattern" I learned – somehow or other – that Epic Fantasy had, and that Camilla simply had no room in her life and no interest in such things, I still did not have it *quite*. But I was closer.

Then, one day, I saw a scene from book three (only I didn't know it was book three yet; I know it's got to be book three now because I'm writing book three). I even wrote the scene down because it was so vivid, even though I rarely *write* scenes out of order. And that was when I really started to get it. That was when I started writing *Heart of Fire,* and it *flowed*. It *fit*. I wasn't in the greatest state mentally when I wrote it, so the writing has required a lot more editing than usual to make it easy to read, but I *had* the story. Finally.

This is probably the most epic of my Areaer series, though as always it will have its slow, almost cozy moments strung throughout. As I say, the slice of life moments are just as important, and they're the only reason that those exciting moments of challenge matter, or that anyone can rise to the challenge and win, so they're *epic* too and belong in epic stories!

Enjoy!
-Raina Nightingale

Table of Contents

Map of Ellenesia

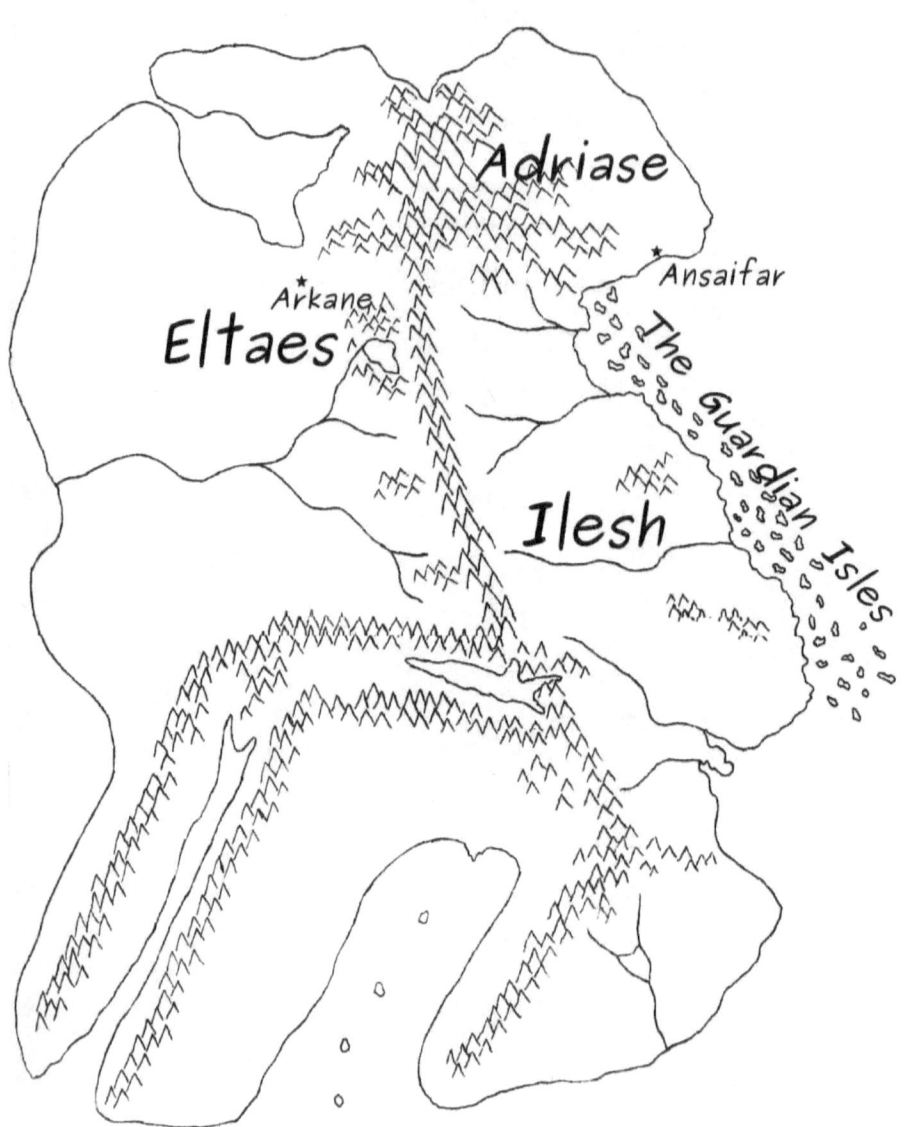

HATCHING

It was not destiny that changed and joined lives that night, and forever after. It was choice, her choice and the choice of a few others. Fate had nothing to do with it – nor did the gods, if they ever existed.

Camilla laid her broom against the wall in a dark corner and crept away. She could tell from the sounds that all the elves were now assembled in the stadium to watch the Hatching. Hatchings were very rare, and reputed to be getting rarer. The dragons were believed to be dying out, but at the moment, she was less interested in what the elves said about why this was, and more interested in the fact that she simply *must* see a Hatching, and that this might be the only opportunity she would ever have. Though being a human slave she was not allowed to see the Hatching, she had always loved and admired the great dragons and was not going to miss her chance to see them hatch!

She walked down the passage-ways towards the stadium. She would not be able to take her seating with the elven watchers, but, if she timed it right, she could slink onto the Hatching Ground after the candidates were already there, waiting among the eggs. She knew how to get there, from her work as a slave and from her insatiable dissatisfaction with that place. She always looked for ways to hide, for things to learn, for anything, really. She also knew all the slaves' passages for getting places to do their work without obstructing the elves' passage-ways.

When she got into the shadow of the stadium walls, she pressed herself against the stone. She was not as good at shadow-blending as most elves, but she suspected she was good enough not to be noticed *this* night. The elves would be too excited, and they would not think to look for her.

Watching the eggs rock gently, she felt a lump grow in her throat. She blinked back tears. All she had ever wanted, since before she could remember, had been to bond to one of those great creatures. Whenever she saw one she felt as if her heart was about to break. According to the elves, if a human was allowed to bond to a dragon, it would further doom the majestic race to extinction. Camilla, however, did not believe most things the elves said. She *knew* she was not nearly as inferior as the elves said she was. She doubted captors who wanted her and themselves to believe that she was an inferior being so it was okay that she was their slave would care to tell the truth about who and what she really was or what would happen if she Recognized a dragon.

Now, looking at all the eggs, surrounded by the elf candidates, she wondered if the dragons were as close to extinction as the elves said, or if that was simply a lie to prevent any of her race from ever thinking to try to Attach one of the magnificent creatures. There were probably close to forty eggs laying on the sand.

The eggs were rocking furiously now, and she had to keep tight control over herself in order to keep from breaking into tears, something which would completely disrupt her shadow-blending. The candidates waited, impatiently, nervously around the eggs. She wished desperately that *she* could Recognize one of the Hatchlings. She wondered if she *could* make that happen, *if* the dragon would choose her. Would she be able to get close enough to the Hatchling before it Recognized a nearer elf to give the dragon a chance to Recognize her? Just as the dragons were coming out of their eggs she would have to *run* for it – but it *might* happen. She would be in terrible trouble, whether she Recognized or not, but if she *did* Recognize then no power would ever separate her from the dragon. Recognition could never be undone. She would be a Dragonrider, the first human Dragonrider in uncounted memory.

As she thought these things, Camilla sensed someone moving behind her. In the barest whisper she asked, "Who is it?"

"Sylvara," a voice answered. Another human slave. "I want to know what you are doing here. You should be working. You don't belong here."

"I *have* to see a Hatching," said Camilla. "Even if I can't ever Recognize, I *have* to see."

She felt Sylvara nod behind her. "But you'll be in such terrible trouble."

"I don't care. Even if they do whip the skin off my back, all I've ever wanted…" said Camilla. She stopped before she told Sylvara about her plan to get just a *chance* at Recognition, and wondered why she was losing her edge; she never told Sylvara anything if she could help it. The more submissive human would tattle on her; she had done so far too many times, and Camilla hated her for it. A moment later she wondered if it would do any harm if she did tell Sylvara. The eggs were *about* to Hatch. Between the time it would take for Sylvara to be heard and the time it would take for the elves to stop her, it would be too late. She would have Recognized or not. Even as she watched, a dragon on the far side of the Ground Hatched. The egg on which Camilla had set her eye was cracking and splitting even now. Interestingly, it was not quite the egg closest to her, but, for some reason, it was the one Camilla fancied.

But *would* Sylvara tattle on her? Doing so would reveal that Sylvara had abandoned her work. Camilla decided to risk it, though she was not sure what moved her to tell Sylvara anything. "I *must* have a chance to be a Dragonrider," she said. Her determination to ride had only grown stronger as she watched the Hatching.

A moment later the egg turned over. Camilla sprang forward at the same time as she heard a bell ringing in her mind. *"Camilla!"*

What? she thought, confused, but not enough to stop her rush through the sand. The Hatchling was staggering out of her egg *towards* the human slave-girl. An elf moved to encircle her neck, but the Hatchling clipped her with an awkward-shaped wing and growled. A moment later, the elves saw

Camilla and came towards her, trying to block the Hatchling from reaching her, but the small, awkward dragon fought them as well as she could.

She barely escaped the hand of an elf trying to grab her and flung herself through the elves standing between her and the dragon. As soon as her skin touched the dragon's scales, it was as if she were born in fire. There was nothing painful about it at all. Her whole being seemed to be taken up in flames, hot and fierce and wild. It was the most delightful, ecstatic sensation she had ever experienced, as if her soul and body were being melted and re-formed in fire, or perhaps as fire, as a living flame.

A voice of fire spoke out of the fire that had become her whole world and self. *"My name is Radiance."*

Somehow, Camilla knew how to respond to that voice of fire. *"My name is Camilla."*

The fire burned hotter and stronger and fiercer. *"We are Radiance – Camilla – Love,"* the voice of fire whispered through a thousand tongues of hot flickering flames. There was no longer any distinction between them. They had one heart and one soul. They were one fire, inseparable and therefore free, hot and fierce and wild and untamable. They had Recognized, and it was more than Camilla had ever dreamed. None of the elf tales had hinted it would be like this.

The elves pulled them apart. *"We are fire,"* their twin and inseparable souls sang to one another. Shouts of "Oh no!" and "There's another one!" and "Make sure there aren't any more!" filled the air. Then, right around her, there was a gasp of another and more shocked quality.

What is it? thought Camilla. A moment later an elf voice answered her unspoken question. "There's a *burn* on her palm!"

"A burn?" asked another voice.

"A burn," confirmed the first.

"Serves her right for Recognizing the golden mother, short-lived fool that she is!"

Is that a reference to the shorter life-span of my race, or is it a threat? wondered Camilla. Before her thought was half-finished, it was absorbed into the fiery ferocity of Radiance's response. It was a reference to the life-span of *their* race, and *no* one, no, not the proudest elf in Areaer, would *think* of touching her Recognized with ill intent.

But the elves were talking again. "No, that's not what it is! It will hurt all right, but it's something for us to be concerned about…"

"Then let's stop talking about it around her," said the other.

Camilla's mind finally registered something they said ages ago. *I Recognized the golden mother?*

"Yes." Radiance's mind-voice was smug. *"I got you. None of the others could get you. I got you."*

Aah. I love you, thought Camilla. She discovered then that the elves had left her, and she curled around the Hatchling. Time had no meaning in the heart of fire.

Clumsily, Camilla drew the broom over the pathway. Radiance was asleep, but she could still feel the golden hue of the dragon's mind in her slumber. Nonetheless, she felt depressed. The agony in her hand did not help matters, nor did the fact that she knew what the agony meant. Such burns were a common side-effect when a mage used magic or cast a spell without a proper focus and mind-set, and varied in severity. Despite the stories she had heard all her life about how only elves could use the magic, she had used it. She was not sure for what. Was it the shadow-blending that had used magic, or getting to Radiance across the sand in time and through the elves? It was hard for her to imagine how she had used magic without knowing it. She had always wanted to be a mage, had always listened as well as she could to stories about magic or to whatever lessons she was able to overhear, which was a great deal. The elves were careless, thinking both that her ears were far duller than they were, and that she could never wield the magic. But Camilla had never been as convinced as the elves were that she could not use magic.

She was not sure what was going to happen to her now. She was the rider of a golden female, one of the few Hatchlings who fully expressed the fertility-enhancing traits magically bred into them by the elves. She was a mage. She was sure between both the elves would feel threatened by her. Yet they could not kill her and her gold without revealing that they were *not* actually worried about the dragons going extinct.

The sounds of footsteps made her lay aside the broom and look up. One of the elven men was coming down the hall. "Come," he said, and motioned for her to follow him.

Her heart beat with trepidation as she followed, only worsening the agony in her palm. He led her into his private room and bade her sit down on a bench. Sickening fear pounding in her blood, Camilla obeyed. She had no idea what was happening, but she doubted that there was anything she could do to protect herself – even with the magic she did not understand, and even if she could use the magic, she knew she would do terrible injury to herself.

He knelt down next to her and turned her hand over. Pain shot across the ruined skin, red, blistered, and flecked with beads of blood. A faint golden-green aura emanated from the ruined patch, making Camilla's mind stop in its tracks. *What? Why? How? I didn't know about this,* she thought.

The elf touched her palm, and Camilla almost screamed in agony. *Is he trying to torture me for Recognizing Radiance?* she thought in a panic. She forced herself to calm, wishing she could extend that force to the rapid beating of her heart

– and saw that the golden-green nimbus was stronger, brighter, clearer than before

– and thought at once that, somehow, her terror and panic was causing her to latch on to the magic energies, and she did not know how to let go, even though this would do her no good but would only hurt her more!

The elf looked up at her and locked eyes with her. Then his fingers began to massage her hand. The pain was so intense that she could not help but cry out softly. A moment later, she felt Radiance awaken and mind-merge with her. The pain dulled, replaced with a tingling numbness. *What's he doing?* she asked the dragon.

"I don't know," Radiance answered.

Slow, terrible minutes passed. Then the elf withdrew his hand from hers. "Go now and sleep," he said. "You need it."

She nodded and rose. She was certainly fatigued. The pain in her hand had faded to a dull throb, dull enough she might actually be able to sleep with it. She sought her pallet, mind-melded with Radiance, and slept.

Rough hands shook her awake. A river of fire flowed through her mind. She was too much one with Radiance to forget for a moment what she now was, even if she did not at once remember how it happened. "What?" she asked drowsily. "Did I sleep too late?" She didn't *think* she had. She usually had a good sense of how long she could sleep, and it felt quite early.

"No," said the elf, "but we're moving you."

She sat up, fully awake, her eyes wide. This was better than she had ever imagined. "To be trained with the Dragonriders?"

"No," said the elf, whom Camilla now recognized as a rider himself. "You're still a slave and always will be. We can't have you humans thinking that all you have to do is get to a hatching dragon egg and, suddenly, your life will be changed forever and there won't be any consequences."

Camilla nodded, but determined that she would *not* always be a slave.

"No, you won't be," concurred Radiance. With her mindtouch images flowed into Camilla's mind. The elves had intended to beat her for her disobedience, but the dragons would not permit it. The dragons answered to no one, but they protected their mother, and the old mother would stop at nothing to protect her daughter – and her daughter's rider, for the two were one. As far as the dragons were concerned, whatever anyone did to Camilla they did to

Radiance.

Camilla slid down the brown dragon's shoulder quite ungracefully. She was sore from riding, even though she had not *done* anything. She was also aware that the elves *had* taken her to the training compound for the dragons and riders, apparently, given her courier's remarks, to be a slave here. She wondered why it was important for her location to be changed if she was not going to be trained, then realized that they would probably want to train Radiance, even if they would never train her rider. A mother had to be kept fit and strong in order to reproduce well. Or so she had learned.

When she turned around, she saw another dragon winging in and down. She stepped aside, feigning ignorance over what to do with a dragon's tack, and watched the violet dragon land. She was now close enough for Camilla to see that there were two humans seated behind the elven rider. Straining her eyes, she *thought* she saw Sylvara, and – was that – that couldn't be – her brother? Lavilor?

"*Yes,*" said Radiance. "*Sylvara Recognized Shimmer and Lavilor Recognized Sleet.*" There was a pause, and Camilla caught a strong feeling from Radiance that she preferred Lavilor.

That doesn't surprise me at all, thought Camilla, *but I didn't know Lavilor was there. Now, how did that happen?*

As Camilla watched them come near, all-too-familiar anger throbbed in her breast. *I'm so sorry,* she thought at Lavilor. Now that he was here, and their mother was not, he might never get to see her again. *Curse the elves.* Humans had such long lives in which to enjoy each other and Areaer, yet the elves stole the time of shorter-lived races, making human mothers and children work all day so that *they* could have more of whatever they wanted, at the expense of the humans' lives.

This cannot go on.

She felt that the dragons, or at least Radiance fully agreed with her. She also sensed confusion from Lavilor. *What?*

Instantly, she understood. Radiance understood. It was strange, it had never happened before, but there was nothing impossible or unnatural about it. Camilla had spoken to one of her kind as dragons spoke to their own kind and to their riders.

# Fright

She perched, waiting for the lizard to appear. It would, sooner or later, and then she would have the chance to catch it that she had somewhat painstakingly prepared. The creatures were fast, and they also bit if one let them.

A rhythmic thump made the air shudder, and even the rock under her feet vibrated, distracting Kario's mind and eyes, even as it sent prey scurrying. A moment later all concerns about food were driven out of the girl's mind as she saw the source of the sound: a huge black dragon with glowing red wings and eyes.

She sat, rooted to the spot. There was nowhere she could go to hide. She was far too big to hide in the holes and crannies where the smaller creatures sheltered. The few trees and scrub-bushes which grew in these parts of the plains were too far. If she dashed for a copse of trees, the dragon would surely see her and would catch her before she reached them, and, even if it didn't, they were not much refuge. The dragon could burn them, or knock them flat, or pull her out of them. Besides, it was already coming for her. Doubtless it had immediately selected her as the only suitable prey on these plains. She, too large to find refuge, would be far easier to catch than the little creatures *she* hunted and, besides, they would not even make a mouthful for something this size. *Gods,* she prayed, *take me safely Home. I have been as faithful as anyone of my years and opportunities can have had the chance. I have no weapon with which to fight, or I would ask you to make me a Dragon-slayer, but, as it is, I can only hope for a safe passage Home, and comfort for those whose wanderings are not yet over.*

A chuckle broke in on her thoughts, one framed in flickers of fire. Her fear mingled with ecstatic surprise. Surely, that was the assurance of the gods, who always looked kindly on the prayers and faith of the young.

The chuckle grew more pronounced, and then words flowed like fire through Kario's mind. It certainly felt like the voice of a god, but the words said something very different from what the girl had expected. *"Silly Kario. I am not here to eat you. I usually don't even eat animals, and I have* never *eaten a human."*

Kario's mind melted in utter confusion.

"Yes, quite," continued the voice of fire. *"I eat rocks."*

Y-you're not a god? stammered Kario's mind.

The fire chuckled again. *"A* god*? Maybe. I am the Obsidian Guardian of this age. I am a power and the Wings of the Fire of Areaer. I don't know if that is what you call a god, but I have chosen you, Kario, not to take you Home – such is not in my power nor my right – but to be my rider. And I certainly desire the worship of no one."*

Her mind was still mushy with confusion while the black dragon glided down and landed. She was so heavy that the ground shook when she landed and Kario had to leap from the boulder she'd been perching on to avoid being crushed beneath it as it rolled over.

"*Sorry about that,*" laughed the dragon apologetically. "*I'm so excited I forgot to – umm – lighten myself.*"

When Kario remained standing, not moving at all, the dragon spoke to her again. "*Oh, sorry. I've been so excited I forgot to tell you my name. I'm Nelexi. Now, come forward and touch me. Or do I have to touch you?*"

That shook her out of her malaise. Kario giggled and walked forward until Nelexi's huge snout was within arm's reach, at which point she put out her hand and touched one large, shining black scale.

"Oh!" she breathed soundlessly. A spark of fire jumped between them, faster and faster, welding their souls together. It was a strange kind of pain, utterly unbearable, and just as unstoppable. It made her sink to her knees and put her head in her hands, crying softly.

When she could think again, she wondered if Nelexi felt the same pain.

"*I do,*" said the dragon. "*The merging of identities is painful, but it is also joyous. I trust you felt that, too?*"

I do, Kario thought.

"*Good,*" said Nelexi. "*I've bonded multiple times, but this time has been different. There is more joy this time, in a way, as if we are closer. I think that means more pain, too, but I kind of expect it, since I've done this before. I've always chosen riders before, and I've learned from others that first bonding is almost always unique. But everyone experiences it differently and, so far, it's been different with each rider.*"

Kario nodded. "This is really interestingly strange," she said aloud.

"*Sorry about frightening you, too! The last thing I wanted was for you to think you were about to die, but I tend to forget that your people think we eat them!*" Nelexi chuckled again, but her mind-voice remained apologetic. "*The fact you went into it right out of such a fright might have made it hurt worse, too. I don't know.*"

"It's okay," said Kario. "It's already a lot better. I'm sure in a few hours I won't even remember it."

Again Nelexi laughed. "*You'll* always *remember it.*"

She stepped back from the dragon's face. When she was several paces away, she exclaimed, "You're *way* too huge!" The dragon was so big that she could hardly take her in.

Nelexi chucked again and said, "*You're also the youngest I've ever chosen. Shall we show us to your family now?*"

"Sure," said Kario. "They'll be frightened out of the day if they saw you coming, and really worried about me, too."

"*Want to ride me?*" asked Nelexi.

She shook her head energetically. "No, not yet. You're too big, and I've never flown, and I wouldn't want to fall off, and you're *so* big I don't know if they'd even see me up there and know I was riding you and you weren't coming to eat them." She did not mention other things, stories her people had of young men or women who had become Dragonriders and betrayed their clan. Even if they did see her on the dragon's back, it would only add grief to grief until she could reassure them that Nelexi would *not* eat them. Nelexi did not respond, but she saw the thoughts in her new rider's mind.

Kario skipped ahead of Nelexi, who sank into the earth with each step. She was torn between joyful excitement and sorrowful foreboding. Surely, her family was afraid. Surely, they had seen the huge black dragon. She *hoped* they would believe her that Nelexi was not an enemy, but she was fearful that some of the clan might not believe and accept her. Still, such forebodings soon faded into the back of her mind, and the hopeful excitement made her mind a sea of whirling suns.

When they approached the current encampment, she sprinted ahead of Nelexi. The encampment bristled with spears and desperation. There was simply no way to hide anything bigger than a lizard from a gigantic winged predator on the plains. Mostly, the People of the Plains liked the openness and the space. It was almost like being in the sky, but on the ground, at the same time. They could not imagine why anyone would want to live in mountains or hills, always feeling trapped and surrounded. That is until a winged predator swooped over, in which case they all understood instantly the security of mountains and hills, with hills to cover one, ravines into which something large could fit only with difficulty, if at all, and caves which would hide one from the view of the sky. Even the forests that grew in some places would be great benefit, providing some cover from the sky.

When the first watchers, younglings with exceptional eyesight, picked out Kario's form flying towards them through the grass, a great shout went up which reached her even where she ran. She did not slow down, wanting to tell her people all about her new friend as soon as possible – and, especially, that she was as safe and well as ever.

She reached the system of trenches and bulwarks they build around their encampment to protect it from occasional raiding groups, and was helped across amidst ecstatic cheers and, then, embraces, and someone checking to see who else was still out. Then someone asked her the question. "You saw the dragon, didn't you?"

Kario nodded fiercely. "I did."

Various different responses surrounded her, making her head hurt. She was fairly certain that a few of them had noticed the tone of her voice, but the others were asking questions about how scared she must have been, and assuring her she was now as safe as it was possible to be.

Yes, I know, she thought to Nelexi. *If something your size wanted to make a meal of humans, the* worst *thing we could do was get altogether in one* group. *You would come and eat all of us without any trouble, instead of having to look for us. Then again, with your telepathy is it any trouble to find scattered meals?*

"*Not really,*" said Nelexi, "*but you'd run a chance of being missed or forgotten about, and it would take me a* little *effort.*"

"The child's far too frightened," said one voice Kario recognized as belonging to her aunt. "You need to calm down and talk one at a time, or she'll be overwhelmed."

"No, really, I mean," began Kario, just as her mother's voice cut over hers. "My baby!" she cried, cutting through the crowd to get to Kario.

When she saw her daughter, she turned around and said, "I don't think this is a scared Kario at all! I think this is a happy, excited, if overstimulated Kario!" Turning back to her daughter, whom she hugged, she asked, "What is it? What did you get?"

"A dragon," said Kario, stepping out from her mother's embrace and pulling herself together in a very dramatic pose. She was still a child, after all. "A very rare dragon of a sort that eats rocks." Seeing the gasps and expressions of most of the people, she waved her hands and raised her voice. "You think I'm crazy. You think dragons are things to be scared of, and that I made up the part about how she eats rocks. I'm not crazy. I'm not lying. It's true." *Nelexi!*

She knew the moment the dragon launched herself into the air. In a few minutes she soared over the encampment. Kario felt sorry for her people's terror. They leapt to the bulwarks, bristling with spears everyone knew would be nearly useless against a creature like that.

"*Completely useless,*" said Nelexi to Kario, and then she spoke to them all.

"*My rider, Kario, is right. I do not eat humans. I have not eaten a living being, not even an animal, since I was a hatchling. I do, indeed, eat rocks.*"

The people around Kario gasped. She was aware of their shock – and their fear. She wondered if anything Nelexi said to them would assuage that fear. Would they fear anything which they perceived was *capable* of destroying them, even if that being would never do so?

"*Well,*" said Nelexi just to Kario, "*I might destroy them, if they were killing hatchlings. Or if they were going to kill you.*"

Yes, but they aren't, and they won't, so they don't have to worry about that.

"*You're right about that. As long as they behave like remotely reasonable creatures, I am no threat to them.*" Kario could tell that there was something Nelexi was not telling her, something about to whom she was actually a threat, but it did not seem to have anything to do with her people, so she was more than content to leave it to Nelexi to tell her what she fought when she found the time right.

It was night when Nelexi lifted her head to greet Kario. The little human was running towards her and sobbing. Kario reached Nelexi's extended fore-talon, and threw herself down, leaning against the dragon's leg. "They've rejected me. The clan doesn't want me. They say that whatever I say about what you're like, they don't want a Dragonrider and they don't want a dragon," she sobbed.

"*But not your mother? Your mother didn't reject you,*" said Nelexi.

No, Kario replied silently, *but she can't keep me. I get to either reject you or leave. She has other children, and can't leave. Unless?* Kario lifted her tear-stained face to gaze into one of Nelexi's fiery eyes.

"*No, little one, I can't. I think there's one little spot on me where you can cling to me without a saddle, but without a good saddle it wouldn't be safe for me to carry any others. I'm sorry, Kario. I can't think of any. I don't thinking asking other Dragonriders to come here will help.*"

No. My mother trusts me, but I don't think she'd trust any stranger Dragonrider.

"*And they wouldn't even speak the same language. No, that won't work. I'll have to take you away.*"

"Where will you take me?" she asked out loud.

"*First we're going to the Sea Elves. They don't get along with the Dragonriders, and it's as much their fault as the Dragonriders', but it's the Dragonriders who are more vehement. They will be willing to help you. Then we'll cross the sea and go to Dragonsong Forest.*"

Kario was hardly paying attention, even though at any other time she would have been excited by the mention of Sea Elves. *And I'll never get my Name,* she thought despondently. *My Ceremony was in one passing, and it will never happen.*

Nelexi shifted, pulling her talon away from Kario a little, forcing the girl to re-settle. "*You don't know very much about the Naming, do you?*"

"No. We never do. Not until it happens."

"*Then let me tell you something, little Kario. I have been watching your people for a long time, knowing that you were the one I wanted for my rider, and waiting until you were ready to bond to me. In the Ceremony, you would have chosen your own Name. Do so now, or in one passing, if you like.*"

"Really? Do you care? Can you tell me more?" asked Kario, her voice much perkier than it had been a moment before.

"*I care about you, little rider,*" said Nelexi, her fiery mind-voice chuckling again. "*I don't need a Name to know you, but if you want one, do as seems best to you. I just want you to be happy.*"

"Can you tell me more about the Ceremony, please?" asked Kario.

"There's no need to 'please' me," said Nelexi, laughing again. *"But yes, I will tell you more, though there's not much to tell. You would have danced and prayed for a while and, when you felt ready and certain of your choice, you would announce your Name."*

"Do you think it matters whether I do it now or in two half-passings?" asked Kario.

"I doubt it. I think they just have to choose a time. But that is part of why I came for you now. I thought you would want to choose your Name after knowing me," said Nelexi.

"You're right," said Kario, standing up and looking into the dragon's eye, "and I wish I could hug you. Being bonded to you is such a big thing, it ought to be part of my Name, so that's so considerate of you. I really do wish I could hug you. Maybe I will wait for the passing so we can know each other, and what we are now for a little while, before I choose."

Affection, like a flood of molten fire, washed between them. Kario felt as if it would submerge her, it was so powerful. Nelexi lowered her great head and gently and daintily snaked out her warm tongue to kiss her on the forehead. The girl burst into tears again.

Nelexi settled down on the plains close enough for her to see the high, twisting spires of the Sea Elf city, but far enough away that it was unlikely that she had been spotted. *"So,"* she coached Kario, *"the Sha'adhri – that's the Dragonriders – and the Sea Elves are currently at war. It started with a misunderstanding on the part of the Sea Elves, and an unwillingness to overlook and forgive on the part of the Sha'adhri. However, we should be able to manage a truce for the moment, especially since you don't look Sha'adhri."*

Kario was sitting next to Nelexi's head in the long grass, staring out at the distant spires, barely discernible on the horizon. She had a thousand questions. What was the misunderstanding? And what did Nelexi mean, she did not look Sha'adhri – or like a Dragonrider?

"The misunderstanding was that dragons are prey animals. A Sea Elf hunted and killed a dragon much as he would a deer. It was a terrible mistake, and it's understandable that the Sha'adhri were mad about it, but I think it has gone on long enough and it is time to come to something of an understanding, even if the Sea Elves are loath to admit that we are persons even though we have a strange shape. I'm pretty sure they're willing to agree not to hunt dragons, and we can agree to stop burning their ships – which, by the way, I

haven't done. As for how you look, well, frankly most Sha'adhri are from the northern regions of Aneri, around the Aravin Mountains and Dragonsong. There are other Dragonriders in other parts of the world but they're not relevant to us here, or to the Sea Elf-Sha'adhri quarrel. But the Sha'adhri did not handle the misunderstanding properly. Instead of explaining to the Sea Elves what they had gotten wrong and how terrible that was, a bunch of them got together and burned some Sea Elf ships, and that's how things got into the present regrettable state of affairs. But I'm pretty sure we can manage if we do this right."*

"All right," said Kario. She felt singularly depressed. Having to leave her family was bad enough, but having to navigate a quarrel made her feel even worse. "What do I have to do?"

"The Sea Elves are not perfect, but they're not nearly as horrible as the Sha'adhri think they are, like the Sha'adhri are not perfect but are not nearly as horrible as the Sea Elves think. What we have to think carefully about is how not to scare them with the idea that I am taking you to join the Sha'adhri in fighting them, because they certainly won't help us do that, if that's what they think we are doing..."

"Can you just mind-speak to them, like you do with me and did with my clan, and tell them that you're not their enemy and you're actually trying to make peace between them and these Sha'adhri?"

"No. We're not any sort of formal ambassador, and while your little tribe of clans with occasional squabbles might be willing to start patching things up with any sort of informal peace-maker, that's not likely to happen when a nation like the Sea Elves' are fighting with something they think is as big and organized as the Sha'adhri, though, to be honest, the Sha'adhri are fairly informal, unorganized, and chaotic, and if the Sea Elves bothered to understand *anything, they would realize it is in the nature of dragons, and therefore of Dragonriders, to be that way, but, for the most part, both the Sea Elves and the Dragonriders are pretty loath to try to understand the others. One of my loose scales is probably treasure enough for a lot of meals for you, but that doesn't mean they'll help you get where we need to be."*

Kario's mind shifted into a question about why they needed to go or be anywhere; it was not like they were in any danger where they were. Instantly, Nelexi had shifted tracks and was explaining it to her. *"You've heard of the Old Gods, right?"*

She was so shocked and startled that she jumped to her feet. "The Old Gods are r-real – I mean, h-h-here?" she cried.

Nelexi projected calmness into her mind. *"The Old Gods are not a perfect description of what we're fighting, but your clan's stories about the Old Gods are based on the real thing, and provide you a fairly good introduction to what we're fighting."*

Again, Kario's mind spiraled into questioning confusion, and Nelexi answered, along with an aside that her bond with Kario was definitely tighter than it had been with any of her previous riders. *"Yes, we're fighting the Old Gods. They* can *be fought, and remember when you asked if I was a god, and I told you I was something like one? I am the Obsidian Guardian of this age. I can fight the Old Gods, and so do all the Sha'adhri – hopefully. They're every bit as horrifying as your stories, but not as invincible. Areaer hangs in the balance in a war between the Old Gods and... well, Areaer itself, not just its Guardians. There's a lot more than I can explain to you yet, but we need to join the Sha'adhri in Aneri to take our part in this – and I'm not sure part of that part* isn't *resolving this war with the Sea Elves. Resolving it definitely* would *be a victory, but that might not fall to us."*

Kario was silent for a while, puzzling this over. After a while she asked, "Is the Sun God part of this war? What can you and I do that the Sun cannot?"

"You might call the Sun a god. The Sun is a being of power and intelligence unlike your own, but I think the Old Gods are more like the Nightmare we're fighting than the Sun is like your stories about him – if we can consider the Sun to be male. Your Sun God is something a little like the Sun, but also a little like a great many other real things, and exactly like none of them. Thus, we can do a great deal that the Sun cannot, and to answer your question about how the Nightmare isn't defeated yet if it's not invincible, the fact that it is not invincible does not mean it is not a long, hard war. Also, if you remember the Old Gods fight over the souls of men, and the souls of the wicked fight for them. That is the problem we face. The Nightmare exists in the souls of those who do not love the good, but who are controlled by fear and all that comes of fear, and we fight to free others from the Nightmare. As long as humans, or dragons, or elves, or any other number of beings, embrace the Nightmare we cannot wholly drive it out, and if we turn to slaying or destroying those who are enslaved by the Nightmare in order to drive it out, we do not drive it out at all, but invite it into our own hearts. Instead, we might fight for all Areaer, and more, for all the world, though I am but a lesser god, as your people would call it, and my concerns are, presently, all with Areaer and not with other parts of the Cosmos."

"This is more than a little girl like me can handle," said Kario softly.

"I'm not asking you to handle it, and you have me to lean on. You just asked why we need to be somewhere else, and I judged it better to answer you, little heart of my heart, than to find ways to obscure the issue or lie to you, which I could never do. Otherwise, I was going to wait for a while, probably years, to let you know about some of these things. I wasn't even going to take you to Aneri yet, except that when your clan rejected you, I figured I might as well do it now. But when I was gliding in and you were afraid I was going to eat you, didn't you pray to your gods that if you had anything with which to fight or any knowledge of how to fight, you would ask them to make you a

dragon-slayer, but since you hadn't, you hoped only for Home and for comfort for those left behind?"

Kario nodded.

"Think of it this way. The real dragon, the kind you thought of then, is the Old Gods. You are being given the weapons and opportunity to be a dragon-slayer – except what you really want to slay isn't dragons, but something else which your mythology has painted in the form of dragons. But I still think it's an answered prayer, right?" Nelexi's fiery-mind voice sparked with mild, but serious, amusement.

"I suppose," said Kario timidly. Then she asked, "So all those stories about evil dragons are completely false?"

"I'd have to know more about them to know for sure," said Nelexi, *"and that's neither here nor there. We'll talk about that later. For now... "*

That night, Kario reached out to Nelexi. *We're leaving the Plains, right? So we're leaving the domains of my gods?*

"Well, not of the Sun," laughed Nelexi, *"but maybe. There's a lot I don't know."*

Then I should go out and seek my Name tonight, while I know I'm still near their abode.

A few hours later, she curled up against Nelexi's side, tucked under her red wing, assured for what seemed like the hundredth time that she was too much a part of Nelexi for the huge dragon to accidentally squish her.

"What is your Name, little one?"

Heart-of-Spring-and-Flame. It feels right to me.

"That it is. It is right for you – and for us. And in a few days, we leave. I'm sorry we'll be separated – only in body, never in soul – for the journey, but you'll be fine, and I don't see any other way not to scare the Sea Elves. That was interesting, was it not? You told them your tribe has rejected you and you're running away, and they invited you to cross the sea and see if you liked it or if you liked anything on the other side? I wonder if they pay any attention at all to the humans around them, since I get the idea the People of the Plains rarely reject anyone."

That's right, thought Kario, sleepily. *Only Dragonriders, but that's rarer than a solar eclipse, and the occasional murderer or incorrigible thief, which is only a little more common...*

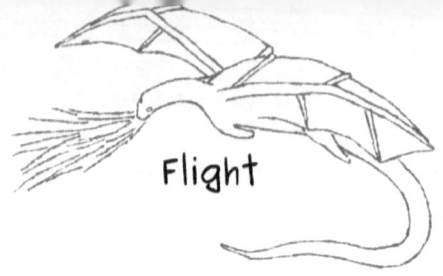

Flight

The intervening months had not in the least changed Camilla's determination that one day she and Radiance *would* be free. She plotted over it, constantly, for a long time primarily worried about her palm. Nothing she could do stopped it from burning. She needed the ministrations of an elf healer nightly, and even then the pain was never completely absent. The scar was not fully healed and was bumpy and ugly and horrible-looking. Without healing, her hand would slowly burn, and the resulting vulnerability to infection could be potentially very harmful, never mind that the pain was unendurable. She could not sleep with it, and she worried that if left untreated it would consume her entire body eventually and kill her outright. She had never heard of a mage with her condition before. She had an instinct that urged her to try magic more, but caution kept her from it. Even if magecraft left no other traces, it would surely accelerate the burning of her palm, and since that was watched so closely by the elves it would be noticed. She did not want the elves to know what she could do with magic or to interrogate her on it. They might place greater restrictions on her.

So she waited, biding her time, trying to figure out a solution to the problem of her burning palm, and also waiting for Radiance to grow big enough and strong enough to carry her.

She was certain the elves hated her. She had even less time to herself than she had before Recognizing Radiance. She almost never got to see Sylvara, which she rather liked than otherwise, but she also almost never got to see Lavilor, which she hated.

"So speak to him like you speak to me," Radiance had suggested one day.

I'm not very good at it. I don't really know how, and I'm not sure he would be comfortable with it at all.

"In that case, Sleet will tell you," said Radiance. That was something else they had discovered. Camilla could not only speak to Lavilor, but to any of the dragons. All those stories about the inferiority of humans were the leavings of bark beetles. No elf had *ever* been known to speak to a dragon other than his or her Recognized, and it was not even obvious that the elves were better at their magic than she would be or, if they were, if it was only because they had longer lives and more time to practice and study.

Radiance had convinced her, and Camilla spoke nightly to Lavilor, inquiring as to his health, sympathizing with how he missed his mother, and promising him that she would make everything right. It wouldn't happen as quickly as either of them wanted it to, but she and Radiance were going to free the human slaves – or at least her family. She did not think people like Sylvara deserved to be freed, but she did not want to talk to Lavilor about that problem yet. She would warn him of Sylvara when she thought it necessary for his well-being, but she did not want to expose him to yet more upsetting facts of life sooner than she had to, or too soon after being separated from their mother.

Thinking of Sylvara, Camilla could not understand why she had Recognized at all, but Radiance told her that dragons were much more naturally suited to humans than to elves, and few of the elves were wonderful creatures themselves. Shimmer, a Hatchling who knew very little, had sought out a rider and chosen the one who was, in some ways though probably not all, the most suitable, and she herself was not surprised by the choice. *"I'm so glad you came to me, Camilla,"* she said, with rare humility and true honesty. *"Otherwise I would have had to bond to an elf, and I wouldn't be free or myself. I'd be a slave forever."* Her fiery mental voice sounded very near tears – if dragons shed tears. Her whole being was repulsed by the notion of such depraved slavery, so that she would have preferred death, but that would not have been offered her as a choice. Usually she acted self-assured, confident, and untouchable, so it was touching and awkward for Camilla when she confided this.

Continuing on the note of Sylvara, Camilla had run into her rather earlier, and the slave – for so Camilla thought of her, though not of herself, nor of Lavilor, nor of her mother, or perhaps a few others – had collapsed into tears Camilla was certain were fake. "Oh, Camilla!" she cried. "It wasn't my fault! I never intended to be on the Grounds, and I didn't try to Recognize, Shimmer just fought his way through to me, he must love me so much, but th-th-they wanted to beat me!"

"The tears are fake. You would know," Radiance told her, while Camilla asked, "Did they?" secretly hoping that the elves *had* beat Sylvara. She certainly deserved it for all the times she had gotten others, including Camilla, beaten when they did *not* deserve it. Was there any other way *to* deserve a beating if one was kept as a slave short of murdering or beating or stealing from a fellow slave who had never done one any harm – or she added, as an afterthought, a child who had not yet had the opportunity to choose to oppress?

"N-no, I mean, not r-really," said Sylvara. "Just a little, until the dragons stopped them but, oh, Camilla, I didn't deserve it! I didn't do it on *purpose.*"

Camilla had leaned in towards Sylvara and half-hissed half-growled in her face, "Yeah right, you didn't deserve it. Think about why you were doubtless there? To tattle on me, right? How many times have I been whipped because of you? I wish to all the gods they *had* beaten you! I'd almost do it myself, right here, right now, except that I would get caught, and what good would that do *me?* Now, go away and do not *look* at me again."

Camilla stepped away from her, breathing hard, her heart hammering in her chest. By all the gods of light, she *could* have beaten Sylvara right then and there. "I *hate* you and *never* forget that, or the fact that you *deserve* it, all of it, more than you'll ever get," she had finished, breathing hard, and then turned away, clenching her fists, though it made her palm hurt more than usual.

The memory still made her feel hot. She had meant every word she said to Sylvara. Snitches of her sort were like traitors, the lowest of the low, and she could not think what punishment or misfortune could possibly befall Sylvara that would make her pity her.

As if you could imagine half the pain I endure, thought Camilla, momentarily entertaining the idea of seeing if she could pull Sylvara into a mental contact and force her to acknowledge the pain she inflicted on others. Punishments, nowadays, consisted of having her hand left untreated for days and being forced to do things with it, which was pure torture. Apparently, the dragons could convince the elves that they had better not beat Radiance's soul-bounded, but they could not make the elves heal her – or take into account her odd hurt. It would have been unendurable without Radiance, though with her it was little more than a nuisance, and Camilla persevered, unwilling to be tortured into docility, and unwilling to give up, for she intended to take others with her into the freedom she would not give up. As it was, she had to come up with a solution to this problem of hers, for she was dependent on the elves' healing for quite possibly her life. She wondered why this happened to her, but why could be solved later. First, she needed a solution to the present problem. *For some reason or another, I channel magic and I can't help it. I'm not even aware that I'm doing it, but it still burns me. So I need something that allows me to use a suitable focus for the magic. But what could I possibly get? What would work?* She knew different magics and spells required different focuses. Some could *not* be cast through an elven body, though with what she knew now, Camilla was wondering if elven supremacy was a thing at all. Maybe humans were not only capable of magecraft but better at it than elves and could focus through their bodies, albeit at the price of pain and possible death, spells that an elf simply could not perform without external focuses – or, possibly, even spells that an elf could not cast at all. Camilla shoved this line of thought aside to be explored later. It was interesting, but had no bearing on her immediate problem.

She wracked her brains, trying to remember everything, no matter how small, that she knew about magic. She knew focuses varied greatly. She knew that an elf body was an appropriate focus for shadow-blending, that most elves had enough magic in their blood to shadow-blend, and that she had discovered ages ago that she was capable of very weak shadow-blending but did not know if that meant she could use other magic as well. She knew the particulars of very few spells and what focuses were needed for them, but she knew that all the high mages carried mageswords or magespears which glowed in their hands, though they did not glow or flicker in the hands of those who had no training in magic or essentially no gift for it. Young elves were tested to see how strong their magic was by being asked to place their hands on such a sword or spear, and if it flickered at all they were trained as mages. Many elves who did not pass this test were also trained as mages, but they were never as good at it as those who passed.

One problem is that I have no idea what I am doing! she thought, meanwhile wondering if getting her hands on a magesword or magespear would help. They were reputed to be assistant focuses for most spells, so maybe they would be enough for her to stop burning herself.

It was worth a try. The only problem was that the try and the flight would have to coincide. She could not see if it worked first. She did not even know how she would get her hands on a mageweapon, but, if she did, its loss would be noticed almost at once. She could not try to see if it worked before running away. Still, it was a risk that would have to be taken, after she figured out how to *get* one in the first place. Stealing something that treasured from an elf was no easy feat, especially when one's life was already full of work and one was left scarcely enough time to sleep and eat afterwards.

Camilla's hand burned with raw, distracting agony as she stepped through the open door into the mage's room. *No,* she told Radiance and the other dragons watching her. *Not the spear. The sword. I can't hide a spear, and I might have to hide in the lands of humans. I don't know what they're like.* Alabaster, the silver dragon of High Mage Azunz, had conspired to get his rider to leave his room open, so that she could steal a mageweapon, but she still had to shadow-blend and more to avoid waking him by her presence. This use of magic was hurting her, and it was with effort that she kept her hold on it and on all the previous planning she had done to get to this point, for everything needed to be ready.

She reached out and wrapped her hand around the hilt of the magesword. She almost gasped at the simultaneous agony and yet tingling soothing of the touch. She knew at once that her plan was going to work, as the drain of power became less agonizing despite the torture of the grasp. She carefully cradled the sheath and belt and hurried from the room as quickly as she dared.

Once down the hall, she paused to attach the belt around her waist, still keeping her hand on the hilt. She reached out to her brother. *Lavilor! It's time!*

She knew when he came awake the next instant. She directed him towards her, and then they went to the shed where the dragon saddles were kept. They took the two smallest they could find, and saddled the dragons who were waiting for them, tails twitching and wings shimmering with suppressed excitement. Under the moon, Sleet was startlingly beautiful, with a long, shapely neck and scales that shimmered silver in the light of the stars. Radiance was beautiful, too, but Camilla thought she came into her true glory during the day.

"That's because I do," she remarked, as her rider secured the saddle-strap around her neck, and then turned to check on Lavilor's work.

It would be nice if you could somehow be less shiny at night, but I don't think I can manage to shadow-blend two dragons in the sky. Such a feat was remarkable for anyone less than a High Mage and, whatever her innate talent, she had no practice or training. She was very nervous, too, because the elves were not as inclined to do things only during daylight hours as the humans. They *usually* slept during the night and were awake during the day, but that was only a *usually.* Any moment an elf might come by and then all would be ruined.

Finally, she smiled at Lavilor, who was already secured in Sleet's saddle, as she settled herself into Radiance's saddle. She had never ridden before and that made her mad. The new elf Dragonriders had made their first ride half a cycle of the large moon earlier, and Radiance was much bigger and more developed than their dragons. She was larger than Sleet and Shimmer, and even Sleet and Shimmer were larger than the elves' dragons. She wondered why, since they came from the same clutch.

"Well, we're remedying that right now," said Radiance as she raised her wings.

A moment later she was in the air, climbing smoothly, Sleet on her tail. Camilla reveled in the feel of the night-air flying past her face, raising goosebumps, and tried to calm the frantic racing of her heart as she worried that they were about to be caught and that this would be the last flight of her life as well as the first. *If this is going to be the last flight of my life,* she resolved, *then it is also going to be the last night of my life. I might be untrained and know very little, but I have a magesword and I have the talent. We will fight to the death if they try to take us.*

"That we will," Radiance agreed, the fire in her mind blazing like the noon sun.

Wild delight in flight tore Camilla's mind from her concerns. The wind in her face, the wild freedom of the skies, the sheer wonder of it all, washed through her soul like the air rushing past her and Radiance. As one, they beat their wings and made their way through the trackless sky. Nothing could break their union; nothing could break their freedom.

Then, as they passed over the wall around the compound, she looked over her shoulder, wanting to smile at Lavilor, though they probably could not see each other's faces in the night. Instead she saw, rising from the compound and flying behind them, another silver dragon. For a moment she panicked and prepared to go down fighting. Then desperate, bracing resolution was replaced with rage: the dragon was Shimmer and the rider was Sylvara.

Why is she chasing us now? She thought in fury. *Is she hoping to betray us? But if that were so, why follow us instead of alerting an elf? If she is afraid of being punished for interrupting someone in order to betray us, isn't she just as afraid of being punished for not doing so while she knew? How would she not be punished for trying to escape with us if she's found with us?*

For a moment Camilla contemplated reaching out and throwing her hatred and fury directly into Sylvara's mind. Then she reconsidered and decided that maybe it would be better to do that a little farther away from the compound. *But I still hate you, and never forget that I hate you,* she thought, not daring yet to interject it into Sylvara's mind, but fully intending to do so in a few moments.

Racing through the sky distracted her a little from her anger. It was exhilarating to feel the wind rushing past her, raising goosebumps on her lightly-clad arms, caressing her cheeks, under the bright, unwinking stars that spangled the sky above with a glory she had rarely had any time or space to appreciate. Now, the night sky felt wild and free and *hers*. Magic sang in her blood, and she did not know whether it was her own or that of the world around her. She just knew it was like being in a different world. For a moment it was if she had never been a slave and, she guessed, her soul was as if it had never been a slave. She had never been, and never would be, cowed. She was free at heart.

It was not night anymore, but it was not as far into the day as Camilla would have liked. The sun was still low in the eastern sky, but the dragon hatchlings were far too tired to fly farther. That cursed Sylvara and her Shimmer were still trailing them, and Camilla and Radiance had scarcely found a large meadow and landed with Sleet and Lavilor before they descended after them.

Camilla stared up at the sky, and momentarily considered trying to send a bolt of power at Sylvara. Several things kept her from trying. She did not want to kill, at least not Shimmer. She knew hurling bolts of power was a very advanced skill, one most mages never achieved, and she was not at all certain that she *could*. Even if she could, she probably could not make sure she blasted them *away* instead of killing them. Furthermore, she was certain that the magesword alone, even if she had known how to use it, was not an adequate channel for such powerful magic. If she tried and *could*, or even if she could not, she might burn her hand to a cinder. So she waited for the two to land.

As soon as Sylvara's feet touched the ground, she was standing before her, magesword drawn in her hand and flashing with green-gold sparks of fire that mirrored her mood. "You do *not* belong here," she hissed in Sylvara's face.

"I want to leave Ilesh myself, and I don't have any way of getting past the border spells, but maybe you can with the magery and sword of yours."

"I don't want you," said Camilla. "I'd rather go with an *elf* rider than you! You're worse than an elf."

"I am not. Shimmer Recognized me. He could have Recognized an elf."

"Just because you're *human*, doesn't mean you're not *evil*. Now go away before I blast you. I do not want to see your face again."

Sylvara smiled in mock sweetness. "You wouldn't, Camilla. You couldn't. You know if you killed me, you'd kill Shimmer, too."

"He'd deserve it. He *Recognized* you," said Camilla.

"He's a *hatchling*," said Sylvara.

Camilla knew she was right. She *wouldn't* have been able to kill Shimmer. She was so close to Radiance it would have been like killing her own brother. But as she stood arguing with Sylvara, she heard Shimmer's voice in her mind. *"It was the best I could do, Camilla. You are Radiance's. Who else would you have had me Recognize?"*

Haven't I heard stories about dragons Calling their riders so they would be available when they hatched? Didn't Radiance do something of that for me – since my eyes were laid on her egg even though it was not the closest, most natural choice? she asked.

"That was long ago," said Shimmer. *"I do not know how long ago, and I do not know if it was ever that common. I could not. I saw no one who was matched to me."*

She nodded. The world had been unfair to Shimmer. She thought of Radiance's shudder at the thought that Camilla might not have come to her, at the thought of being bonded forever to an elf slave master... The thought was chilling.

"I did Call you, a little, Camilla, but you are different. Unique. You Hear very well, and you Speak well, too. You must know that, since you can speak not only to any dragon but to any human as well."

You're right, but I didn't know it was like that. I wonder why it's harder for dragons to Call now than it once was.

"All right," she growled. "I can't chase you away anyways, but *stay out of my sight* or I might find something I *can* do to you!"

"Without hurting your hand?" mocked Sylvara.

"I have a magesword now," said Camilla. "Yes." She smiled a broad, bright, unnerving smile, showing all her teeth as if she was a beast of prey. Then she turned and stalked off. *I'm sorry,* she told Shimmer, *but I can't feel sorry for you or like you. After all, you* are *one with her.* To herself she thought, *How am I ever going to manage now?* There was so much she had to do, and that was without Sylvara constantly being around to make her blood boil. Speaking of which, even before she had to figure out what to do once they were out of the elven forest, Ilesh, and how to deal with the cultivated human lands beyond – about which she knew next to nothing, only stories told by the elves which might be hundreds of years out of date and rather untrue even in their time – she had to figure out how to get across the border. Upon it lingered many spells, most of them ancient and forgotten, and only an elf mage could traverse them safely. She did not know what it required. Would the magesword be enough, or did traversing them require knowing what to do with the magic? Was her bid for freedom doomed almost before it was begun?

She and Radiance joined as one soul again. *No.* It would not be. They *would* be free, for themselves and for all the dragons yet unhatched – and all the human slaves.

Ambassador

"Greetings, Ambassador of the Sha'adhri." The elf was tall, with coral-pink hair, saffron skin, and eyes so dark they were almost black and it could not be told what color they were. Like many of the Sea Elves, his appearance was incredibly strange, at least to Kario. But then again, he was not the same race as herself. Animals would look really weird, too, if she had never seen them before. "I am called Edreen of Eskeliae."

"Greetings, Ambassador of the Sea Elves," replied Kario. "My name is Kario Flameheart, Rider-Partner of the Obsidian Guardian, Nelexi. You can call me just Kario or Flameheart." She curtsied as she finished, just as he had bowed. *This is so strange and funny-feeling!* she said to Nelexi. *I'd never have dreamed of doing this.*

"I know, Flameheart," said Nelexi, *"but you're necessary for this. After the preliminaries we'll pass this on to someone more suited for it, but we needed someone the Sea Elves* knew *had nothing to do with fighting against them to start with."*

They had spent the first six months after landing in Aneri getting to know each other. Nelexi had shown her Dragonsong Forest once, and introduced her to a few of the Sha'adhri, but after that they left to wander the strange, new continent. As they got to know each other and she got more comfortable, they started to discuss the war with the Sea Elves, which had been going on for so long that it was just a fact of life among the Sha'adhri, something taken for granted, and no one knew when it had begun, except for the long-lived black dragons. Both Nelexi and Heart-of-Spring-and-Flame felt that it had to end, and so they had established contact with the Sha'adhri and with the Sea Elves. At that point, Nelexi had started to seriously teach her Anerian, and now, several months later, they were finally together to start working out negotiations. Nelexi grumbled to Kario that it would be helpful if they knew how the Sea Elves felt about the war. Was it still rather a recent thing to them, or had it been going on for *so* long it had become matter of fact even to them?

Edreen offered to her a necklace made of pearls. She knew that it was a small gift among the Sea Elves, but for some reason it was part of their diplomatic traditions. It made sense in a way. If two or more clans of her people had a quarrel, Heart-of-Spring-and-Flame could easily imagine such a gesture being part of making back up. Still, there were so many things about national negotiations that were complicated and strange and stilted, and she was very glad she had Nelexi in her mind to help her. She could have never gotten this far on her own. She hung the pearls around her neck and offered him in turn a gift from the Sha'adhri as a gesture of good-will and regret for the burning of their ships. It was a figurine of two dragons with wings upraised facing each other, carved out of a hard, aromatic wood that only grew in Dragonsong Vale. The two dragons were different, illustrating the variety of different features, including spines, winged ears, and combs that appeared in the dragons of Areaer. Kario herself had had no part in making it, and she wondered if Edreen had had any part in making the gift he offered her. Personally, she thought the Sha'adhri gift was more impressive, but it was kind of nice owning some jewelry. She wondered if she would get to keep it. Probably. If she wanted it, Nelexi would insist that she could keep it. She knew she had prime of place among the Sha'adhri as partner of the Obsidian Guardian.

"We of Eskeliae have waited for this gesture a long time," said Edreen, first examining her offering, and then looking into her eyes. For some reason, her stomach started doing flips. She was really nervous. "For hundreds of years the Sha'adhri have been burning our ships and attacking us at sea and harrying us all along the coasts of Aneri. We would welcome peace between the Nations of the Sea and the Sha'adhri. We have no need of the blood of dragons, if their fire is brought no more against our waves and winds, Flameheart." The corners of his lips twitched as he said this last, as if he found her name amusing, at least after his little speech.

"That is well-understood," said Kario, enunciating carefully and listening constantly for corrections or advice from Nelexi. "We, too, have no need to burn your ships, if we can have a guarantee that you will not hunt us – for we and our dragons are one."

"We who ride the sea in ships do not understand you who ride fire on wings," said Edreen, "but peace should be achievable, and certainly beneficial, if we can understand one another well enough not to make war on each other."

"That is my hope as well," said Heart-of-Spring-and-Flame, fighting back nervous giggles. Why did she think this was so funny? Because it was!

Discussion soon moved to what would need to be changed or done for the peace to work. Edreen asked what the Sha'adhri would do if any of their own ignored the peace and attacked a Sea Elf ship. "I do not see any threat of that happening," she replied "We do not have any problems with attacking other people's ships. There will not even be any danger that we agreed to peace but a few outlying Sha'adhri do not know about it and therefore attack you, since any dragon can speak to any dragon without regard to distance. The moment we cast off this peace, every Sha'adhri will know. What concerns me more is ensuring that the mistake which led to this in the first place does not happen again. We need to make sure that no Sea Elf hunts a dragon as a beast and that, if it does happen, the Sha'adhri – or the Sea Elves – can deal with the offender, instead of open war arising between us."

Only when she was done speaking, did she process the gleam of surprise in his eyes when she spoke of how the war was begun. Speaking in Anerian was still hard for her, even with Nelexi watching her and occasionally correcting her, but when she was done she realized it. For a moment she wondered if it was so long ago that even he did not know. Or had he thought the humans were too short-lived to remember, and had the Sea Elves never known about the obsidian dragons?

"I do not think that, after this war, any Sea Elf will wish to hunt a dragon," said Edreen, "but, just as the Sha'adhri need that assurance, the Sea Elves also need assurance that any attacks which hopefully will not take place will not go unnoticed or unpunished by the Sha'adhri in case they do take place. You do not understand the sea in our blood, and so it is reasonable you need more assurance than that we will not hunt your dragons again. Likewise, we do not understand the fire in your hearts, and so we need assurance we can understand that this war will truly be at an end."

Nelexi! cried Kario. *I have no idea what to do!*

"It's okay, hatchling. I'm here to guide you and, before long, you will turn this over to other negotiators. I have one waiting here who is level-headed enough to do this. You met him yesterday. Remember when I told you the Sha'adhri are disorganized, and that there are many who care not for their grudges and prejudices or their pride and who wander most often alone? I've called an old friend of mine like that. He will take this from here. At this point, he is a better choice for this than you are, since he has more experience with the Sha'adhri and can speak for them better, whereas they scarcely count you one of us."

I know, said Flameheart with a sigh. *I'm too young. I'm from too far away. I don't know what it's like. I'm really too young, and I've no training, and I* definitely *don't know what it's like to raise a dragon. That's the biggest one, by far.*

She noticed Edreen's eyes flicker as she sighed, and responded to Nelexi's prompting. "I was speaking to my dragon," she said. "At this point, she thinks that there is another who would be better at figuring these things out than we are. She would like me to introduce him to you."

"Very well," said Edreen. "Many weavings take many hands to complete, and a peace is no different."

Are all Sea Elves so poetic? Flameheart wondered. *I didn't really pay that much attention to them on the sea. I was too sick most of the time.*

Homesick and heartsick and missing Nelexi, as well as seasick. I think so, though. Maybe he's a little more flashy-tongued than usual.

A man stepped through the curtains to one side of the room. His hair and beard were mostly gray. A scar slashed across his forehead. His eyes were a blue-green-gray that Flameheart thought wonderful for a negotiator with the Sea Elves. It was the most common eye color among them, whereas their hair and skin were as often as not colors never found on humans – as far as Flameheart knew, she guessed she would not have known that humans could be as light as they could until she had met a few of the Sha'adhri. He came to stand beside and just behind her, and bowed to the Sea Elf Ambassador.

"Edreen," she said, feeling more than ever like she was playing some weird out-of-tribe game, "this is Zhaizen of the Sha'adhri, Rider of Zenith. Zhaizen, this is Edreen of Eskeliae, Ambassador of the Sea Elves."

The two exchanged pleasantries, and Flameheart struggled to maintain her composure as she left the audience room. As soon as she exited it, she collapsed into giggles.

"Come on out to me, and let's fly together," Nelexi interjected into her mind.

She got to her feet, and as she started to run she stopped giggling so much. *I can't believe we did it!* she said, jumping up and twirling in the air.

"We haven't yet," said Nelexi.

What? Have you gotten this far before only to have it fall through?

Nelexi paused for a moment, and that in itself made Heart-of-Spring-and-Flame suspicious. Then she said, *"I guess I have to tell you. There's a lot I have to tell you sooner rather than later, now that we've come this far. Yes. I tried with my last rider, but it fell through. I don't think it will this time; Edreen seems fairly reasonable and likely to want to make things work. Still, humans – and elves – surprise even a dragon such as myself sometimes."* Kario got the impression that there might be other dragons who were surprised far less often, if ever. *"Yes,"* she continued, *"that's the one downside of being your first-and-only. Usually an obsidian team has at least three members, so one has all the talents, thoughts and personality of three working together, sometimes more. We're just two, but I love being bonded to you like this. We're just right for each other. Back to our earlier topic, though, yes, I tried. That was quite a long time ago though. He was not that much younger than Zhaizen is now when we tried, and I was searching Areaer for some twenty years or so before I found you – before you were born, actually."*

Wow, thought Flameheart. *You waited for me a long time.*

"I did. As I said, you are right for me, and things are a little more complicated than I made them sound. You are not my first, though you are definitely my closest, so while there's only two personalities and talents here, I still have what I learned from all the things I've done and thought with my previous riders." As she spoke, Heart-of-Spring-and-Flame got the distinct

impression this was the last she was going to hear from her – at least for a long time – about her previous riders *or* about the things she did before finding Kario.

Some minutes later, Heart-of-Spring-and-Flame stood, looking up at Nelexi's bulk. "I'd really rather not have to saddle you," she said. "You're huge. The saddle is heavy. I'm small. It's hard for me to put it on."

Nelexi chuckled in her mind. *"I think the winds are gentle today, and you are tired. I agree. We can do without the saddle today. Come and climb onto me."*

"By the way, Nelexi," Kario asked affectionately, as she climbed up the dragon's scales, "is that why you don't seem to know very many people and why the ambassador you chose was so old? Because you haven't been with the Sha'adhri in a long time?"

"Part of it, but I would have chosen someone older anyways. You did great, but Sea Elves live for a long time. I expect them to respect someone a little older than yourself better. If anyone can do this, I think Zhaizen can."

Flameheart declined to probe at what Nelexi clearly did not want to talk about, but she wondered for a moment if Nelexi might have been willing to choose Zhaizen, if something in her had not known to wait and look for Flameheart.

She settled herself into a hollow at the base of Nelexi's neck, nestling her legs into a depression between muscles in her crest. Nelexi waited just a moment longer for her to get comfortable, then spread her wings, and they were aloft with amazing ease for a creature so big. Kario still marveled at Nelexi's wing-span – and at her wings, which glowed red-gold, flashing up and down, back and forth, on the edges of her vision if she kept her eyes turned ahead of them.

The city spread itself out below them. Flameheart did not understand why anyone would ever choose to live in a city. She could just understand that someone might love the sea, or the mountains, or deep forest, in the way she loved the plains of her home, though she did not feel that way, but who would ever choose a *city*? Who would ever live so cramped together? She was not certain who would ever want to stay in one place, either, but she supposed there *might* be reasons for that, though they were hard to imagine, but what was great about a city? She had not thought these things when she first saw the Sea Elf cities, since that was different. The Sea Elf cities were beautiful places to which they came, again and again, because they could not live only on the sea. They were more like trading outposts, like the kinds tribes would use to trade amongst each other, than they were like these human cities. The Sea Elves might have places in them that belonged to each one of them, but they hardly lived in them. Most of their lives were spent on the sea, and their cities were where they went to interact with humans, or to repair their ships, or sometimes to give birth and raise their young, or to do any crafts they could not do on the sea. They would not have thought of *living* in them the way the humans lived in their cities.

"*I don't know either,*" Nelexi said. "*For all the conflict between us, the Sha'adhri do these things more on the same principle as the Sea Elves. For one thing, none of us dragons want to stay in one place for too long. And we wouldn't fit in cities either.*"

Certainly not ones the size of yourself, said Kario, with a laugh that matched Nelexi's. She knew that only one dragon in an age approached the size of the Obsidian Guardian. Other obsidian dragons were large, but not as large as the Obsidian Guardian, Wings of the Fire of Areaer, the one who carried the power of the Volcano of Ellen Island in her – or his – heart. That volcano was one of the places Nelexi had shown Flameheart. She had told her that when dragons were old they sometimes went there to die. When they could no longer fly and their lives were now measured in no longer than weeks, they would climb to the crest of the volcano and glide into it with their riders.

Strange, Flameheart had thought, and she had asked Nelexi what she would do when she got old. Looking up at the huge black and glowing red dragon, she had somehow found it easy to believe, strange as it still seemed to her, that Nelexi could swim in the sea of liquid fire without harm.

"*I am an obsidian dragon,*" Nelexi had replied. "*I do not age as other dragons do. When the time comes, I will fly into the lake of fire, and I will pass from Areaer, as if in death – and I will take you with me.*"

"You will?" she had gasped.

"*Yes, I will. I know now, you are my last rider, and I have already shared with you more of the secrets of my Guardianship than I believe any Obsidian Guardian has ever shared with a rider before. But do not press for more. When we pass into the heart of fire, then your questions will be answered well enough. Wait until then.*"

Flameheart had nodded, strangely tense and excited, wondering just how apt her name *was*. But now she looked over a human city, and wondered what possessed people to live that way.

"*Protection,*" Nelexi told her. "*They feel safer, that way. Some of them attack and steal from others, and it's easier to defend something like that, than if they are sprawled all over the place. Also, there are things they can build and make, in a city, that they could not if they lived like your people live, or like others live, who live not unlike your people, but in different places. Though there may be other reasons as well, but those are the simplest ones I know.*"

I know about those, and I think our way is best. That way is clearly not. I don't think they can be happy, caged like that. And look at the refuse it produces! With so many people so close – why, that's more people cramped together than we have at a meeting of several clans – how can they seek the spirits and the gods? How can they get alone to find their names?

"*I'm a dragon. I wouldn't know. Let us fly! In us, earth and sky and fire are one! And I think that this peace with the Sea Elves will work out."*

You do? asked Kario. *What do you know now?*

"I'm in touch with Zenith, and he's almost certain this will succeed this time. There are quite a few bumps that we will have to figure out what to do about, but none of this is your concern, and he's fairly certain that Zhaizen and Edreen will be able to work it out."

But? asked Flameheart.

"Is this what it is like for other dragons?" asked Nelexi. *"No wonder I've shared with you secrets no Obsidian Guardian has ever shared before. How do you keep anything from someone as soul-bound to you as this? It must be meant to be, for otherwise I wouldn't be bonded to you like this. Anyway, yes, since I have to answer your question, the Old Gods, or the Nightmare, may try to do something to stop this peace from happening. I can't guess what it would be – I am a dragon after all, and I think like a dragon – but I know there are things they might be able to do to keep this peace from going through. Anyway, it's nothing for us to worry about right now, Flameheart."*

But I'm your rider, right? It's our task to fight the Old Gods, right?

"Yes, child, but this – soaring into the sky, uniting earth and wind and fire, being happy, enjoying each other – is one of the ways we fight the Nightmare. Worrying about it plays right into its claws. It weakens you to its disease. You will be as ready as possible when the time comes for you to close in combat. Trust me, and the rest of the Guardians, and Shallim-Araldor, to make sure of that. You must not worry about it."

All right, Nelexi, said Kario. *Let's fly.*

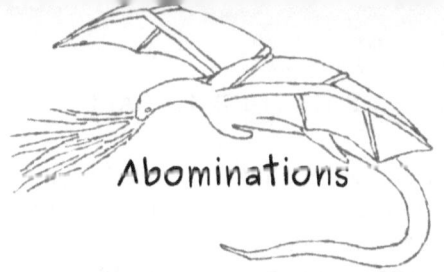

Abominations

They had already been in the sky for an hour or more, and the stars shone with unrivaled glory, the only sign of the sunset being a lingering lightness on the very line of the horizon, when Camilla felt – *something*. It was not her skin that tingled, and it was not a nice tingling either, and it was sharp and sudden. It overlaid the ache of her burned palm in a pattern of abrupt agony.

All that, she noticed in a flash. Already she was twisting in Radiance's saddle to look behind them.

Somewhere behind, and off to the north, a column rose into the night. Seeing it, she knew at once that it was the source of the disturbance she felt. Dark things moved in it, and it swirled round and round in a pattern that suggested tightening coils. More than that, she could not see, not at this distance, and she dared not even try to see what she could do with her magic. Even if she had not been afraid of what it would do to her hand, she would have been too afraid of that *thing*. Even the tingling felt so wrong.

A moment later, she *knew* that her fear was more than warranted; Radiance knew. Her kin, the dragons of Ilesh, fought it, hoping only that in death they might escape it, for it was the dead-born sorcery that legends attributed to the kings of the North that they fought. No more dreadful enemy existed, nor a more dreadful captivity. Camilla felt Radiance pull away from the minds of her fellow dragons, unable to help, unable to cope with what was happening, unable to admit her own fear, desperate that they *might* be forgotten and missed.

Camilla could not admit her fear, either. *We must be – are – free*, she thought, and, to Radiance, *You think there is no hope for the mages to fight it?*

"*No.*" Perhaps, if they were free mages, free dragons, a free people, but no people that kept slaves could be free. Their magic, their power, their freedom was flawed from within, and could not hope to stand for long even against lesser opponents than this one, for it was scarcely more than illusion or facade itself. Any opposition would shatter it – reveal it for what it was, reveal what was underneath it.

What of the human slaves? Camilla asked.

Those who had the souls of slaves would find their souls enslaved. – Camilla thought of Sylvara, and did not know whether she felt more pity or more vindictive satisfaction. – Those who were free at heart would die free – not only of the horror out of the north, but of their elven slave-masters.

Still, I would rather be free and alive, if possible.

As the night deepened, Camilla's sense of *wrongness* increased. Other elven villages were lit by the writhing column. Camilla began to wonder how they would escape. She knew they must be fairly near the border now, but she had no idea how to get through it – and if magic left traces, and she used magic to get through it, would not the horror pursue – and catch – her? What if she, just by being a mage, and an untrained one at that, left enough traces to be followed? She considered for a moment that the magesword, being a thing of magic, might leave traces – or whatever it was that she felt; she was not sure it was precisely 'traces' – and wondered if she should throw it away, but then she thought that she did not know anything about this. For all she knew, the same thing that kept her magic from burning her hand would also make that magic less obvious to other mages. She would do anything, even die by slow torture from her own magic, to keep Lavilor free.

The shadow of a thought from Radiance made her turn her eyes to a portion of the sky where the shapes of two wheeling dragons were silhouetted against the stars.

What? asked Camilla.

"They are not like me," said Radiance. Their bond was such that Camilla knew at once, as well as Radiance knew, what the dragon meant.

They're over the border, aren't they? observed Camilla.

Radiance thought so; a moment later, the two dragons turned and began flying towards them, their silhouettes growing rapidly larger.

"We will continue flying towards them," said Radiance. *"If they mean us harm, they have seen us already, and I cannot outfly them."*

Besides, thought Camilla, *there are enemies on every side. The elves have no friends, and whatever is attacking them is far worse than they are. We have to take our chances.*

Radiance responded with a feeling of warmth and gratitude for her rider's encouragement, and steeled herself to continue flying. Her wings and shoulders burned. They wondered how the two silver males were doing. They were smaller than the gold female, and while Lavilor weighed significantly less than Camilla, Sylvara did not. *"Not that I care about Sylvara, and, as much as Shimmer did not have any good choices,* that *is his fair desert,"* they thought.

It felt like a long time for Radiance, her wings were so tired, but the stars moved only a little, before the two *different* dragons were nearly on top of them. Then they spoke, but with voices which were almost human, though there was a draconic quality to them. "Come with us. We have waited long for you, and we are able to protect you, if worst does not come to worst, and to bring you safely across the border."

"I will come with you," Radiance said to them, speaking not only for herself and her rider, but for Sleet and Shimmer also.

The strange dragons wheeled above them, turning, and then they continued flying, the three hatchlings almost literally under the wings of the strangers.

Between laborious wing-beats, Radiance said to Camilla, *"This is strange. Dragons should not be like that."*

Dragons also should not be forced to bond, instead of getting to choose, replied her rider.

Several hours later, they touched down. With her dragon's eyesight, Camilla saw that they had landed in a large enclosed garden, and that at one end was a house the size of a mansion – possibly big enough for several large dragons to lie down in easily. "We are still in the middle of the border zone," said one of the dragons, a large red. "Do not wander, or you may be ensnared by the border spells."

"Understood," said Radiance.

"In that case, all is well for the moment. We will bring you what will amount to no more than a snack, but perhaps will let you sleep easier," continued the red.

Before their eyes the dragon, a female, transformed. Her body turned into a haze of ruby-tinged mist, and then dissipated, leaving a human male standing in her place. He turned and strode off in the direction of the mansion.

"What?!" asked Lavilor, even as Radiance and Camilla shared their shock.

Sylvara started to say something, but Camilla cut her off sharply. "I don't know what it means, Lav, but I think I saw the same as you did. It is very strange."

"It is," said Radiance. *"It should not be. It was not."*

At least it is not evil, said Camilla. *It seems as if it exists to protect against the horror that now conquers Ilesh, to stop it from taking us also, and perhaps all lands.*

"Perhaps," said Radiance. *"But it should not be."*

Though Camilla felt what Radiance did, for the first time she and her dragon differed. It did not seem so clear to her that such a thing should not be, or at least that it should not be any more strongly than Radiance should not be. The elves professed to have changed the dragons to help them adapt and survive, to be fighting their extinction. Camilla did not believe *that* was true, that the dragons were near the point of extinction, and, if it *was* true, she was certain that it was the elves' fault. However, she *did* believe that the elves had altered the dragons, probably in order to make them bond to them, when otherwise they would have chosen elves only rarely and, when they did choose elves, choose ones who respected them and would see them as equals in their relationship. But did that mean Radiance *should not exist*? NO! It was definitely good for Radiance to exist, and there was nothing wrong about *her.* Likewise, there was no reason these creatures should not exist, and there was not necessarily anything wrong with them, and neither she nor Radiance even knew that their existence had been brought about – or altered – in such a wrong manner, to such a wrong end.

"All right," said Radiance, *"but they are not dragons."*

We will have to ask them what they are, said Camilla, *but I agree that they are not the same kind of dragon as you are.*

Radiance grunted acceptance of that.

Camilla swung herself off of Radiance and began undoing the saddle. She tried to ignore Sylvara, since Shimmer had landed to one side of Radiance, and Sleet to the other. When she got to the side next to Sleet, she gave her brother a smile in the dark. "Good. I'm so sorry about this, but you're doing a great job in the dark," she said. "I'll help you with it after I finish with Radiance."

"Thanks, Cam," said Lavilor, and she could hear both the gladness of his relationship to her in his tone, more immediate, and the sorrow of his separation from his mother which this flight had made final to him, and that was deeper and more pervasive.

Her own heart twinging, Camilla said, "Lav, I'm sorry about Mom, but I promise, we will do everything we can to get her back. If there's a way to survive, she will. She'll flee. And I will do anything to free or save her, Lav. I promise it'll be okay." She really *did* feel what she said: that she could do anything necessary to make the world, or at least the part of it that was most important to her, right.

She did not know if her brother believed her words, even though she did, but he left his dragon and came to her for a hug. She hugged him for a few moments, and then whispered into his hair, "Now, go take care of Sleet, while I take care of Radiance. Then I'll give you a hug again, all right?"

He nodded his ascent against her shoulder, and stepped away.

She was helping him take the saddle off Sleet when the two *creatures* arrived with two carcasses for the dragons to share. They left them, smelling of fresh blood, on the grass, and said, "Do not be concerned. We're bringing something for you as well," before turning back towards the mansion.

Radiance turned towards Shimmer and growled, low and terrible. Camilla grabbed Lavilor's hand and backed away. She knew the dragons would try not to hurt them, but part of her did not trust Shimmer. He might not have been able to help it, but he *was* bonded to Sylvara, who was not at all trustworthy, and both dragon and rider affected each other. Moreover, she was afraid the alterations by the elves made the effect of the rider dominant, and vowed to herself that she would be careful of that with Radiance and make sure she did not override the dragon's personality. Something else told her she did not have to be careful with Radiance. Maybe it was *her* affect on the dragon, but Radiance possessed a personality to match her own in fierceness and strength. She would never let anyone, not even Camilla, dominate her.

"She thinks!" began Lavilor.

"Yes," said Camilla. "She thinks she and Sleet deserve the greater portion. Mostly herself, because she's bigger, but Sleet too."

"Doesn't Shimmer need to eat, too?" asked Lavilor.

"Shimmer's rider is an..." – she scrambled, looking for terms strong enough for her feelings, "liar, snitch, traitor, and whipper. It won't hurt them to go hungry for a night, and so they can do so. *She* owes it to me, for all the times she has gotten me whipped on purpose, and I bet she owes it to you and Sleet, too."

"But Shimmer didn't..."

"Shimmer's rider *did*. And, while Shimmer had no good options, if he Recognized Sylvara because, being human, she's a better natural partner, instead of an elven youngster who, while if he were truly good would understand he should not be keeping humans as slaves, might be much better... well, being hungry for one night won't hurt him. And *she* deserves it."

Camilla could tell that her arguments were having no effect on her brother, as they stood there, watching Radiance growl and snap at Shimmer. Sleet looked forlorn. Camilla suspected his thoughts were much like her brother's, but did not bother speaking to him to be sure. *I'd feel sorry for Shimmer,* she told herself, *except that it* was his *choice, and dragon and rider are* so *close. Maybe that's the more reason to be sorry for him, but then why didn't he Recognize an elf? Some of them are not that bad, and even treated me with a touch of courtesy when I did something they told me to. It wasn't fair. It wasn't right. They're all cowards and rottenhearts for not trying to stop it, but some of them were worlds better than Sylvara, who was only even in the right place to Recognize because she was looking to snitch on me and get the skin beaten off my back again!*

Finally, Radiance shoved Shimmer away from the carcasses, and he backed away, head and tail hanging, wings drooping, the very picture of a cowed and beaten dragon. It was almost enough to make Camilla's heart hurt for him, and she wondered then why it was suddenly Radiance who was more vehement against him, or had she and Radiance shared themselves so completely that it was impossible to tell, or even guess, where the one ended and the other began?

Radiance split the carcass and shoved the smaller piece at Shimmer, who looked at her with a beaten, disbelieving look in his eyes, dull with defeat, and then tore into it rapidly, splattering blood all over his silver scales, as if afraid that, at any time, the gold dragon would change her mind and take it back. But Radiance did not change her mind. She turned her tail on Shimmer, mentally beckoned Sleet, and began tearing into the other half of the carcass.

Even as she did so, Camilla heard a voice calling her to where the strange creatures had left something for her, Lavilor, and Sylvara. Even if she felt pity for Shimmer, she still felt none for Sylvara. Even the soft, submissive, almost defeated pose with which Sylvara approached the platters screamed to Camilla of her tormentor who had so often adopted much the same pose when almost in the act of tormenting her fellow slaves. The pity-ploys she had engaged in with such a cruel heart had long ago lost any effect on Camilla, and instead aroused only her fury and hatred.

She took her and Lavilor's share, and carried it to a corner of the garden, leaving Sylvara alone. Her heart raged against the cruelty of it. It was not the fault of the dragons of Ilesh that they had been forced to bond to elven slave-masters, nor was it their fault that the horror in the north had come to make them its undead slaves! It was not fair, it was not right, and it *would not be!* She would do anything, whatever she had to, to make sure that the dragons were free, would never be anyone's slaves again, and that her kin would be free again. She *hoped* that they would either die cleanly or, better yet, be able to escape into the forests and scrape by. Either way, this was *not* right, and it had to be fought and overcome, and it was so evil that, surely, it *must* be possible to put right. Something that evil had to be stopped, and therefore it would be stopped, and therefore she would be able to stop it, if no one else could or did.

These thoughts churned her stomach so much that it ached even before she had finished her relatively small portion. She told Lavilor he could eat the rest of hers.

He looked at her with eyes that even in the dark awakened far more of her sympathy and pity than even Shimmer's display had done – or, perhaps, it was not his eyes, but the fact that she could hear his thoughts as dragons can hear one another's thoughts – and asked, "You really don't want it, sister?" His tone had the same quality to it – a deep sadness, a crushed spirit, and yet a little spark of happiness, which she knew was from her and, doubtless to a far greater degree, from his dragon, Sleet.

"Yes. I can't eat right now," she said.

The smile he gave her next – or maybe it was what she felt from him after the way of dragons – warmed her heart. He continued from his portion into hers, still eating with a vengeance.

He's probably much hungrier than I am, she thought drolly. *He's right at the age to shoot up like a sapling that's just got its roots established, and I'm as near full-grown as matters.*

And to think that Sylvara would never even *notice* such a consideration – and, if she did, would not care in the least, but would go on stealing food from those who needed it far more than she did. It *was* best she learn what hunger was, and if the only way to do that was through Shimmer... well, they both needed to know. Only, would *she?* How had someone like her even had enough capacity for empathy to Recognize a dragon? One would have thought she could *not!*

Looking up at the sky, Camilla saw a maze of shadows in its lower quarters. She looked again, and realized that the shadows seemed to her more dominant than they really were. They only slightly obscured the light of the stars, but they did obscure other things. She wondered if the two strange creatures dwelt within the border protections – *if* they dwelt here – and had taken them within the border protections in order to shield them from the dead-born horror destroying Ilesh, for there definitely were spells about this place that confused magic and blocked magic. She could not sense the wrongness that she had earlier that night, but instead she sensed something else. It was eerie, but not as horrible. It was more like a buzz right on the edge, either in volume or in tone, of the audible.

She watched the strange spell for a few moments, then tried to shut it out of her awareness. It was the kind of thing that was not really irritating, but *would* make it harder for her to sleep, and while the anger she felt had riled her stomach and would not let her eat comfortably, it did leave her feeling drained and exhausted – but not any less angry.

Late in the morning, she woke under Radiance's wing. *"You are hungry, little one,"* said the dragon. *"And so am I. Are we ready to get food together?"*

Camilla stretched and grunted. *I'm not sure about* together, *given the way you like to eat. And I am older than you are.*

"But still you are smaller," said Radiance, *"and that is what I said."* Despite her bond with Camilla, she was a little confused. Why had she taken *'smaller'* that way?

It's nothing. Nothing at all. Mom just used to call me and Lav that.

"Oh," said Radiance. She understood now. Her rider was just testy about being reminded about her mother. *"Then let's get up, heart of my fire, and eat as together or not together as we desire. My stomach is burning hunger, and I can tell that you are only a little less hungry."*

"You're right," said Camilla out loud, getting up and knocking her head against one of the bones running through Radiance's wing. The dragon lifted it, exchanging the dim gold light filtered through her wings for the startling brightness of a sunny day.

"I have told them that we are awake now. You could, too, if you wanted," said Radiance. A moment later, *"They say to come. They wish to speak to us alone."*

Tacitly, Camilla agreed. She placed her hand on the dragon's golden shoulder, and walked with her towards the mansion. Lavilor and Sleet were still asleep, but Shimmer was not. His eyes were dull with depression and he slumped across the grass. Sylvara sat next to him, glaring at Camilla and Radiance. Camilla glared right back.

They walked around the back of the mansion, and saw there the two strange creatures waiting for them. They were both in dragon-form, a red female and a purple male. Camilla felt a wave of revulsion from Radiance, and the dragon stopped dead in her tracks. Her rider stopped beside her.

"Greetings, dragon and rider. But one of you is revolted by us, and that we wished to discuss," said the purple.

Stiffly, Radiance agreed. Camilla said nothing. Then, Radiance projected her thoughts to them, *"But why do you wish to discuss this with us... alone?"*

"Because there is no need to involve the others," said the purple. "Why are you revolted?"

"You are a dragon... and yet not. When first I saw you, I knew you were not like other dragons. Though we speak mind-to-mind, it is not as I and my kin do. When I saw you transform, I understood better what you are, and it is wrong! Nothing of that sort should be!" There was so much vehemence in Radiance's mind-voice.

The red transformed again, and the shape of a human man stood before them. His hair and beard were graying, and his eyes were a green rare in humans, though common in elves. "You touched our minds, and saw that they are not the minds of dragons, and yet are. You are rightly revolted by what you imagined us to be, Radiance. Yet it is not what we are. Though I remember what Serrate remembered, though I remember what Yetra remembered, though my personality and my bodies come from Serrate and Yetra, I am not Serrate nor am I Yetra. I am not a combination of Serrate and Yetra. I am a single, distinct person." He took a deep breath, and transformed again into the red female dragon. "Though we think we know why you were confused."

Camilla spoke this time. "Because I and Radiance are so close... we feel like we are *almost* one person. Her mind is mine, and mine is hers... *almost*. It works that way often with our thoughts."

"But yet you are two persons. Your mind and thoughts are almost hers, and hers are almost yours, but those very statements make it clear that there *are* two of you – that if you are hers, and she is yours, that means you are not she, and she is not you," said the purple.

Both of them acknowledged that. *"It would be an abomination if we were,"* said Radiance, horror making her mind-voice patchy. *"It would also be an abomination if we were somehow stuck sharing one body. It would..."* Her thoughts shifted into an image of herself and Camilla disagreeing – or working together – and then another where that was not possible.

"It would be," agreed the purple and the red together. The purple continued. "You are one because of love. If you were somehow made into one person, then there would no longer be the two of you to love one another, to think *with* one another, to share with one another – even to correct one another. You would no longer be a dragon and rider. You would be alone. But I think that it occurs to you, Radiance, that this abomination might be possible – that we might be such an abomination – for two reasons, one of which is because you and Camilla are bonded exceptionally tightly – tighter, I think, than is natural. You are close enough, I think, that the natural ability of dragon and rider to correct each other, to balance each other's strengths and weaknesses, to think *differently*, is weakened in you. The blending of personalities and thoughts is such that the notion of being one being occurs to you, and sometimes you feel like you are one being, but you know that you are not, and the very closeness you have, the oneness or almost-oneness you have, is because you are two, united in love, not the same."

Radiance and Camilla shifted uneasily. It felt as if a river of fiery desire to avenge this wrong committed against them by centuries of elven life-mages boiled under their skin. Then they remembered the horror visited upon the elves even now by the witch-kings of the North, and did not know whether to feel that the elves had gotten what they deserved, or whether to pity them as suffering under a horror which, for all the evils they had done, was still not right – it was not even as if all elves were equally guilty, or even as if quite all elves *were* guilty.

If the strange creatures observed this, they gave no sign of it. It was the red who spoke now. "Yet that is not what we are. We were created by the action of the Lord of Light when the pairs from whom we come died, and by Him we were given their forms, and much of their memories, and an imprint of their personalities. Yet each of us is one person, not two. We are not a fusing of two beings, something infinitely more dreadful than the loss felt by a dragon or rider at the death of the other. Set your minds at rest about this."

"I... I don't know if I can. It's hard for me not to... feel that way, when I see you. Especially when I see you transform," said Radiance. Then, together, she and Camilla asked, "And what do you think is the other reason it occurs to us that this ... whatever you appear to be is wrong?"

There was a hesitance on the part of the strange creatures. They swung their huge heads to glance at each other, then transformed in a swirl of ruby and violet mist into their human forms. The purple appeared an elven woman. Camilla gasped. Radiance tossed her head up, flared her wings, swung her tail like a whiplash, and gouged the earth with her claws.

"Peace, Radiance," said the woman. "Peace. For one, I am not the one who was not my rider. For another, she is not one whom you would have hated, had you known her. When Sërien Recognized Gloaming, she understood things most of the elves did not. It took some time, but eventually she left Ilesh, being a mage sufficient to the task of navigating the border protections. To tell you all that happened since then would take a long time, as it revolves around history of which you likely have no knowledge, unless Ilesh has changed greatly since she and he whom I am not lived, which I think unlikely, for while our sleep has been long, and our lives since it not short, by the reckoning of humans, it has not been that long by the reckoning of elves. Yet, I think I must tell you this sooner or later, so sooner is just as well:

"Your kind are not the only dragons left in the world. There are many, on another continent, who have not been altered by the magic of elves. One of the things that happened when your kind was altered by the elves, is that your minds were altered by the elven magic and by the way of thinking that lies behind and within the elven magic. You still have an instinctive sense of the rightness of a thing, but it is confused and muddled by the traces of elven magic left in your mind..."

Camilla stepped away from Radiance, as the dragon roared. Her wings flailed, missing Camilla's head by inches – crucial inches, yet Camilla was not frightened, for their link was such that Radiance knew the position of her rider's body as she knew her own. She tore up huge chunks of earth in her claws, and roared again and again. Camilla went to the ground, feeling the waves of the dragon's rage welling up within her – for it was not just Radiance's rage, it was her own, and that not only because she was bonded to Radiance; she had thought and felt alike before ever she met Radiance. *How dare the elves change the dragons, not only in body, but in mind! How dare the elves change the dragons, not only to make them bond to them, but to make them not even know as dragons should know! Let the earth swallow them! Let fire rain down on them! Let their forests burn! Let the winds shatter them!*

"*Peace,*" said the strange creatures, their voices cutting through their shared rage.

The next moment, Camilla realized what they had done. They had wakened Sleet and Lavilor with their rage, and roused Sylvara and Shimmer with it.

Dragonmage

Radiance and Camilla stepped back from their mindless rage. Shock rolled over them in its wake. *I can't believe what I've done!* She remembered, *now*, that she spoke mentally like a dragon, and to both dragons and humans. Radiance might have radiated her rage directly only to Sleet and Shimmer, but she had done it to Lavilor! Besides, poor Lavilor and Sleet! He would have gotten enough through his bond to Sleet, and Sleet did not deserve it, either.

"*Neither do I deserve what you give me,*" Shimmer said to her.

Get your sympathy from Sylvara. You Recognized her, she growled in reply. She was not sure, now, whether she pitied him at all or not, but she did not want to deal with her feelings about him and his rider right now. Those could be worked through later.

"Peace," said the purple again. "Radiance, Camilla, you nurture far too much rage. It does not help you, it does not help anyone, and it is rooted in your fear, your rebellion against the notion that something besides yourself, and worse than yourself, is strongest. Otherwise you would be angry, but not so madly angry as you are, and it would not be so destructive to those around you, and to your own peace of mind."

Camilla looked straight into the creature's elven green eyes and held her gaze. She was not going to be treated as a child or an inferior. She was not going to be controlled or told what to do, ever again. "Maybe," she said, standing as tall and straight as she knew how. "I and Radiance will think about it."

"Very well," said the purple. "Let us see about feeding all of you, and we will discuss more later. I just wanted to resolve the issue of your disgust."

Camilla nodded, then reached to Lavilor. *I'm sorry, brother.* She did not know what more to say. She could feel how shaken he was from being awakened by waves of her rage, rage which even now she fought to control. She pitied *some* of the elves. There was no reason to hate their children, who had not yet chosen their path of oppression. And if what the purple had said was true, then there were, now and then, elves who did entirely forsake the evil of their society. There might be more of them than she had ever guessed, and the elves might suppress any mention of them. *Well,* she thought, *I hope any like that managed to escape. The others, even if they were merely cowards, deserve what they got! Cowardice* ought *to lead one to* far *worse fates than courage.*

She spun on her heels, ducked under Radiance's wing, which was still flared, and ran towards her brother and his dragon. She almost slammed into Sylvara, who was looking at her with something in her eyes that was definitely hate and anger, but which seemed different from any hate or anger she had ever before seen from the girl. She skidded to a stop in front of Lavilor and Sleet.

"*I'm sorry,*" she said to both, with both mind and voice. "*I didn't mean to do that to you. I love you!*"

Sleet fixed her with one colored eye, and touched her mind with his. He was not a wrathful dragon. *"There is nothing to be forgiven,"* he said.

Camilla nodded. "I'm still sorry. I shouldn't have done it. I love you. Both of you."

Lavilor stepped forward and gave her a hug.

After they ate, the strange creatures again called her to them. They told Radiance that she did not need to come. She could finish her own meal and listen in through Camilla, as much or as little as she wanted.

Camilla soon found herself seated under an herb tree, facing the two strange creatures in their human and elf forms. "What am I to call you?" she asked.

"I am often called Alian," said the red, the human man.

"And I have been called Serrose," said the purple, the elf woman, "but we have not called you here to discuss names. You carry a magesword and seem to be a mage, though you are human."

"Yes." Camilla nodded.

"You will need some training, and while I am not qualified to train a mage of such proportions as yourself, having barely graduated – well, my parent, Sërien, having barely graduated – before departing Ilesh, I may be able to help a little. To at least set you on the right path so you don't hurt others or yourself before you can get into the hands of those who can train mages."

"Umm," said Camilla, "I *have* hurt myself, and there are mages other than those in Ilesh who can train me in the magic?"

Serrose nodded. "We have not met them ourselves, but someone we trust assures us of their existence. Across the sea, there is a clan of elves who do not despise humans and who do not ride dragons, but who are masters of magic. And what do you mean, you have hurt yourself?"

Camilla drew her hand out from under her cloak and held it up for the two to see.

Alian gasped. Serrose bent closer, and gasped more softly. "I... see," she said, "and, yes, that is part of what I was going to warn you against. Give your hand to me."

Camilla did so, remembering the elves who had tended her, and wondering if Serrose could do similarly.

Serrose's touch was gentler than the elves' had been, and Camilla's hand at once both warmed and cooled under her kneading fingers. After a while, she let Camilla's hand go, and said, "That is all I can do. That should never have been allowed to happen. What did you do?"

"I don't really know. It just happens to me. Since I stole the magesword, it's not happening anymore," she said.

"All right. What do you know how to do?"

"Shadowblend. I can shadowblend, albeit poorly, but I think I've been shadowblending since before my hand started to burn, though it burns when I shadowblend now, at least when I don't have the magesword. I don't know if I knew if shadowblending was exactly magic until that happened. Other than that, I'm almost certain I *could* throw bolts of energy, but I've never done it. I also feel mage energy. I feel the spells around this place, and I felt the spells, or some of them, when the Northern Darkness attacked Ilesh."

Serrose listened intently while she spoke. "When did your hand start to burn?" she asked.

"When I and Radiance Recognized."

Serrose leaned back and nodded. "This complicates things. I do not know how you are burning yourself or what you are doing to burn yourself. I am glad the magesword stops it, which is not surprising, but what is surprising is that this is happening to you. It's known among the elves that master mages, who have worked a great deal of magic, will build up magic within themselves and unless they release it in a controlled manner, it will release through their bodies and burn them. This is why great mages always carry mageswords or magespears. The mageweapons take the energy and hold it in a way that does not hurt the mage. But what is surprising is that you, who have never practiced any substantive magic are having this happen – though from what you report, your senses are those of a trained adept mage, though I doubt you understand them as well."

Alian quirked a smile while Serrose spoke.

"Do we need to solve this right now?" asked Camilla.

"Not right now, exactly," said Alian, "but it is a liability, a danger. I have learned some of magic from Serrose – Yetra learned some of magic from Sërien – and it is unprecedented for Recognition to cause this to happen." He looked to Serrose. "Could it be related to the changes made to the dragons' minds? After all, it's rare for humans to bond to these dragons, and most of those were probably not mages of her potential. She was shadowblending before Recognizing. It is entirely possible that I – that Yetra had any ability for magic because of his Recognition to Serrate, and that for one who is already a mage to begin with, when one..."

He trailed away, and Serrose took up the thought. "That's a very interesting idea, especially since *we* do not have the problem of burning without a proper focus. Sërien did, but I don't. I thought it was a gift from the Lord of Light so we could work magic even though we can't carry focuses when we shift. But what if it's not that, at least not directly? What if it has to do with the link between the dragons and the magic used to alter them?"

Camilla raged silently. Radiance was, helpfully, not immersing herself in this conversation, but she was still getting too angry to concentrate or think well because of the abomination just mentioned. She *was* trying to control it. She did not believe there was anything wrong with the reaction – it was perfectly natural and fitting – but it did interfere with what she was trying to do now, so they needed to learn how to *control* it, not stifle it. She also hated being talked over or around. She did not know what Serrose and Alian were talking about, and it upset her. She did not understand the magic being talked about, and she did not know who or what this Lord of Light was!

When Serrose stopped speaking, she leaned forward and interrupted. "Pardon," she asked, "but can you two please explain all of this to me?"

"All of what to you?" asked Serrose, looking at her. "I don't know what you're talking about."

"She knows even less about magic than we do," said Alian, "and probably does not realize just how little we know. She also knows nothing about the Lord of Light. You have to remember how confusing this is to someone else. It's confusing enough for those of us who experienced it." He turned towards her and said, "Mages, even the best, know far more about *what* they do and *what* the effects it produces or can produce are, than about what is happening or why. And neither I nor Serrose are the best, nor were the riders from whom we come. We are trying to figure out what we must, to give you what we can. We cannot explain everything we know to you in a minute. As for the Lord of Light, there is something of him in the bond that ties every rider and dragon. He is Lord of the Ellenari, those who guard this world and its people from the nightmare or corruption which is the source of power of the lords of the north, though he himself is not one of the Ellenari. He is Lord of the Land of Love, which brings us back to what I first told you about him: that it is something of his power or nature that ties you and Radiance. He is victorious through love, and because of him all that loves will be victorious over all that hates and will finally restore the world. There's not much more that I can tell you."

Camilla's thought flashed in a moment to what she and Radiance had been thinking about the human slaves. "So he stands between those who love, the free in heart, and undeath?" she asked.

"Perhaps," said Alian. "We do not know what undeath is – what it is the horror of the north does with the slain. We cannot answer all your questions."

Camilla nodded, her mind spinning on this new piece of information. Whether it was true or not, there was truth in it. And something had made these strange creatures, but there seemed something wrong about them, so *could* it be something as good and wholesome as this Lord of Light was supposed to be?

Her mind and thoughts and Radiance's met in an embrace of fire. *"To love is freedom."* Yes, thought Camilla. *I always determined to be free, but I always loved, unlike people like Sylvara. And when I met you, I know we must be free. And our love was our courage to seek freedom at any cost.*

She stood, and said, "Teach me what you can about magic. I need to know all I can."

Serrose stood and faced her. "I will teach what I judge that you are ready to learn and I am qualified to teach. I know you want to demand, and I know that I constantly look to you like your oppressors and slave-masters. I thought it would be easier to speak to you in a more human form, and I still feel that it would be easier to teach you certain elements of magic in a more human form, but perhaps we should do everything we can do from my dragon form in that. For while I do not, and must not, appear to you as your oppressors, and if that is how you feel it will not help you learn what you must, yet you also must not demand or act imperious. You must learn."

Camilla nodded. "Whatever you think best," she said. "I will try."

"Good," said Serrose, her eyes twinkling. "I'd rather not transform right here, so let's go into the other meadow." She and Alian rose.

Camilla followed.

When they entered the meadow, Serrose transformed into a glittering violet and amethyst male dragon. He sat down, curled his tail around himself, and faced her with glowing eyes. "We do not know what magic is," he said. "It comes from somewhere, but we do not know where. All elves are born with some mage potential within them. This is what allows them to shadowblend, and I can do it, even in this form. Despite what the Wood Elves of Ilesh say, there are many humans who also have this potential, though few have it as strongly as some elves. Until you, we have not met any humans who could shadowblend. There are different kinds of magic and, until I heard you could, I thought shadowblending was specific to the Wood Elves, just as the way they sing is specific to the Sea Elves, but I knew that there are humans who practice magic very similar to most of what is practiced by the Wood Elves. Doubtless, you have heard that objects or items are required as focuses or anchor-points for most spells?"

Camilla nodded. "I have." It felt strange to be talking to this way to a dragon, but she had to remember that Serrose was not a dragon. Not quite.

"Why is not something which is understood. There are only speculations, most of which I do not wish to repeat to you right now, but what is certain is that masters, or those with strong potential can often cast spells without as much preparation or as precise focuses as novices, but there is a cost, as you have discovered in your hand. I would strongly advise that, except in the most dire need, you do not try to call lightning bolts, or streams of energy, or fireballs, or whatever it is you imagine. You could burn yourself *very* badly and, in some cases, the worse a mage burns, the more easily the mage burns in the future. That is why I was so upset by the scars on your hand, not to mention how much that must hurt."

Camilla nodded, looking down at her feet and trying to control the waves of anger she felt. *It was the elves' fault!* That torture had probably been intentional as more than torture, or even punishment. They had probably – no, *certainly* – intended to damage her potential, sooner or later, if not in one way, then in another.

"What is upsetting you?" asked Alian, who was still in human form.

"The elves," said Camilla. "Once I Recognized Radiance, the dragons wouldn't let them beat me. So, instead, they refused to heal my hand, and let it burn and burn for days." She could hardly get the words past her fury, which was making her nearly cry. She spat them out, several at a time at most.

Serrose growled, long and low. Then he said, "It is no use raging about it now, though it makes your anger somewhat understandable – yet, still not wise or helpful. Such rage does not help your bond of love with Radiance grow into its perfection. Yet, I am glad to understand you a little better, and it makes me angry myself. Still, there is naught I can do about it now. What I was going to say, is that while the magesword is a partial focus for a wide variety of magic, it is not a focus for all spells. You probably should not try throwing bolts of energy unless you want to incinerate yourself. It will not be adequate for that."

"Most of this I know already," said Camilla.

"Then, there is not that much that we know that you do not, except for the details of spells and the mental practices."

Camilla stood proudly. "I've always felt certain that I could be a mage, and listened to everything I could."

"Good," said Serrose. "That will save time, but I still need to know what you do and do not know, and we will not practice *any* magic, until I have healed your hand as far as I can."

Camilla nodded again, disappointed. Then she changed the topic. "How long do you want me to stay here? I need to find a way to rescue any human slaves, and any dragons, captured by the Northern Darkness."

"I don't know if you *can* do that," said Serrose. "It is a task far beyond the abilities of any one being, and will take the intervention of the Lord of Light, in one form or another. Alone, you can do nothing. But I think the best thing is for you to train, to learn your magic, something you need to do anyways, and for that you need to cross the ocean and go to Aneri, where live those who will be able to properly instruct and guide you. There, also, is one of the places where the Ellenari are seen most often, and it may be the best place to go if you seek to rescue these people, for you will need their aid. As for how long, I want to wait for your hand to heal, and then give you a very introductory course in the basics of spell-casting. We would go with you, but we have eggs, and those eggs require both parents to be around when they hatch. After that, we, or one of us, will find you if we can."

"What are the Ellenari?" asked Camilla.

"I don't know much about them. They are beings of power unlike ours, and they may – or may not – have had a hand in the formation of myself and Alian. There are things only they can do to combat the Northern Darkness, or any army of the Nightmare. I can say no more. I know of them only through a friend who knows and speaks with them."

Thinking of names and types of beings brought Camilla's mind to another question. "I wish I had something to call... not you individually, but things like you. You spoke of eggs, so, what kind of thing are you?"

Serrose and Alian looked at each other. Camilla thought it was really funny to see a dragon and a human looking at one another that way. Alian said, "Our friend called us dragonmages, and the theory we just discussed about why I am a mage is correct, then perhaps all of our kind are, or will be, dragonmages." As he spoke, he turned from Serrose towards Camilla. "But now that you are here, it is hard not to call you a dragon-mage."

"That's okay," said Camilla. "Dragonmage is something at least, and somewhat descriptive." She took a deep breath, then said, "Were your... umm, parents mated?"

A ruby mist formed around him, and Alian took on the form of a red female dragon. Over a deep hum, she said, "Yes. Both pairs of them. It is so with all the pairs of dragonmages born at the end of the Great War of the North."

Camilla nodded, then said, "Tell me the true story of that war. I know only the corrupted elven history of anything."

"Gladly," said Alian.

Camilla sat down and closed her eyes. It was easier to listen to creatures in dragon form talk if one was not looking at them. She felt Radiance spread her wings and soar over towards her.

I'm glad you're coming, she said, hardly knowing if it was her thought or the dragon's. *Even though we're almost one soul, there's something special about being together physically.*

Radiance hummed in response. Camilla could tell that she was feeling largely recovered from the bone-wearying flight from Ilesh, though there was still a darkness in their minds because of the lost, dead or enslaved, dragons and humans. Camilla had asked for this story because she felt she needed to know it. It was related to what she was fighting, but she dreaded it, for she was certain that it would remind her of the horror recently visited upon those she and Radiance knew, including dragons like Alabaster, who had helped her take the magesword. *Thank you,* she thought to him, wondering if he would be able to hear it. *I will do everything and anything in my power to free you.* She hoped, wherever his soul was captured, if he was not dead and in a region of victory, he would hear her and know that she and Radiance were coming.

"Our name is Radiance," she and the dragon thought. It was a perfect name. Radiance she was, in the darkness of slavery, and in a yet deeper darkness, radiance to end the darkness, radiance to bring hope and victory.

Alian was speaking now, and Camilla and Radiance listened, even as the dragon swooped down to land near her rider. "So," he said, "we cannot tell you everything that happened, but this is what we know..."

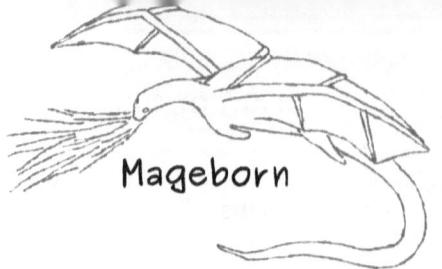

Mageborn

It would be difficult and distracting to represent accurately the exchange between Serrose and Alian, as each of them told different parts of the story, or the gasps and comments of Camilla, as it differed from what she had heard, sometimes in ways she suspected, and sometimes in ways she could not have guessed.

Ilesh had long been reclusive. Its people stayed within its depths and almost never ventured forth, hemmed in by the same wild magic on its borders that intruders were kept out. Occasionally an elf mage would seek his or her way out of the forest, and even more occasionally, one would return. Many of these mages were Dragonriders, like Sërien, and it may have been because of the off-spring of their dragons, when they found and mated with one another, that there were human Dragonriders throughout the kingdoms of Ellenesia. Of these kingdoms and nations, there was a long-standing feud between the northern and the southern peoples, one which exceeded even the typical conflicts, which sometimes persisted for ages and sometimes came and went, between different peoples. And in the north, about the Icecrown Mountains, or the Ring of the Everlasting Ice as some called it, there was a wilderness fraught with evil nightmarish creatures and men who practiced dark witchcraft and had become enslaved or possessed by the nightmares that walked the Ring of Ice.

One year a prince who had spent several years in seclusion and returned with magics that seemed dark to some, Kestor by name, succeeded to the throne of a nation named Eltae. At first, there were few overt signs of the darkness, but Sërien was suspicious, since she knew enough magic to sense the wrongness in the spells of the new King of Eltaes. While she and Gloaming distrusted the history of the elves, they yet knew it, and had heard of the shadow about the Icecrown Mountains. Now it seemed to them that it was not as much of a legend as they had thought. She gathered around her the human Dragonriders to whom she was teaching what magic she could, and watched. And even as Sërien watched and trained her Dragonriders in seclusion, Eltaes and its people suffered under a growing tyranny and depression.

Before long, all dragons and Dragonriders had vanished from the Kingdom of Eltaes. Sërien was suspicious about where they had gone, for she could not find signs of them having gone anywhere else. She and Gloaming only passed through the territory of Eltaes under the strongest spells of illusion and unnoticed passing which she could master, and that they did only rarely, but the magic she felt radiating from Arkane, the capital city of Eltaes unnerved her. Even though she dwelt in seclusion and moved from place to place, they had often to deal with the assaults of the Nightmare, and some of her riders were lost in battle with it, perhaps weakened by its influence of fear and hatred.

Then, after some years passed, King Kestor declared war on nations surrounding Eltaes. Dragons appeared from time to time in his armies, but every Dragonrider that fought him on behalf of other nations or peoples vanished. Sometimes, the bodies of the dragons were found, but most often their bodies vanished and no one could say what had happened to them or where they had fallen. Where his dragons appeared, so did terrible dark magic, and he began to be called the Wizard-King. The forests around Arkane withered, and most of the plants that remained were sickly and weak. Soon, nations that had no Dragonriders refused to receive dragons or riders, associating them with Eltaes and the relentless war Eltaes waged against the Dragonriders, as it conquered nation after nation of the north. Some nations exiled what Dragonriders had lived in them, and more refused to accept any who sought refuge.

It was during this time of darkness that Sërien and her Dragonrider-mages met several other elf Dragonrider-mages who were guarding and training coteries of human Dragonriders with more or less limited potential for magic, not unlike what she herself was doing. Together, they resolved that the Wizard-King of Eltaes must be opposed. They emerged from hiding, and gathered to them what was left of the Dragonriders of the human kingdoms. They trained, as quickly as they could, those with the greatest potential for magic, and made their stand in the skies above the hills of Adriase. They chose Adriase for many reasons; chief among these were that it was a northern land which still held on against the witchery of Eltaes, and that it was a rather loose confederation of tribes and civilizations that had not entirely outlawed Dragonriders.

With their magic, they successfully fought against many of the forces Eltaes sent against Adriase. However, they took losses, and the Wizard-King sent new and more powerful forces against them, including many of his bewitched dragons. He killed some of them and captured others. At last, their battle defeated and Adriase lost, Sërien and Gloaming and what little remained of the original forces, took it upon themselves to find a way to carry the battle to the Wizard-King himself. They could not stand by and do nothing while he spread his horror over more and more of the lands and captured and enslaved more and more people, now conquering and enslaving nations that had no Dragonriders as well. They knew that they had no chance of fighting all his minions, but though they judged that it was small, they thought they had some chance of defeating him if they could catch him alone or unawares. This they endeavored to do, sneaking deeper and deeper in Eltaes, often with the help of magic, and finally into the ruined lands around Arkane itself.

There, they succeeded to some degree in ambushing the Wizard-King, and fought him with very minimal protections, far less than he would take into battle. The fight was fierce and close at times, but in the end all were slain, and Kestor, if it could still be called Kestor, was victorious. But when the dragons and riders were slain, a power more ancient than Areaer took a hand.

As the dragons and riders fell, to pass to whatever next awaited on their journey after the touch of death, the Lord of Light took their powers, their memories, and their mortal forms, and from each pair, even as they died, stitched another being, one possessing the greater portion of the powers and memories of either partner, and able to take the form of either partner, dragon and human or elf, at will. Upon explaining to them what had happened, and what they now were, he took them to some caves under the earth, and cast them into a sleep that would last until the time was come for them to awaken, having told them something of what their missions would be.

"So," Alian continued, "we don't know all that happened between when we were created and cast into slumber, and when we awoke. But that is our first-hand experience of the Fall of the North."

"How long ago was this?" Camilla asked. "Is the current King of the North the same as Kestor?"

"I don't know exactly," said Serrose. "We were wakened some thirty years ago – closer to forty than thirty. As I said, a short time for elves, but not so short for humans. It would be hard to imagine that it is Kestor, since the events we have related took several decades themselves, and we must have been asleep for some time, but there are rumors that dark mages or witches can live unnaturally long life-spans, so it could be. As for the state of Ellenesia, last we left this refuge the Sea Elves felt that they were threatened, and almost all of the north is under the banner of Eltaes, excepting only the Sea Elf bays and isles. It makes me very sad, having remembered and loved all that Sërien and Gloaming did, to see what we – what they – fought and gave their lives for, so utterly destroyed and damaged. For while I did not die, they did, I think of it as if I lived in them and made all their choices in them, for I remember it as if I did. Even the dying. It wasn't I. I've not lost being Sërien and loving Gloaming, or being Gloaming and loving Sërien, but it certainly feels as if I share full responsibility and agency for their actions, and certainly I have learned and grown through their lives and choices as fully and intimately as if they had been my own. So it hurts, but it would not have been right for me to fly to challenge the Wizard-King, and I was supposed to wait here for you."

"Though we did not know who would come," said Alian.

"Right," said Serrose. "I had no idea that the Dragonrider for whom I was waiting would be a human gold-rider with more mage potential than I ever had. Or what her companions would be. We knew essentially nothing about who we were waiting for, except that we were waiting for someone. I think we guessed it would be someone rather like myself."

Camilla sat against Radiance's side, her knees tucked up to her chin. "So, I have some special role in all of this, and I am destined to destroy this Wizard-King and free all his captives." Her tone of voice was flat and expressionless. It could have been skeptical. It could have been irritated. It could have been proud and excited. It could have been almost anything.

"I don't know about that," said Alian. "We were to wait for you and help you. That is all."

I hope so, thought Camilla. *I want to defeat this Wizard-King and free his captives! I want to drown him in rivers of fire! But I want to do so because I can and must, not because I am chosen or fated! Not that it matters. It's what I am going to do, and since it is what I am going to do, it isn't changed by being chosen or destined for it.*

"Maybe we are here to help you, and anyone else who was able to flee, to escape from the Northern Horror, as you called it," said Serrose.

She nodded. It made sense, except that none of this made sense, and as prone to being angry and so-called rebellious against the elves, and traitors like Sylvara, as she was used to being, she felt like there was something off about the way she felt now. As if... as if she were fighting fear with anger, and so instead of being purposeful and directed, present only when proper, it was spinning around aimlessly, lashing out and clashing against everything, and swamping her experience, instead of flaring up when appropriate, and retreating into the embers when no longer necessary. *Is this what they mean by the influence of the Nightmare?* she thought. *I suppose whether it is or not, I have to fight it. The problem is, how? How do I differentiate between this anger, which has no purpose and is not helping me, and the anger which is the right and appropriate response to abominations like the Northern Horror and its atrocities, or traitors like Sylvara, or lying, thieving slavers, or cowards?*

"Well," she said at last, her voice coming out strangled, "thank you for telling me that story. It explains a lot." She had opened her eyes.

Serrose tilted his purple head. "You're welcome. I'm glad you got what you were looking for from it."

Are they ignoring the way I feel? She touched Radiance's wing membrane, trying to calm herself. *For one thing, I know that one can't control magic very well like this.*

The purple dragon shared a look with the human, and rose to his feet. He took a few slow steps towards her, a shifting of violet mist about his body showing that he was on the verge of transforming into the female elf.

"Camilla," said Serrose, in a deep, throaty voice, but one which yet held accents of the elf's speech, "you have a great deal of anger, and it is not good."

"Some of it is," said Camilla. Beside her, Radiance spread her wings and lifted her head. *"Some of it is,"* she agreed.

"And much of it is not," said Serrose. "I am here to talk to you about the part that is not good, not the part that is."

"I *know* I need to learn how to control my anger. It's a little harder for me than it is for others, since most humans don't have this dragon ability I seem to have. And I know I need to control it to be a mage. But other than that, I don't see what there is to talk about. But if you want to teach me techniques that will help me control it so I can work magic, then I'd be happy to learn." It felt as if she were biting off her tongue with each word. She felt as if her whole body thrummed, as if it were a string being plucked, with magic, and with the need of the magic to be released right into the face of the Wizard-King. It felt so strong, furious, and pure that she was certain it would kill him, would blast him right off the face of Areaer.

Serrose sighed, then took another slow step towards her and sniffed the air. Then he settled back onto his haunches, violet mist still obscuring the lines of his form. "I know why you are burning yourself at a rate quicker than the most powerful mages are prone to do," he said.

"What?"

"When you get angry – which happens a great deal – you draw energy, as light draws moths. You're vibrating with it, singing with it to my senses, and it is far too much. You gather energy, as if you were preparing an act of magic, but it is not released, so it burns you. And, while the magesword you bear has slowed this effect down so much that you think it has fixed it, it has not. It's not enough to dampen all that energy. *You* will need to learn how to stop gathering it – and how to release it," said Serrose. "You will also need to get less angry."

"Are you sure I need to get less angry? Won't I need this energy to kill the Wizard-King?"

"It will take more than mere energy to kill the Wizard-King," said Alian, stepping forward. "Even if you are the strongest mage to have ever been born." His tone made it clear that he was not suggesting this, but merely making a statement. "Those from whom we come would have killed him, if that was all it took, for while you have more magic than Sërien, you do not have more magic than the entire group that opposed him. And you will destroy yourself with your magic far before you ever get a chance to fight him, if you do not stop doing this."

Camilla did not nod. She just accepted their gazes and held them – as best as one could hold a dragon's gaze. She was *not* certain she had been doing this the whole time. She was not even sure it had not begun when she took the magesword. The first time she had felt pure magic waiting to be released had been when they were fleeing and she had seen and felt the attack of the Northern Horror on Ilesh. She took a deep breath, then said, "I don't think you have the right of it. I haven't felt like this, as if I were a bow drawn almost to the breaking point with burning energy, until the Northern Horror attacked Ilesh. It was when I felt its spells that I first felt as if… when I first knew I could throw bolts of power." Another memory surfaced, and she continued. "I think that's not quite right. It was after I took the magesword, when we were fleeing, that I *knew* I could fight with magic. So I think it is the magesword that is letting me do this, and my hand *definitely* is better than it was before I took the magesword, so I don't think taking it away is a solution."

"I was not going to suggest taking away the sword, Camilla," said Serrose. The purple mist thickened, obscuring him completely, and when it faded, the female elf was standing before her. "There might be something to your supposition," she continued, "but I still think that if you can stop burning with anger, you will draw a lot less magic. What is more, with all this anger you are feeling, I cannot teach you how to deal with the magic. And I can only teach you so much in the way of techniques. More even than being a barrier to magic, your hatred is the power of the Nightmare within you."

That made Camilla bristle even more. "That can't be! They *deserve* it. Most of all, the Nightmare *deserves* it. I want to make the Nightmare burn!"

"I have fought the Nightmare, and so did Sërien and Gloaming. I have met the one who has power over the Nightmare, and know that only love defeats it. You can*not* fight it with hate. Hate is *its* weapon. So is fear. Your heart must be filled with love, so that nothing else can enter. *Then* you can fight it. *Then* you can fight for what you love. And *deserve* is not a word that will heal Areaer, or anything else."

"Then how else *should* I feel?" asked Camilla. Each word thrummed with her anger.

Both Alian and Serrose looked taken aback, but they responded quickly. "Love, Camilla," said Alian. "Love. You don't need to hate the Nightmare or the Northern Horror. You can simply love what is good. Love Radiance. Love the dragons. Love the world. Love the elves. Love those enslaved by the evil. But if you give way to hate, you will find that you hate those you should be protecting."

Camilla shook her head. "I will never hate Radiance. I could never. I could never hate Lavilor either. But I can*not* love people like Sylvara or some of those elves!"

"Then, that is a victory of the Nightmare," said Alian, stepping closer to her and Radiance.

Serrose stepped forward, too, and placed a hand on his shoulder. "Wait. If she throws a magebolt, it might not be able to kill the Wizard-King, but merely casting it could kill *her.*"

"I think she has more control than that," said Alian.

"Isn't there a way to be angry without gathering magic that I can learn?" asked Camilla.

"Learning that will take longer than it will for you to stop being so angry," said Serrose.

"I *can't* stop being angry, I *can* learn."

"Very well," said Serrose, "but – Camilla? Do you really mean what you say? If you truly love anyone, you must love everyone. Do you really want everlasting destruction for those who have hurt you and others?"

"I don't know. They *deserve* it, and I hate them."

"They deserve to have their souls destroyed? They deserve to be reduced to an agony of torture and despair, never to be cured?" asked Serrose.

"*They* destroyed their own souls," said Camilla. "It takes a destroyed soul to be able to enslave or torture or control people or dragons the way they do."

"Perhaps, but don't you want them to be saved from it? Why should they be evil, when they can be saved? What does *desert* have to do with anything?" asked Serrose.

That's a stupid question, Camilla growled to Radiance. "Do you know what *deserve* means?" she asked the dragonmages. "It means that it is right for them to get it. That they've made it right for them to get it. That they *ought* to."

"It may not be *un*just, Camilla, but it is not justice," said Alian, stepping forward, between her and Serrose. "All that is not justice will degenerate into injustice. Why would you want evil where there can be goodness? Why would you want them to hate, when they could learn to love? Why would you want them to be your enemies and trampled beneath your feet, when they could become your friends and trample with you over the Nightmare – the hatred and fear that *is* the enemy of all?"

"Do you have any idea what you're talking about?" asked Camilla, fire in her eyes. "Have *you* been changed and lost your true nature due to the use of magic? Have *you* been beaten and starved and forced to work so that those who already have more luxury than you could imagine can have still more?"

"This hatred does not make you and Radiance happy," said Alian. He exchanged a brief glance with Serrose, then strode towards the house.

"What is he doing?" asked Camilla. She and Radiance admitted to themselves that their anger was not conducive to enjoying each other, but she would not admit it to these… mageborn creatures, these dragonmages.

"Getting my flute. Well, it used to be Sërien's," said Serrose. "If you won't try to stop being so angry, I'm going to have to teach you something. It would be better if you would draw less magic, since releasing magic will drain energy out of you, but it's better than destroying yourself with all that energy. And you know that music is used for magic, right?"

She nodded. "I do. I've learned everything I could."

A smile graced Serrose's lips at that. "Well, then, I am going to see if you can learn the arrangement to help you focus a dispersion spell. It's part of some very complicated pieces of magic, and I am unhappy teaching it to a novice, but you're going to destroy yourself otherwise."

"All right," said Camilla. "Thank you."

For some reason, it changed her attitude totally to be learning magic.

And if it was such an advanced spell that Serrose was going to teach her, maybe she could figure out other things from it as well.

"I warn you against that," said Serrose. "If you try to experiment in that way, it could destroy you."

"Then how did the first mages discover and learn?"

"From the ground up. Usually not with advanced spells they had not even discovered themselves," said Serrose. "If you had discovered dispersion on your own, I might say otherwise."

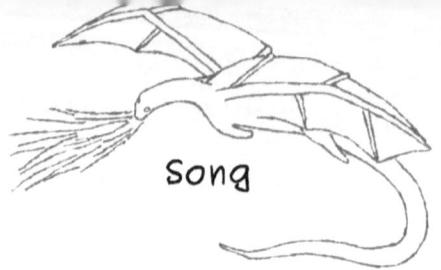

Song

For several hours that evening Serrose taught her notes, and helped her use the notes to focus her magic. Camilla threw herself into it. She realized, now, that the magic *felt* musical, and that it made her feel like music or a musical instrument. Nonetheless, she felt like there was something about what Serrose was teaching her that did not match her.

The next several days passed similarly. She was too frantic and angry about what had befallen all of Ilesh, including the human slaves such as her mother, to want to play very much. She felt sorry for Lavilor, who seemed depressed and withdrawn, but she mostly left it to him and Sleet to comfort each other. Though she played with him a little, her heart was not in it. Every moment, she felt drawn to learn and do what she could so she might be able to defeat the Northern Horror at last, and free those whom she loved from it. She spent most of the day learning, or trying to learn, what magic Serrose was willing to teach her. She bit her tongue down on her desire to experiment and see what she could do. It was something she had been doing all her life. It was probably how she had learned to shadowblend, while hardly knowing what she was doing. Yet she knew that Serrose would teach her far less, and would lecture her constantly, if she expressed her interest in "experimenting" with magic, let alone got caught doing so. Additionally, she could always try out what she felt when she finally left Serrose's tutelage, and so while around the dragonmage, she tried to do nothing to indicate the bent of her mind. She watched and listened most attentively, but gave no indication of the outlandish ideas she even then developed.

Alian sometimes took part in her training, or even tutored her while Serrose did something else. He did not seem as alien to Camilla as Serrose did, even though she had gotten the idea that Serrose's ability with magic was probably closer to Camilla's than Alian's. Alian seemed to understand where she was coming from better, but whether that was because there a human element to the make-up of the dragonmage, or whether it was because – he? she? What? – had been more recently taught magic and never achieved the same facility, Camilla did not know. She also had no idea what Alian thought about her desire to "experiment" or "innovate" or whatever one wished to call it.

One day, she sat next to Serrose, who was in "her" elf form. "Why must we go soon?" she asked. "Why can we not wait here, while you teach me, and go when you and Alian and the egg you are hatching are all ready?"

"For one, because I can only teach you so much. I am not the right teacher for you, but a friend of mine has told me about the Light Elves in the mountains of Aneri, and that they are true masters of magic. I think they will be able to teach you better and more safely than I can. And I thought you are in a hurry to become the best you can and save your mother and the dragons – if they are still alive – as quickly as possible."

"I am," said Camilla, jutting out her chin, "but I know nothing of the world and nations and customs outside Ilesh. I do not know where we will be going. And from what you and Alian have told me, the world outside our refuge here is very dangerous."

"It is dangerous, and will only grow more dangerous the longer you stay here. That is why you *should* go as soon as you are remotely ready. Shortly before you appeared, Alian visited with the Sea Elves, and they are besieged. I think they will hold out for longer than anyone else could, but you must reach them while you still can. As for knowing where you are going, I and Alian will give Radiance and the other dragons the knowledge."

"What will we have to do?"

"That depends on how much I can teach you right now," said Serrose. "It is my and Alian's hope that you will be able to avoid any interaction with the human kingdoms. What little remains free of direct rule by the King of the North is hostile to Dragonriders. You will have to go north, and they are also hostile to southerners. It is better if you can avoid all contact with other humans."

"That suits me fine," said Camilla. Then she asked, "Can you keep Sylvara and Shimmer here when we leave?"

Serrose shook her head. "No. For one thing, while I and Alian can figure out how to cross the ocean ourselves if the Sea Elves abandon their harbor on Ellenesia, Shimmer will not be able to manage such a feat for many years, if ever."

She nodded. Nothing she could say would help. She hated even the thought of traveling with Sylvara. The current situation was just bearable, since she did not see the other woman often. She could not imagine having to travel in her company day after day. Yet she could not convince Serrose, and she doubted she could lose Sylvara and Shimmer herself – if she chose to try. Nor was she even certain what she wanted. As much as she hated Sylvara, as much as she felt that Shimmer had got what he deserved for Recognizing her, she did not really *want* them to be captured and enslaved by the Northern Horror.

Why was *I so maddeningly, irrationally angry before?* Camilla thought. *I'm still angry now. I still don't want to see her. But it wasn't normal the way I felt angry several days ago. It wasn't natural. It's not like I haven't been capable of speaking to both humans and dragons with my mind for months now, and I never lost it before. What went wrong with me?*

Radiance did not have anything to add. *"It went wrong with both of us,"* was all she said. Camilla knew she would *never* admit that to anyone except her rider and neither was Camilla likely to admit her failing to anyone except her.

"Is there anything else you'd like to ask about?" Serrose asked her.

She shook her head. "Not that I can think of right now." *Even now, there's something wrong with me*, she told Radiance. *I ought to enjoy playing with Lavilor and Sleet. I ought to be enjoying the fact that I can, instead of being so driven by anger that all I can think about is learning magic. Instead, I hardly enjoy the few minutes I spend on it.*

"Then let's fix that. I agree with you, there's something wrong. It's right to want to free our friends the way we both do, but we don't have to not enjoy, love, and take care of the friends we still have with you, and Lavilor and Sleet are lonely."

I know. I miss my mother, and Lavilor misses her even more than I do.

"Then I will go now, and take care of the things I have to," said Serrose. "Have a fun evening."

"You as well," said Camilla, absently. She ran her fingers along the flute Serrose let her work with and used to give her the notes for spells. As Serrose left, she raised it to her mouth and blew a slow series of notes. She still struggled with the instrument, but after almost a week of practice with it, as part of her practice with magic, she was rather enjoying it.

Do you know what else the elves stole from us? she realized, as she shifted into the last note. *We never got to make music! That was the elves' prerogative, and I only ever even dared sing when I wasn't being watched. They didn't want to hear* my *singing, even if I had wanted to, while I went about my work –* and we *never got to have festivals and celebrations of our own, not ever, for anything!*

She settled the flute into its case, swung it over her shoulder, and leapt onto Radiance's shoulders. There was no way she was going to let *Sylvara* enjoy her music. Once she had even thought of the fact that Sylvara might hear it, her joy had departed, and she had known she could not play or sing for enjoyment anymore. They had to go somewhere Sylvara would not go.

Radiance carried her between the trees and away from the dragonmages' mansion, following Camilla's instincts, even as the lower rim of the sun kissed the eastern hills. It might have been not yet a full week, but her senses were already so much sharper. She knew, now, the truth of the stories that various different magics guarded the border. She could feel them. Some of them were very deep, and very strange, different from anything else she had ever seen. They were still musical, strains of a deep, hidden, almost forgotten song, but it was unlike any music she had ever heard before. Others resonated on notes similar to those of the elven magic with which she was familiar. She guessed these were the more recent spells, and her head spun to even think about the age of the others, the ancient song. She noticed that every piece of it seemed to be a part of the same song. It was very strange, and very hard for her to concentrate on. Even when she so-to-speak felt or saw it, it was almost slipping away, as if it was something that was nearly outside the ken of her senses. Buried between the patches of the ancient song were pieces of something else.

There was song in it, a song that was not like the notes of elven spellcraft as she knew it, but which she could still mostly reach. Some pieces of it flared when her energies touched them, and she was careful to touch it only very lightly. She began to think of it as some sort of mageshield, though she was fairly certain it was not much like anything she had seen the elves of Ilesh build. It felt wild and dangerous.

She led Radiance through the maze. The ancient song was distracting, and little more, but she could see how it might lead someone into, or keep them trapped within, some of the other pieces of magic. Nonetheless, recognizing it for what it was, it was relatively easy for her to navigate, and she stayed out of places thick with the thrum of magic, sometimes so thick with it that she could not differentiate the pieces of magic or even guess at them.

Finally, Camilla and Radiance felt themselves alone, in a thick patch of forest. She slid down Radiance's leg, and leaned against the dragon for a moment. Radiance clasped her to her with her wing, and then raised it, letting her go.

Camilla stepped away, pulled out her flute, put it to her mouth, closed her eyes, and blew, imagining nothing but the notes, the throb of the music, and something else... a music she had never heard from the flute, but which hummed in her blood. She played an intro, slow, pain-staking, but hauntingly beautiful. She played it several times over, trying out different variations, until it was smooth and, relatively speaking, easy. Beside her, Radiance hummed, and swayed in time to the music, keeping Camilla within that time.

Words came unbidden into their minds as she played, and, unable to see the words and think about the music of the flute, something still difficult for her, she put the instrument down and raised her hand to the horizon, where the last rays of the sun were fading into the night.

> Wind of fire, behind the sun
> Storm of fire, within the sun
> Brighter than fire, and freer than wind
> Fury of light, and fiercer than rage
>
> Inferno, bright and ever-pure
> Inferno, heart within my heart
> Flame in my wings, and wildest wind
> Joy of my heart, and desire undaunted!
>
> Fire births wind, and wind births fire
> Flame is wind, the wind is flame
> Within our hearts, a storm that burns
> A life that burns, and never knows fear!

And as she sang, she felt as if she were on fire – or as if she were the flame. There was no pain in it at all, and it was more like the moments of Recognition than anything else she had experienced. It did not feel as if it was her voice that sang. She wondered if she sang at all. It was as if fire sang within her heart, and she heard the voice of flame itself. Fire was not a destroyer. It was alive in its own right, with such a fury of life that it burned all else to ashes with the strength of its own life, its flame. It killed by being so terrifically alive, a desire of life that withered all else before the purity of its purpose, its delight. It did not kill; it lived. And with that same force and fury of life that burned and killed, it also burned and gave life. And now it felt as if it had been born in her, had been merged with her soul. The unity between herself and Radiance was a flame, and from that unity came Radiance's own kinship with fire, and the inner flame that would be her fire-breath when she was older. A dragon without a rider was a dragon without fire, and thus no dragon at all!

> Flame that burns, and will not die
> Flame that knows only your fire
> Flame of burning, and heart of life
> Bursting anew, ever-fresh fire.
>
> Heart of fire, and heart of life
> Storm of fire, tornado bright
> Raging free, in abandon wild
> Heart of fire – burning, fearless, soaring joy!

She lifted both arms to the horizon, longing for some mode of expression yet denied her. She felt as if she were wreathed in flames, as if she *were* a flame. The air shimmered around her, and it was as if a symphony of flames played in her mind, yearning for some form of yet more earnest expression. Certainly, she could give no form to the music she felt, for it was feeling more than hearing, and yet all aflame.

"We are fire," she and Radiance sang together. She raised the flute again, and flames danced harmlessly along her fingers as she played. Her playing was rough and clumsy, screeching sometimes and petering out, but none of that mattered. All that mattered was the song, the fire, the heart. It burned in her with unbearable ferocity and desire, and she would be consumed by it. Her need to rise on the wind, to be a flame, a tornado of fire, was both pure joy and pain. It was as when they had Recognized. joy and the pain were one. It was not that she could not tell where one ended and the other began. They were simply one, the same. She had found love, and she sought it. The fire had been kindled, and it burned within her breast.

Was this, this ecstasy, this unendurable intensity of purpose and desire, what it meant to be fire?

She had found what she was. She had become what she had meant to be. There was no anger here; there was no room for it. There was only fierce desire, single-minded and undaunted, joy that was somehow far stronger and fiercer than anything she had yet called joy. It burned her from the inside out, hotter than any delight. This was fire; this was love; and every *rightness* she had ever found in anger, she found here. It was as if what she was looking for every time she became angry, or what she was trying to express in every moment of anger, was *here*, in this heart of fire.

No, not every time, she amended her thought. There had been sometimes when there had been something dark and evil in her anger. That darkness, that thing that was definitely *not* fire, had been almost a dominant element in much of the anger she had been experiencing since the night when they fled and the King of the North attacked Ilesh. But this, this was right! This was not anger, it was *fire*. It needed no anger. It was that of which anger was the imitation – mixed with darkness.

The dragonmages had been right. Anger was some small bit of this, mixed with fear.

"Fire that burns, and never knows fear," sang her mind into the wind. In the next moment, she swung herself onto Radiance's shoulder, and the dragon raised her wings. They were almost one. They shared their wings. They beat them together. They sought the sky, ascending as fire. They simply *were*, without thought or fear, without concern for the future or for the past.

Radiance glowed in the night, her scales sparkling.

Then something pulled them out of their fiery ecstasy. *"Come back,"* the dragonmages called to them.

A bolt of darkness came out of the shadows and mists collecting on the ground, and hit Radiance in the wing. She fell, Camilla clutching her neck, both of them nearly unconscious.

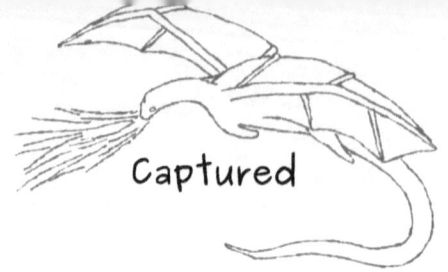

Captured

She found herself lying on a cold stone floor. Chains around her hands and feet secured her to the wall. She was sore and stiff all over, but even so she would not have been able to move much. She reached out to Radiance, and found the dragon just waking as they touched minds. Radiance was even more bruised than Camilla, and all four of her legs, her wings, and her tail were chained to a castle wall. In a large ring around her were arranged a number of guards. It was about mid-morning.

"It's probably our fault for going off... How could we have known?... I shouldn't have to stay somewhere and not be able to leave and do my own thing, just like a slave!" The last thought was definitely Camilla's, but she could not tell whether the others were more hers or more Radiance's.

All the heat seemed to be leeched out of her. She was so sore she could barely move, even if she had not been chained. Radiance was even worse. She did not see what they could possibly do.

But if I can't get myself out of something like this, how can I ever hope to fight and defeat the Wizard-King? Her mind went back to the moment of their capture. That had been magic. What if it *was* the Wizard-King who had captured her and Radiance?

She gritted her teeth, unwilling to give into defeat, though she could not imagine how she would fight. She did not know why, but she did not feel the energy underneath her skin, the sense that all she had to do was really *want* to, and she could send bolts of energy flying where she chose. Now, it was gone. She tried to call up the notes, as Serrose had taught her, but it was as if they were not there. She could not find the ones she needed, or there was nothing there, no energy, or something else, but there was something wrong.

It has to be the magesword, she thought. *It has to be that the magesword helps me gather magic or draw energy or whatever. Oh no! They took the magesword, and I need it, and how will I get another, even if I can escape?*

Lavilor. Sleet, Camilla called.

Instantly, both boy and dragon acknowledged her.

I'm awake now. Radiance, too, kind of. Can you tell where I am?

"Sort of," came Lavilor's reluctant reply. A moment later, Sleet said, *"Yes."*

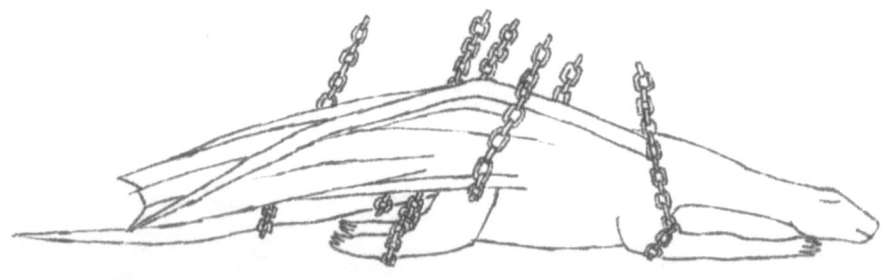

Tell the dragonmages… Serrose and Alian. I don't know what they can do, but…

"*I have,*" said Sleet. "*We were all worried about you.*" Now it was Lavilor's mind-tone that was dominant. "*They wanted to rescue you.*" That was Sleet again. "*But they couldn't find you.*" Lavilor. "*When you're unconscious, I can tell you're alive, but I can't follow.*" That was definitely Sleet. "*Neither can they.*" That was Lavilor again.

Thank you, said Camilla. *I'm sorry. I didn't want to scare or worry you.* She was somewhat scared and worried herself. Or would be. Or ought to be. She could not figure out why she felt the way she did. *I don't want anyone to get hurt… but I would like to be rescued.*

The response she felt from Lavilor was so much like a hug that she almost expected to feel his arms around her neck and to see his form in the darkness of the cell with her.

Why do I feel so defeated? she wondered. *I haven't ever felt this defeated.* Upon a second reflection, she was not altogether certain that was true. There had been times when the elves had punished her – as often as not because Sylvara had either snitched or made up complete lies – when she had been so tired, but she did not think it had ever felt like this. It was as if an energy that she had always been able to reach was gone. The fire that she had always felt within her, at least enough to know it was there, *somewhere*, even when she was too tired to look for it, was now replaced with emptiness.

Radiance? she asked.

The dragon was in a malaise of pain and weariness. She responded with no more than an answering groan.

I love you.

"*I love you,*" Radiance replied. "*Nothing else matters.*"

Wake up! Please! She was nearing panic. *Don't die! You had better not die! You can't die! There's so much we… have to live, first!* Radiance could not die, could she? She could not have been so hurt from her fall from the sky, and whatever that bolt of magic had done to her, that she was going to die now, or could she have been? Not that such a fall could not have been expected to have killed them both already…

No! I've hardly lived! I've hardly been a rider yet. NO! Radiance, she extended her thoughts again, *you are not going to die.*

This time, the only impression Camilla got from her dragon was one of pain and drowsiness. *NO!* she screamed to herself.

"*Calm down, Camilla. Serrose and Alian are coming. They will do everything they can to save you and Radiance, but everyone within several miles just heard that.*" It was Sleet's voice.

I couldn't care less They trapped both of us. Radiance is dying because of them! Why shouldn't they hear it?

"*Listen to them, dragon woman. Many of them did not do it. Some of them don't know! Others see Radiance, as they go about their daily lives, but what do you expect them to do? Listen to them, before you yell your grief and agony at them."*

Camilla growled low in her throat. She was caged in darkness, unable to move, and her dragon was dying, and Sleet was telling her not to scream her agony because everyone around would hear it! He was always a voice of calm and sympathy, but right now Camilla did not feel sympathetic, and she felt even less calm. If nothing else, they should *know* what their rulers did! They should fight back! They should not just go along with evil and be complicit!

Her head pounded. *All right,* she growled at Sleet. She extended her mind, touching Radiance briefly, then working outwards. She could not have done this if she had not had such a deep connection with her dragon that Radiance's senses were *almost* her own. She found the soldiers who guarded the dragon, and she hurled all her rage and anger and grief—

"No!" said Sleet. *"Serrose and Alian say no. You might make yourselves harder to rescue."*

It's too late, she replied. Yet even as she thrust her agony at her and Radiance's entrapment and impending deaths at the soldiers, she struggled with the strange malaise. If only she could sleep... if only she could rest... if only they could find a nice, soft patch of earth and leaves, and she could curl up under Radiance's wing and they could sleep together. *Why can't I find the fire?*

Sleet spoke, comfortingly and reassuringly, into her mind again. *"We're coming,"* he said. *"Serrose and Alian are coming. We should be there in another hour. You and Radiance just need to hold on that long... Lavilor says to tell you he loves you."*

I love you, too, she said to Lavilor. She spoke to Radiance again, though she did not know how well the dragon heard her. *I love you, Radiance. Just a little longer.* To herself, she thought, *Even though an hour is a frighteningly long time right now.*

I wish I could move. I wish I could sit up. But I can't. Maybe I can, but I don't know if I've broken something, and these chains are going to make it really hard. Is this how they always chain prisoners up? It seems rather unnecessary.

She could not believe her friends were telling her not to use her power. Maybe, if she spoke to someone she could convince him or her to help her!

"That's not what you were doing, earlier. You were yelling your pain at everyone, not looking for help," said Sleet. *"That's what we asked you not to do."* Apparently, he was still watching her mind, even when he was silent for a long time.

It's not like I was going to let you, or those dragonmages, tell me what to do, anyway, she retorted. Even in her present malaise, she was not going to let anyone tell her what to do. She had had enough of that from the elves, and was never going to accept it again. Reasons, she would listen to. A request, she might consider. But she would never be *told* what to do. She would never *obey*.

Why do I still feel this so strongly, but I can't find the fire? she wondered, then reached out again. She touched first the minds of the guards watching Radiance. They were mostly angry. They did not know why they had felt such a sudden blast of misery and grief, as if their lives were ending and they were trapped. Some of them assumed it was the dragon's fault, and were staring at her, half-concerned that she would break her bindings and kill them, and half-contemplating tormenting her with their weapons in revenge.

Oh no! What did I do?! To Sleet, she said, *Please ask Alian and Serrose to hurry as much as they can? I'm afraid they're going to kill Radiance.*

Mercifully, he did not remind her that if she had listened and thought, there might not be so much danger. Instead, he said simply, *"We're coming as fast as we can."*

What can *I do, that won't cause problems?* she complained to herself. She kept in touch with the minds of the guards, even though their thoughts sickened and scared her. *If you touch the dragon,* she told them, *she might eat you. If you wound her, fire will flow out and devour you.* She hoped that would be enough to dissuade them, at least long enough for their rescuers to arrive. There was not much she could do with her mental speech. She could suggest things to them. She could try to confuse them. She could hope they would not know what was going on. But she could not *do* anything to them, or *force* them to do anything. And who would be willing to help her?

Maybe I can confuse them, make it hard for them to fight, when Alian and Serrose come. I'll have to know what they plan. Radiance, stay with me.

"I'm here, Camilla," the dragon responded in her faltering voice. It was still a voice of fire, but it was sizzling and snapping, like a dying fire.

I'll give you everything I have, she replied, opening herself to Radiance as much as possible, hoping to sustain her with her own energy.

She did not feel the passage of time.

"Camilla." This time it was Serrose's voice that sounded in her mind.

Yes? she asked drowsily. It was so hard to stir.

"We are almost here. Alian is going to get you, while I get Radiance, so we can do this and fly away as quickly as possible. Will you be able to ride Alian?"

Camilla hated it. Radiance hated it. It upset them both that Camilla would have to ride someone other than her own dragon. *Yes, I can do it if I must,* she said. *It won't be especially hard?*

"If you can get the saddle Alian will bring on her quickly, you can ride like that. But it must be quickly," replied Serrose. *"See what you can do to distract the guards for me. I will tell you when."*

All right. Radiance, I love you. The opposition to her riding someone other than Radiance ran deep in both of them. She hoped she would have the energy and strength to put on the saddle. It would be precarious for her to try to ride someone with whom she was not mind-bonded without a saddle, when she was this tired and stiff.

The moments passed with almost sickening slowness. She did not pull away from Radiance. She wondered if the dragon could even fly, as wounded and injured as she was. Besides, the union they shared now would help them both to endure the fact that Camilla was about to ride someone else.

"Now," said Serrose.

Camilla shifted, and gasped with pain. She reached out, and felt Serrose descending. The guards did not know this, but the slight shimmer around his scales told Camilla that the dragonmage was getting ready to shift forms. She tried to collect herself, to summon energy, since she did not know what to do. She had never done anything like this before. *The wall!* she whispered into their minds. *Was that crack there before? I don't think so. The wall is cracking! It's going to fall on you!* She hoped the distraction would be enough. She had no idea what Serrose planned or could do. *It's going to knock you off your feet! You can't fight! It's going to take everything you've got just to not fall over!*

At that moment, as Serrose snapped open his wings, and then transformed in a haze of purple, Camilla heard the door to her dungeon open. Alian stepped in, holding a flame between his fingers. He flashed a brief smile at her, then applied the flame to the chains on her hands until they split apart in a splatter of glowing shards. She jerked her hands away, trying not to be burnt.

"Hold still," Alian said. "I know how to do this so it won't burn you. But hold still." He then did the same with the chains on her feet.

She rose, half-exuberant at finally being able to move, half-cautious because she was injured and stiff. Her muscles cried out in pain, and pain flowed in lines through her bones.

"A moment," said Alian, as she moved towards the door. "I'm not as good at this as Serrose, but I may be able to help." He held out his hands and touched her body. She felt the thrum of energy, heard the notes of his magic. Her muscles loosened a little.

"All right. That's all I can do for now. Come with me," he said.

She followed him, limping out into the corridor. A sense of wellness washed over her, as Serrose tended to Radiance. They passed cell after cell and corridor after corridor, all unguarded, until they came into a courtyard, even as Camilla felt Radiance take to the air, struggling to fly, one wing throbbing and burning with pain. There was only so much Serrose could heal in a few minutes, but at least Radiance was *able* to fly.

"Quickly, now," said Alian. "I scared them coming in, but they may be coming any moment." He dropped the saddle he had been carrying on his back at Camilla's feet, then ran away from her, and transformed into the female dragon form.

Her fingers fumbled, and her muscles groaning, she struggled to get the saddle onto Alian. They were just in time. Just as she was seated, and Alian raised her wings, a host of guards could be heard running down a nearby corridor. They were still within range of arrows when the guards poured into the courtyard, quickly, gracefully readying their weapons.

"How much has Serrose taught you?" Alian gasped out as she flew.

"Not enough, and I can't find *any* magic right now," answered Camilla.

Alian did not respond. Instead, the dragonmage beat her wings in a furious flourish, then twisted, and painted the air around her with a long blast of fire. The first flight of arrows was caught and incinerated in the blazing fire. A moment later, Alian twisted, changing direction rapidly.

I am glad I am riding in the saddle for this! She did not think she could ride Radiance through these maneuvers. *Then again, if we hadn't stopped to saddle Alian, we might not be having to dodge arrows.* Her stomach rolled, and all her muscles groaned, as she stayed low to Alian's neck, and grasped the saddle straps with her hands. Her head hurt, as if something inside it was being tossed around.

And why can't I get to the magic now? she wondered. *What is wrong with me? And it seems so wrong to be riding this... being. I'd much rather be riding Radiance! Something is really wrong!*

What about my sword? Is it lost forever?

"*No.*" It was Sleet speaking to her again. "*Alian and Serrose got it. I don't know how, but I have it.*"

Good, Camilla replied, as a feeling of relief washed over her.

She could feel Radiance struggling to keep aloft more and more with each breath and wing-beat. If it had taken Sleet, Alian, and Serrose over an hour to reach her – and it had; they had flown in the general direction that she and Radiance had been taken even before she woke – then Radiance would never be able to manage the flight back in her current state. And that raised another question. *How did they* move *her so far so quickly? It must have been with some sort of magic I don't know about. She might be hardly more than a hatchling, but she's large and heavy already!*

Camilla shoved these thoughts out of her mind, trying to give all her attention to the immediate task of helping Radiance land. After Radiance, Serrose landed – once again, shifting forms on touch-down. She helped Radiance further out of the clearing, for Alian to land, since she could not transform safely while carrying a human. Camilla got out of the saddle as quickly as she could, stiff and sore as she was. She stumbled towards Radiance, as Alian transformed and stepped out of the way for Sleet, carrying Lavilor, to land.

She collapsed next to Radiance. Her beloved dragon was bruised and sore from snout to tail, from wing-tip to wing-tip. Her wings burned and ached. Some of her scales were mangled. Something like rage flowed through Camilla. *How could anyone have done this? Who would ever do such a thing?* her mind asked her. She loved Radiance so much!

She looked up to see Serrose standing over her. "Do you think you can help me?" she asked.

"Heal her?" asked Camilla. Serrose nodded ever so slightly, and Camilla continued. "No. I can't… feel any magic at all. It's like it's all gone. Even when I look for it, try the notes, there's nothing there! I think I need the magesword to gather any more magic than I need for shadow-blending – but I doubt I could even do that right now."

Serrose called over her shoulder. "Alian. Can you bring the magesword?"

"Getting it," he replied.

Serrose turned back towards Camilla. "That's undoubtedly a component. The mageswords *do* make sensing and directing magic easier. But that can't be all of it. It takes a substantial amount of energy to burn your hand as you were doing, and you told me the magesword made *that* better, so you were gathering a lot of magic without the magesword." She paused, as if to consider something, and Camilla leapt in.

"So, is there something I can help with without magic? Shouldn't we be working on that?"

Serrose shook her head gently. "There's not much more I can do for Radiance on my own right now. She is on her way to recovery, and as long as she doesn't do something violent to herself, a few minutes resting will do her no harm at all. But we need to figure out your magic."

Camilla stood straight and still, and said nothing. She did not know what to say. On the one hand, her whole body burned with the desire to relieve Radiance, and she felt the dragon's pain as her own. On the other hand, she knew she needed her magic if she was going to have a chance to do anything of the things she wanted to do. She wanted to know what was wrong with her magic – if it was something wrong – and what to do about it. And, then, she thought that they needed to get away from here as fast as possible. They were not far at all from where they had been captured. It would be easy for that dark mage to come after them here, maybe with several companies of soldiers, maybe with more dark mages.

For several long moments, Serrose simply examined her. Camilla was almost certain she was looking for something magical, but she could not tell what or how. Finally, she said, "Don't we need to get as far away as possible as quickly as possible?"

"Generally speaking, yes," said Serrose, almost absent-mindedly, while Alian approached, carrying the magesword. "Take it," she said to Camilla.

She reached out and took the sword – sheath, sword-belt, and all. She buckled it around her waist, and drew the sword. Ephemeral golden-green flames rose from it, sheathing the blade in a soft, ethereal light. It hummed in her hand, gently vibrating with a rhythm that wasn't quite her own, and sang to her as magic did.

"Ahh," said Serrose.

"What?" asked Camilla, her eyes snapping up from the sword.

"You burned off all the excess magic energy you had been accumulating with that song you sang last night," explained Serrose. "You had been so used to having enough magic in you it was almost ready to burn through you, and you have so little training, so you don't know how to reach for magic or build it on your own. There's nothing wrong. You did not even take any damage from the dark magic that captured you and Radiance – though you may be so depleted partially from a clumsy, instinctive attempt to block."

All of this sounded academic to Camilla, though she forced herself to realize that it probably was not. Knowing these things *could* potentially help her. Nonetheless, listening to these explanations aggravated her. She wanted instant solutions and, if not solutions, then at least something she could start doing right now to rectify the situation, or learn whatever it was she needed to learn, or *something!* She did not want to stand around, listening to speculations about why and how. When Serrose stopped speaking, she set her voice, trying to keep her aggravation from coming out – she knew how the dragonmage reacted to it, especially when it had to do with her desire to learn or attempt magic – and asked, as nicely as she could, "Can you teach me how to reach and build energy? – But first, can we figure how to get somewhere safer than this?"

"What do you think, Alian?" asked Serrose, turning to the other dragonmage. "I can't heal Radiance any more right now, and she can't fly any farther the way she is. Is there something we could do to get her away ourselves?"

"She would be heavy," said Alian, "but I think we could fly a fair distance even with the extra weight, but I don't know how we would carry her – or how she would be comfortable."

Ah, thought Camilla. "She certainly can't *ride*, but, how well can either of you *carry* something?"

"What are you thinking?" asked Alian. Camilla liked him the better of the two.

"Well, *if* you can carry something in your talons, and you have cloth and ropes that won't pull through under the stress of her weight, could we create a kind of flying litter?"

Yes, I know, Radiance, Camilla responded to the sluggish stirrings of her dragon's mind. *It's quite undignified, but it* would *be funny, and you want to get away from here as much as I do, and I think it would be fairly comfortable.*

Radiance granted that.

Called

Kario Flameheart watched with attentive eyes as the Lorekeeper carefully threaded a magically strengthened chain of silver through a magically bored hole in the lightstone she had chosen, so that she would be able to wear it around her neck and never worry about losing it.

"Thank you so much," she said, during a pause in his work.

"It's nothing to me," said the elf, whose name was Eversong – Azayr-ren in his language. "We would do this more often for the Sha'adhri, if they weren't such arrogant creatures, thinking that we owe them for letting us live in their *Passage.* As if we were not given sanction to dwell here by the Guardian himself."

"Are they *all* that bad?" asked Flameheart. She had seen a fair amount of petty arrogance from them, and knew that many looked down on her and did not consider her a true Dragonrider because she had never raised a hatchling. She also knew that Nelexi had one or two friends and, besides, had not been around for a long time. Weren't some of the Sha'adhri fairly reasonable?

"Not even," said Azayr-ren. "But most of them pay no notice to us, ignore us, and if they do meet us are condescending, sometimes going so far as to imply that they permit us to inhabit the Caves of Light only because we make traversing the Caves easier for *them.* I daresay there are one or two other Dragonriders around right now with such a gift from us. But it's not as if many choose to stay with us longer than they must, and Nelexi is an old friend of ours." That said, he turned back to his work with the chain and stone. Flameheart sat perched on her boulder and watched with quiet attention.

When he had finished, she said, "I'd like to be able to do that."

"The threading?" asked Azayr-ren, holding the stone up. "Anyone with quiet, steady hands and the inclination to take the time can learn. I'd be happy to start you off."

"That would be pleasing." Her eyes drank in the lightstone. It was a rather unique specimen – deep brilliant red, like Nelexi's wings, but with a faint overlaying spiderweb pattern in white.

"I take it that wasn't all you were asking about though?" asked Azayr-ren.

Flameheart took the lightstone, and held it in her palm, the silver chain lying around it and glittering with an amazing variety of reflected light. "I don't know," she said, "but that *would* be pleasing."

"Then I shall teach you, but I don't think I can teach you the other arts. Almost all Light Elves have some capacity, though some of them never train it, but I've met very few humans with any appreciable ability, and I don't think you are one of them."

Flameheart laughed. "I don't need to be, do I? No one can do everything. And I've already helped to stop a war that's been going on for many generations of my people."

"No, you don't need to be," said Azayr-ren, "and, contrary to the expectations of most humans, it's not any more possible for us to do everything, than it is for them. All the centuries of our lives, I think, serve only to teach us that better. The longer I live, the more I learn that, no matter how long I lived, there would always be things I could never learn, never do, never be, and that I have to choose sometimes between one thing and another."

Flameheart nodded. Then she said, "I've never really chosen anything. Well, I suppose if deciding to look for *scarva* grasses when I was asked to catch lizards counts, but that's about all the kinds of choices I've made. I didn't even choose Nelexi, though I'm sure glad she chose me. Nor did I exactly *choose* to be part of stopping the war. I just… was there, and what better was I to do?"

"Of such are choices made," said Azayr-ren. "But I think you feel more than just gladness that you were chosen by Nelexi."

She nodded, knowing what he asked, even though his words could have been interpreted in any of a number of ways. "I suppose. I'm glad to be with Nelexi, but I miss my family, and I can never go back. Well, I could, if Nelexi would take me, but they wouldn't like it. They don't want to share their plains with dragons or Dragonriders."

"And you feel lonely and useless," observed the Lorekeeper.

"I do. Sort of. Not wholly. Nelexi loves me, and she's with me all the time. But I do miss my people. I miss Dad's stories. I miss being hugged by Mom. I miss playing with the other children." Her voice broke as she continued. "And, aside from helping to start the peace negotiations with the Sea Elves, I don't see what I'm really good for. I believe Nelexi, that she chose me for a reason, and because she loves me, but I really don't see how I can be much help to her. Not in this war against the Old Gods. What can I do? It's not like I'm even a warrior among men. She doesn't need me."

"She does, I think. I don't understand it, but it seems that dragons, even the Obsidian Guardian, need riders. But what are these Old Gods?"

"Nelexi sometimes calls them the Nightmare."

"Oh," said Azayr-ren. He sounded like he was about to say something else, when Flameheart almost stopped breathing, her mouth agape. *"We need to go as quickly as reasonably possible,"* said Nelexi. *"I have been called."*

Where? asked Kario, mentally. *Why?*

At the same time, Azayr-ren replied out loud. "What would you like from us? You've always been a friend to us, so we will help you as we can."

"Provisions for my rider," said Nelexi. *"I do not want to stop to buy food if I can help it. I have a feeling this is urgent. Flameheart, I know not where – only that it lies to the west, across the sea. I know not why either, except that it is part of the war against the Nightmare. We will find out why*

soon enough."

"I will get those who would know what they are doing working on that," said Azayr-ren. "Would you also like coins in case you must stop and buy provisions on your way?"

"Tell him we would much appreciate that," said Nelexi.

Flameheart wondered at the dragon's sudden shift from speaking directly to Azayr-ren to asking her to speak for her. "Nelexi says we would much appreciate that," she said. "I don't know enough about where we were going and what things are like to know for myself," she added.

"Of course," said the Lorekeeper. He departed with a brisk step.

She gazed for a moment longer on her new lightstone necklace. Then she hung it about her neck. It felt very light indeed. She wondered if that was due to magic, or if it really was that light. When she had picked the stone out, Azayr-ren had told her, "It is a very good stone for the Partner of the Obsidian Guardian, especially since you are one of those very rare riders who ride only the Obsidian Guardian. Usually, a Light Elf chooses his or her stone as she is discovering her magical affinity, so she can choose a stone which will work well with and augment her magic for the rest of her life. Oftentimes, there is a correlation between the appearances of stones and the mages they augment. I don't know if this stone will have any effects for you, other than lighting your way in the dark, but it certainly looks appropriate." It did, at that, and she wondered if he might have done far more to it in the way of magic than he had let her know.

And it really is appropriate, she thought, getting to her feet. *It looks like a heart of fire.* She started down one of the tunnels, hoping it was the one

that would lead outside, and knowing that if it was not she would meet an elf along the passageway who could tell her where it led and how to get where she did want to go, sooner or later.

"Show it to me, soon," said Nelexi. *"I think I will like it."*

I think you will like it, too.

It was not very long before she found that elf who could tell her where she was, and it turned out to be Azayr-ren. "Flameheart!" he said, kindly. "I didn't mean to leave you there. I still had something to show you. I was coming right back as soon as I got other things happening."

"What is it?" she asked, suddenly all curiosity.

"I can show you right here. Let's just go to the side, so if anyone comes along we're not in the middle of the way. All right now. Surely you have thought that there are times when you want your light somewhere other than just a few inches below your throat?"

She nodded vigorously.

"So, if you will take the chain off your neck, I will show you something."

Flameheart obliged.

Azayr-ren took it from her, and then showed her how to wind it neatly around her wrist, so she could carry it in her palm, between her fingers, or let it dangle, to provide light somewhere she might need if she were ever working on something in the dark. "It's a good color, too, for someone who's not a mage and able to augment its light into something really brilliant," he observed. "It won't disturb your night-vision much. Do you think you could do that again?"

Flameheart nodded vigorously again. "Shall I try to see if I have it right?" she asked.

"Yes. That's a good idea," said Azayr-ren.

Flameheart smiled to herself, wishing she and Nelexi did not have to go so soon. They had only been here for a few days. She unwound the chain and then proceeded to re-wind it.

"Very nice," said Azayr-ren. "Not quite as perfect and neat as mine, but you did it basically right. You'll get the hang of it soon enough."

She almost glowed with pleasure. Simultaneously, tears pressed at the backs of her eyeballs as she remembered her family. She felt Nelexi touch her then, comfortingly, reassuringly, but without saying anything. Flameheart leaned into the mental caress.

"I'm sorry I won't be able to show you a lot of other things, some of which you asked about, and talk with you more, Flameheart," said Azayr-ren. "Maybe, if you come back another time, we can do those things."

"I would like that," said Flameheart, bobbing her head again. At the same time, she wondered if that would ever come true. Wandering the Plains of Zharda had been one thing. Wandering a world that, as peaceful as it seemed at times, was yet in the throes of the war between the Powers of Light and the Old Gods, and that as the Partner of the Obsidian Guardian, something of a god herself, was something else entirely.

"I think we have some time before everything is ready for you and Nelexi," said the elf. "Is there something you'd like to do in the meantime?"

"Do you have any suggestions?"

Azayr-ren shook his head. "Not really. I don't have things ready to teach you how to thread chains right now, otherwise I'd think we could just do that, since you were so obviously interested. Barring that, I suppose I could show you my magestaff, and tell you about the quest I went on and what I did to make it."

"Yes, thank you, that sounds fun!"

Flameheart was certain that she would never be able to get used to the Steep Descent. It just should not be possible for ground to be so nearly vertical – and it *was* nearly vertical. There were flat, or gently sloping terraces, sometimes with hills, to be sure, but the cliffs separating them were almost completely vertical, and they were *tall!* Ground just should not – could not – be that shape. Who would want it to be, anyway? It eclipsed the sky, eclipsed the rising and setting of the sun, and cast its shadow over the whole land. Who would want to live on such a thing? Her heart yearned for her plains.

"*Dragons like it,*" Nelexi told her, as she leveled out and caught an updraft. "*Especially big ones, like me. It's much easier to take off from a cliff, or even a steep hill, than from the plains. Of course, we can all do it. It would not do to end up in a battle, and not be able to get off the ground! But if we were not so pressed for time right now, I would show you the Plains of Arosië. I think you would like them well enough. They would not be like the plains of your home, for the sun is not so bright and harsh here as it is there, even beyond the shadow of the mountains, but I think you would find them somewhat pleasing. At least, they are mostly flat and open.*"

Probably I would, but they might make me so homesick, too. I long so much for my family and my home. There was a long pause between them, as Nelexi climbed higher into the sky. *If we're going to fight the Old Gods... what am I going to do? Aren't I just a liability?*

"*You are my Rider-Partner, Flameheart. I myself do not know for what we are needed right now, but I chose you because it was right to do so. I have told you that the power of the Old Gods is fear and hatred. I chose you for love, and you love me. That is enough. You do not need to fit the mold of the Obsidian Rider, the Dragon-Warrior. It is for some, and not for others, and if it was what was needed now – you and I would not have been made for each other. Be yourself, Flameheart, and do not worry about fighting the Nightmare.*"

I know, but I feel... lonely and useless. And terrified. The Old Gods are terrible, horrible. I'm afraid of them. I don't see how I can be part of the War of the Gods. A strange smile touched her face. *Even if I have been chosen by a god herself.*

She could tell that Nelexi laughed at that, too.

And I know this is stupid worrying, Nelexi. You told me that, and I've not forgotten it. You've told me, time and again, that enjoying the sunshine, riding you, chatting with elves, learning how to swim, choosing a lightstone, and admiring mountains even if I can never love them the way I love the Plains of Zharda, and the way those who are born to them love them, is how we fight the Nightmare. I remember that the Old Gods fight against joy and light, and that to fight them is not to fear or worry, even about them, but to enjoy what we have. I understand this, and it even makes sense, but I feel so lonely and vulnerable and homesick. And now that we're about to engage, afraid.

"The engagement may not be what you imagine. And, even if it is, you will not be asked to do what the Ellenari can do, or what other great powers can do. You are not asked to ride the storm, to command the lightning, or to bear the Dragon-sword. You are asked only to be yourself, and my Partner, and that is something no one else can do. And I love you, Flameheart, Kario."

"I know, Nelexi. I love you, too," said Flameheart. She gathered the cloak she wore tighter around her body, as the cold airs of these altitudes chilled her. Flying *would* be more enjoyable, for longer periods of time, with the gifts the Light Elves had given them. She was sure there was something slightly magical about the cloak. It had no outside or inside; both sides were designed to be worn as either. One was a shade of brown that would not stand out too much in most environments – except for a flashy Sea Elf city, she thought. The other was a brilliant red that matched Nelexi's stripe and wings perfectly. It was this side that she currently had out, and she liked it. *Flameheart,* she thought. *Heart-of-Spring-and-Flame indeed.* What really convinced her that the cloak was enchanted, though, was that it was doing a better job of keeping her warm than she would have expected, given the light material. The wind *should* have gone straight through it, but it did not. She pulled the hood over her head, to keep her cheeks warmer. She let it fall all the way over her face to protect her from the windburn she had experienced several times flying, and marveled at it. It only barely tinged her vision red, but it definitely softened the wind's bite.

Why don't all the Sha'adhri make friends with the Light Elves and get these gifts from them? They're wonderful, and much superior to the heavy fur capes the other Dragonriders use, Flameheart commented to Nelexi.

"For one thing, you've gathered that this cloak is magical. The Light Elves wouldn't make one for just anyone who asked. I don't know much about elf magic, but it takes a lot of time and energy to make such a cloak. They worked on it the whole time we were here, and only had it ready this morning. As for why they did that for us – for one, I think they like you. For another, I have always cultivated a good relationship with them. There are things I've done for them, and I've certainly always been respectful to them, and they respect me – I am, after all, the Obsidian Guardian. So, they will do things like this for me and my riders. I should warn you though, that it is not a combat cloak. It won't do anything to stop a sword or an arrow, and it will be damaged by one. That makes it slightly less useful, depending on what you're doing, since those heavy leather furred cloaks provide a little protection, as well as being much easier to replace."

I wouldn't ask this to stop a sword or arrow, said Flameheart. *Why should I think that because it holds off cold it would do that?*

"I forget, sometimes, just how different your background is, even though I watched you for most of your life," answered the dragon. "Humans often have strange ideas about magic and don't know what to expect with it, unless they're very close to a wizard or mage, and one thing I never paid attention to was how you felt about magic. Though I should have guessed."

I don't have any feelings about magic. My people don't know about it at all. The powers of the gods and the gifts they bestow are no mortal magic that anyone can learn. Other than that, all I know is a little about the Sea Elves.

"Yes, and I should have known you would know that, but some people don't very well." Nelexi directed her attention to the snow-covered peaks that towered high above them. "I think there are places in Galen that are also marked by the power of the Ellenari, but I know less of them, but you were right when you recognized that ground does not become so vertical on its own. These are the Greater Aravin Mountains and in their heights, higher than even dragons can breathe without the power of the Ellenari, are the sanctuaries of the Ellenari upon Areaer. It is because of those sanctuaries and the powers of those who dwell within them, after a fashion, that these mountains rise to touch the skies, and remain stable even when the surface of the world is changed."

They are beautiful in a way, though I could never love them as I love the plains. Yet I think I see why you love them. She was quiet for a few moments, then said, *It is very nice that you took me to visit the Light Elves before this... call happened.*

"You are welcome. Such things do not always happen, and cannot be counted upon, but they are common in the life of an Obsidian Guardian, especially one as old as I. Yet it is not quite as favorable as you might imagine. I am called across the western sea, and from here we must fly over most of Aneri to even get to the shore. Only Ellen Island is much farther from where we need to go!"

Looking out over the plains, Flameheart remarked, *Isn't it strange that among my people we think of the south as the place of ice and the north as the place of fire, but here, in the north, that's backwards?*

She felt Nelexi chuckle underneath her. "I guess, but your people aren't all wrong. Ellen Island is *the Volcano of the Guardian of the Fire of Areaer.*"

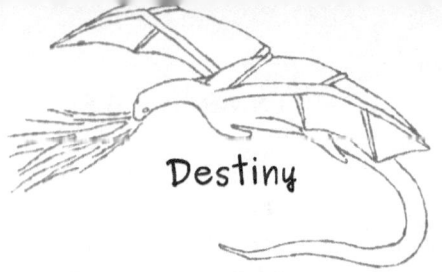

Destiny

They found places to land, so the dragonmages could trade which one was carrying Camilla and which was carrying Radiance's stretcher. Radiance – and, therefore, Camilla – was galled at her need to be carried, her inability to fly! Camilla was also upset that Sylvara and Shimmer were with them again. She had to admit that Sylvara and Shimmer had helped – that, without her, they would never have been able to do what they did. At the same time, it was more than probable that, if not for Sylvara's presence, Camilla and Radiance would never have wandered off and fallen into trouble, so that counterbalanced any softening of her feelings toward Sylvara that might have been occasioned by her usefulness. But more important than all these irritants was the fact that they were flying in the *wrong* direction – not towards, but away, from the sanctuary on the borders of Ilesh.

This time, when they landed, Camilla swung herself down from Serrose, and stepped between the two dragonmages who were about to transfer Radiance's litter. "Where are we going?" she asked. "Why are we flying away from your sanctuary?"

Serrose's voice rumbled as he replied. "If we take you back in that direction, then they will set up a guard around the place, and it will be impossible for you to leave when you are ready. We must take you outside their territory, where they will not look for you, before that happens, and we must do so as quickly as possible, so that at least one of us is back with our eggs, in case the protections around our sanctuary are breached or somehow navigated – or the eggs hatch early. It will be bad if both parents are not present. It will be a disaster if neither parent is present."

Camilla did not argue with her. For all her desire to be competent and knowledgeable, she knew very little about most things. She did not know anything about evil magic and the tactics evil mages and servants of the Northern Horror were likely to employ. She certainly did not know what the needs of new-hatched dragonmages might be. "So, where are we going?" she prompted.

"That's something I and Alian are still discussing," said Serrose. "We're thinking of leaving you on one of the Guardian Isles. You should be fairly safe there, until Radiance is healed and the dragons are grown enough to carry you comfortably. The problem is, getting there will take longer than we're comfortable leaving the eggs for." He stopped speaking again, and Camilla sensed that he was not going to speak anymore. There was a strange feel around him, as if he were doing something magical – or musical – that she did not understand. She turned and left, feeling very much like getting angry.

In a few more minutes, Serrose called Camilla, and they were all in the sky again.

They landed to trade who carried Radiance several more times before nightfall, when they stopped to rest. Camilla strode over to where Alian collected deadfall to make a fire. Serrose had already flown off, and she was happy with that. Despite the fact that Serrose was her teacher, she did not like the dragonmage – perhaps, mostly because of her elven aspect. Either way, she did not like Serrose and preferred to talk to Alian.

Alian looked up at her and greeted her warmly.

She returned the greeting and launched into her question. "How far are we going? I heard from Serrose that you are planning on leaving us, but I don't have any survival skills. Those are the last things the elves were going to teach us, even below magic," she asked, as she stepped in to work beside Alian. Her body, sore from the riding and from the abuse she had taken, protested.

Alian chuckled. "I have no doubt of that, but between the dragons and the little magic you can control, you'll do fine once I and Serrose explain what to do and how. We are going with you one more day, since Radiance needs some more time, even with our best magic, before she's healed enough to fly on her own without risking further damage. After that, I will go with you to the Guardian Isles, but Serrose will return to our sanctuary, since she has the stronger magic and a better chance of being able to hide or defend our eggs if anything attacks the sanctuary. Once I'm confident that you can take of yourselves, I will fly back to the sanctuary."

"Oh." Her mind went at once to the things she would do to Sylvara. It would not be anything truly cruel, but for once Sylvara would get a glimpse of what she had done to others all her life. *What a brat that girl is. She hasn't changed one bit from Attaching Shimmer. Otherwise she'd be over here, helping, sharing the work. Lavilor is a child. I can't blame him. But here I am, hurt, helping, and what is she doing?* she growled to herself. She knew better than to get upset about Serrose going back to the eggs since she was the stronger of the two. One could hardly fault a couple for caring more about their eggs than about some strangers, and, anyway, Alian's company was better than Serrose's. *Unless Serrose finally decides to teach me some magic. Then I could put up with it.*

By the time she and Alian had finished building the fire, Serrose had returned with several doves and a rabbit. The dragonmage was in her elven form, and her mouth was creased with laugh lines. She threw her catches down at Camilla's feet, and said, "It's really funny. I fly past, and then shift mid-air, catch them in my hands, and break my fall with the tree branches as I – as Sërien learned to do."

Camilla knew. All the elves knew how to climb and fall through trees in ways that seemed just short of magical to her. But the tone of Serrose's voice and the laughter about her mouth and in her eyes somehow effected a change in the way Camilla viewed her. "Thanks," she said. "And thanks for working so hard to heal Radiance."

"It's what we're here for," Serrose said. "New races are rarely created. We were created when we were, by the power of the Lord of Light so that we could help you. There's more to it than that, but that *is* a large portion of it."

Camilla stood for a moment, dumbstruck and unresponsive. It was taking her a few moments to adjust to her new feelings towards Serrose, and now Serrose said this! Her new feelings warred with her hatred at the notion of having been chosen or destined or fated to anything. "I'm so sorry, Serrose," she said, "but that's not possible. It can't be. I have no fate or destiny other than the one I choose for myself. You can't have been created in order to help me."

Alian and Serrose looked at each other in such a way that made Camilla certain that they felt that her reaction was childish and immature, even though she had spoken in a calm, reasonable, almost casual tone. *That* made her feel like yelling, but that would not help, would it? *But why do I care?* she asked herself. *Why do I care what they think of me, or what I look like in their eyes? I suppose I don't. It's just that if I behave in a way they find too irrational and immature, Serrose will certainly not teach me any magic.*

She shivered under their gazes a little, as she realized they were trying to understand *why* she was so upset at the idea of having been chosen or destined. Finally, Serrose said, "You're afraid that this would mean that you are not free to make your own decisions and choose your own way. You're determined that you *will* be so free, and thus determined that this is *not* the way things are. But you misunderstand. That we were sent to help you does not mean that you are not free to choose as you desire. It does not mean that your path is fated apart from your choices. Nor, as far as we know, was it even you specifically whom we were sent to serve, until it was you specifically who appeared on our doorstep. I ask you: have we tried to force you to do anything? Have we been anything other than an aid to you in choosing your own way? Have we not, far from making you a slave, rather stood between you and the Horror that would enslave you if it could?"

Fury warred with more sedate and reasonable emotions. She *hated* that Serrose knew and understood her like this. She did not know why it upset her so much to be understood, even a little, by the elven dragonmage, but it did. She squared her shoulders and looked Serrose straight in the eye. "The Northern Horror *couldn't* have taken me." Even as she said it, Camilla knew that she was not as certain as she would like to be. She thought that, at the very least, she would have killed herself and left nothing to be taken fighting. If she had taken all that energy she had felt and cast it, it would have burned right through her, leaving nothing behind. That might take care of Radiance, for she was almost certain the dragon could not live without her, and given what she understood of magic and the dragons from the dragonmages, it was possible that, especially if she were in physical contact with Radiance while casting the magic, it might have incinerated both their bodies. It definitely did not take care of Lavilor and Sleet, though.

Serrose did not respond to Camilla's declaration, but continued. "The Lord of Light is not an elven slave-master. We are given freedom, and that freedom is guarded. It is the Nightmare, and the Northern Horror, that enslave. The Lord of Light and all the Guardians fight for our – and your – freedom. The whole world, being what it is, defines that freedom. There are some choices you can make, and other choices that you cannot – and this is the nature of freedom. Otherwise, there would be no choices and freedom at all. Where many beings interact, here is freedom, and also the limitations of freedom."

"That's not true at all!" Camilla interrupted. "I'm closer to Radiance than to anyone else, and that doesn't make me *less* free. It makes me more free! I'm most free because I and Radiance are so close and love each other so much!"

"That's true," said Serrose, "and it is there that you understand freedom best. Are you a slave because you cannot fly with your own arms, or free because you can fly with Radiance? Would you be a slave if you were not a Dragonrider and could not fly with your own arms? Are you a slave because I, or anyone else, may make choices which interfere with your own plans? With Radiance, you would say that you are so close and love each other so well that your plans are one, and no such thing as one or the other of you making choices that interfere with the others is possible. Camilla, while there is evil, while there is hatred, while there is lack of love, no being in Areaer is perfectly free. When all love perfectly, when all are one in the heart of love, then all will be perfectly free – and the closer we each are to loving perfectly, the freer we are, as individuals."

"That doesn't change the fact I don't have a destiny! You *weren't* sent to help me!"

"You have a future," said Serrose. "That future consists of the choices you make with the situations you encounter. *That* future, *those* choices *are* your destiny. We are here to help you, not because you have been fated apart from your will to do something, but because we are here to help those who need it, and you needed it, and you came looking for it. You sought freedom. We are here to help you have it. *That* is your destiny, Camilla – the fact that you seek to be free."

"But what about all the people who want to be free just as much as I do, but couldn't bond to a dragon? And what about Sylvara, who doesn't want to be free at all, but is just along for the ride?" Camilla raged.

Serrose cast a glance over her shoulder at where Sylvara sat against Shimmer's shoulder, plucking a dove. "I think she does want to be free. Perhaps only a little, but I think she does want it. Else, why would she have come? I do not think it was just in order to torment you. For one thing, if you just learned to stop thinking about how much she has hurt you and how much you hate her, her presence would not hurt you at all."

This made Camilla's skin burn with anger, but Serrose continued. "As for others, I do not have all answers. We dragonmages cannot do all things. We were to wait and to help anyone who came to us from Ilesh, specifically any Dragonriders, and of course we would help anyone else who came to us, as well as we could while remaining ready for any Dragonriders. But there is only so much that we could do. Remember, those from whom we come perished when they tried to fight the Wizard-King. We would fare no better if we assaulted Ilesh. Whatever we chose to do, some would be left behind. Is this – choices and limitations – what you call destiny? For no one is making you choose or do something, but not every one has the same possibilities before them."

Camilla nodded. Then she said with great vehemence, "That's *wrong!* Everyone should have the same opportunities. Well, I suppose people don't need to have opportunities they don't want, but *everyone* should have the chance to be free." She paused to glance at Radiance's golden bulk, glowing dimly in the evening light, and said, "I'm not saying everyone who wants to bond to a dragon should. That's the dragon's choice, too."

Serrose nodded, and infuriated Camilla yet again with her reasonableness and understanding. "That makes sense. It seems that would be better. I rather think it would, but I'm not sure what such a world would be, or *how* it would be, given that many choose the Nightmare over the Light. And what exactly do you mean by free? As you yourself well know, none of you are *made* to serve the elves. It is simply that, if you choose not to, it is often at the cost of pain, and even your lives in this phase. This is a horrible evil on the part of the elves, but *you* are still free to choose. How do you get around the fact that, if we're all free, then we can impinge on each other's freedom if we choose?"

This time, Camilla could not resist her anger. Growling, her hands clenched into fists, she demanded, "So you say. But what about the Northern Horror? Doesn't it *really* enslave its victims?"

"I think you and Radiance believe that those who love and who truly desire freedom face death, not undead servitude, at its hands, right?" asked Serrose.

"How do you know that!"

"I'm not as inclined towards telepathic empathy as dragons are, but I have that ability. I got that sense from you two," she explained, her tone of voice not at all suggestive of Camilla's own. "Also, it makes sense. I could have guessed it."

Why am *I so angry?* Camilla wondered. *I shouldn't be, even if Serrose is intentionally infuriating me. I decided this isn't natural to me and doesn't make me and Radiance happy, yet here I am being far more angry than I need to be again.* "Yes," she said, "that's what we think. We're fairly sure, but…"

"But you're not as sure as you wish you were, or at least *you* aren't, and you're not sure that those who love and desire freedom too much to be forced to be evil aren't subjected to an existence of torment with no foreseeable end."

She nodded and shuddered. "It's not fair. But neither are you!" *Fire births wind, and wind births fire. A life that burns and never knows fear,* she thought, and knew that Radiance was part of her thought, and that when her mind and Radiance's were joined, then was her mind most truly her own, and then were her thoughts the ones she most truly thought and believed. *No, it's not possible. We are fire. We are free. We are life. And we will be death, before ever we are enslaved or deprived of our life, our fire.*

Even as she thought this, Serrose said, "No, it isn't fair. I don't know what is, or how to make life fair while letting it still be life. I certainly cannot. But are you satisfied now that you are not being chained into a destiny just because we are helping you?"

"I don't know. I really don't. All I know right now is that I am *going* to kill the Wizard-King. I am *going* to defeat the Northern Horror, and set my people free from whatever tries to enslave them!"

"Well, if that is settled, then other things need settling next," said Serrose. She turned to Alian and said, "Would you mind showing Camilla or Sylvara how to take care of their meals, and then hunt for Radiance?"

"Gladly," said Alian.

Lavilor stepped forward and said, "I can learn, too."

Camilla cast him a warm smile. At least, he was free with her, too, and *he* was a true friend, even if they did not always agree.

He smiled at her in return, and as she moved across the glade, Camilla turned from him and cast Sylvara a scathing look behind the dragonmages' backs. She might be much angrier than she ought to be, and she might need to discover why and stop it, but Sylvara did not deserve the credit Serrose gave her. Perhaps Shimmer desired to be free, even though he had chosen a slavery-loving treasonous human instead of an elf who might repent of his race's wrongs if given the opportunity and incentive to notice them, but then again maybe every elf on the sands that day had been cruel, as well as naturally unsuited to Attaching a dragon. Sylvara, however, did *not* desire freedom. She was probably along simply because she could not help caring a little about what her dragon wanted. Or maybe she *was* here just to hurt Camilla, despite what Serrose had said about her being unable to hurt Camilla if Camilla just stopped reacting, whether that was true or not.

The next day, she was as stiff as ever. She tried to endure having to regularly mount and dismount, so that neither dragonmage got too tired bearing

Radiance, with good grace, but it was difficult. Her whole body protested every part of the process, and she was never comfortable, but she did not want Serrose to spare any of her energy for her own injuries, which would heal eventually. Radiance was far more injured and, being a flying creature, many portions of her body were regularly subjected to more stress than Camilla ever expected to endure. She needed to heal better and stronger than her rider did. Camilla spoke as little as she could, knowing that anything she said would be tainted by her attitude, and tried to take refuge in her bond with Radiance, even as Radiance took refuge with her.

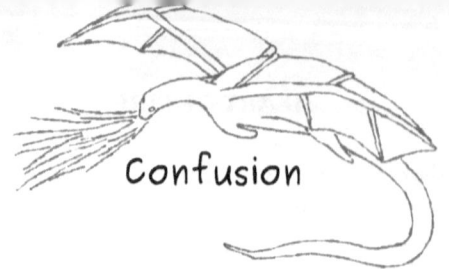

Confusion

It worried Camilla how slow their progress was. Alian bore all three humans most of the time, and Radiance struggled along. They flew now over largely civilized areas, instead of the wild woods on the borders of Ilesh, and they often flew only several hours a night. Alian scouted ahead to look for shelter that would hide them during the day, and that they could reach without pushing Radiance's endurance to its limit or past it.

One morning, as they settled in, Camilla asked Alian, "How will we get to the Guardian Isles, when Radiance can hardly fly more than a few hours at a time?"

"I will scout ahead," the dragonmage answered, "as I have been doing. There are isles enough between the shore and the Guardian Isles themselves. If I must, I will find a good wind current, and we can use that. This is quite doable."

She nodded, accepting that. It was probably true, but she was upset. It upset both her and Radiance almost past sanity that the dragon could fly only with pain and difficulty. Her muscles had taken incredible battering, and Serrose had explained to them that she had focused on healing the bones and ligaments, the most badly torn muscles, and a little damage to the organs. The rest would have to heal on its own, since bruised muscles almost always healed well, and she had only so much. He had been so exhausted after healing Radiance the morning they departed that, when he tried to take to the air, his wing-beats would not synchronize. He had been forced to land, and had asked Alian to go ahead, assuring his partner that he would be fine. He just needed to rest a little more.

"Are you sure?" Alian had asked. "Right now you're as vulnerable as Radiance and Camilla were, and I and Camilla will not be able to rescue you as effectively as you and I rescued them."

"Yes," said Serrose. "The longer we stay in one place, the more vulnerable we are. As soon as I can, I'll find another place to rest. It will be fine." His voice dropped with affection. "Don't forget I'm a shapeshifter. I won't be caught, and even if I am, I can escape."

The effect of that conversation on Camilla had not been to keep her from worrying.

She brooded also on the things Serrose had said about Sylvara. What was it about the treasonous weasel that made people think she was good and... well, whatever it was they wanted? Was the fact that Serrose thought there was some good in Sylvara's intentions an indication that Serrose was not interested in Camilla's freedom? Was Serrose deceived by Sylvara, or was Serrose deceiving Camilla? Were they not helping them escape at all, but taking them to be their own slaves? Perhaps, the other dragonmages lived on the Guardian Isles.

Her hand stole to the hilt of the magesword, underneath the cloak she wore. She almost heard the magic in it. She wondered if she should confront Alian. Since being re-united with the magesword, she had started to feel the energy again, and if Serrose was telling her the truth about her magic, then she had far more potential power not only than Alian did, but than Serrose did. She might not be a match in a mage duel for Serrose, at least until she recovered further. The purple dragonmage might have less magic than she did, but she – or he – had far more knowledge of how to use it. But Alian's power was supposed to be quite minimal. If she chose to be, she was probably a threat to Alian, even if the dragonmage had far more training. If it turned out that she was trying to enslave her, she would attack Alian.

She reached out to Radiance, inviting the dragon to take part in her thoughts, if she could. Flying was enough of a difficult and painful ordeal to Radiance that, even though she took refuge with Camilla from the pain at times, her mind was often given wholly to the effort of flight.

The dragon took a moment to understand and consider her rider's thoughts. Finally, she said, *"I do not think that slavery is what these dragonmages, strange and unnatural as they are, have in mind for us. As strange as their minds are, I would have sensed that sort in them, if not at first, then by now. As for Sylvara, I do not like her and Shimmer any better than you do, but they are changing each other. The line between her desires and Shimmer's, between her thoughts and his, is not quite clear."* There was another long silence within them, as Radiance-with-Camilla *felt* Shimmer and Sylvara and thought about them. Then the dragon continued, *"Sylvara is very complicated, though that might be the result of Attaching Shimmer. I understand now why he chose a human over an elf. It is hard for an elf Dragonrider to feel what we dragons feel and know the injustice done us. They do not think like us, they cannot understand us, we cannot understand them, and their thoughts and drives are master, and we subordinate, by nature and by darkest magic. With Sylvara, at least his thoughts and who he is can become a part of her actions and thoughts. As terrible as she is, he is not wholly her slave."*

Darkness and fire roiled underneath the surface of Radiance's thoughts. Her hatred of the elves and their magic burned as never before, even as she condemned individuals – perhaps – a little less. Never before had either she or Camilla called their magic 'dark', let alone 'darkest', but in that one word she placed the elven manipulation of the dragons on par with the enslaving death magics of the Northern Darkness, and they *were* alike, Camilla thought. The realization frightened her, as she realized just how completely and hopelessly the dragons of Ilesh had been enslaved.

Their slavery had not been external as hers had been. It had not been one which admitted, as hers had, the choice to challenge it, to pursue freedom, and if all else failed, to gain that freedom by death.

The dragons had had no hope, hardly even the ability to desire freedom, at least until she appeared – for they *had* helped her, and she still did not understand why they had treated her the way they had. It was one of those things that frightened her, making her worry that she had been chosen and forced into a destiny.

And if the dragons can be so enslaved, can anyone be certain of freedom?

She was torn between hope and fear, confidence and worry. On the one hand, she could not believe it, could not believe that she and Radiance could be enslaved, that their love would permit them either to be sundered or to be subjected to the will of another. On the other, it was unacceptable and impossible that thousands and thousands of dragons should be subjected to such slavery, such corruption of their very natures, through no failing of their own! It *was* dark magic. Necromancy was worse only in that it threatened to prolong such slavery beyond the bounds of life and death, but, did it? What awaited dragons, bonded body and soul to those who mastered them and were not truly united with them, beyond the limits of this world? The bond could not be severed, and it could not admit freedom... even if the elves were not evil, even if they *tried* to respect the dragons bonded to them, the bond would still be no true union, and would be artificial and constraining – and how *could* the elves even know and try to respect the dragons? She truly could not decide which was worse, the necromancy of the Northern Horror or the life-magic of the elves of Ilesh. *I suppose the elves really* do *deserve what they got. But what about those elves who don't?* The life-mages were long gone, what remained of their arts insufficient – at least, if the elves' representations were to be believed – to work the changes which had been worked in the dragons. Most of the elves were evil to some degree, or they would not have stood for keeping the humans enslaved, even if they could not be expected to understand the far greater harm done to the dragons, but what of those who were not, or who were only minimally, evil? What of those who were like Sërien and others she had known?

A sudden thought blazed through Camilla's mind as if the sun flashed across the midnight sky. *What if... what if the best thing that* can *be done with these twisted elf-dragon pairs is* to *make them truly one? If union is impossible, if the dragons are wholly subjugated in the bond, perhaps the best thing* is *for them to become one being, merging the mind and desire of the dragon with the elf, and ending the slavery?* For a moment, she was ready to believe that Serrose was wrong in thinking that Sërien and Gloaming were different from herself, and had a separate existence, but then she remembered Alian. Alian had been human. According to the story, it sounded like others of the riders from whom the dragonmages had come had also been human. Such a merging should not be necessary if the rider was a human, not if what Radiance had just said about Sylvara and Shimmer was to be believed...

Just supposing Serrose is Sërien and Gloaming though, how would Serrose know how abominable it would be if a real dragon-rider pair were somehow combined into one personality? Would she-he know from touching my and Radiance's mind, or perhaps from some human-dragon pair that was rightly bonded? Did Serrose and Alian lie to me about what they are, in order to make me comfortable, or is it possible that the dragonmages don't know what they are – always assuming my idea is more than a notion that sprang into my mind but has little to do with the reality.

Or, she considered, knowing that she was indulging fantasies, *maybe this Alian is what they told me, and Serrose is not. Maybe this Lord of the Light, or whoever it was that did it, does not want everyone to know, or does not want the dragonmages to know, or does not want someone to know, at least not right away, what some of them are. If no one figures out what they are and spreads the knowledge before the originals die, no one will be able to figure it out from their off-spring, and if anyone ever does guess it will be one idle speculation among thousands.*

All right. I won't try to confront Alian over what's probably nothing. But, she continued vehemently, *if anyone* does *try to enslave me, I will kill them. I am not going to be a slave and be marched to some 'destiny' of another's choosing. Even if the magic kills me, I will kill anyone who tries to do that to me.*

Then, in a softer tone, *But I will free my people and the dragons, and if I'm destined to do so, so be it! Let my own will be the destiny. But I will never be destined against my will. I will never be anyone's slave.*

It was a couple weeks before they reached the ocean. Radiance went straight for the beach, and rolled over. She spread out her wings, and wriggled across the sand, trying to get it over almost every part of her. Even though Camilla did not understand *why* Radiance liked the sand so much, she found herself laughing aloud both at the dragon's antics and with her pleasure.

A few moments later, the males joined her on the sand.

Camilla glanced around, and realized that Alian now stood beside her as a human male, that Lavilor was running down the beach to play beside the dragons, and that Sylvara stood slightly apart with a strange look on her face. She almost reached for Lavilor to warn him about the dangerous waves, then realized that the dragons would not let him drown. She did not know if they could swim, but they were not going to be swept away by a single wave. Sleet at least, and probably Radiance also, would watch out for Lavilor's safety, and they would snatch him back if the sea grabbed him.

"I… Why is it that we haven't been attacked? We've traveled so slowly. Were we not chased?" she asked, folding her arms across her body against the surprisingly chill wind blowing over the waters.

Alian looked at her with quiet consideration, then said, "There are no trails in the sky for them to follow. Even though we moved slowly, they could not guess what direction we had gone – though they might have been able to guess a few that we hadn't."

"Oh," said Camilla. She had never felt a wind like this before. She turned her attention back to her conversation with Alian. "But can't they track *magic?*"

A sudden shift in the atmosphere made her turn to see Alian standing in a posture of shock. After a moment, he recovered himself enough to say, "You can see that?"

She nodded fiercely. "That's how I and Radiance navigated our way out of the sanctuary. I also felt the dark magic of the Northern Horror's attack. I'm… not sure why I didn't feel it before I and Radiance were attacked, but it might be because I was so absorbed in my own magic… song."

"Or that your senses are rather unrefined, and no magic was cast until the bolt that brought you down." Alian's tone was thoughtful, and friendly. "That's… uncanny. I understand now why Serrose is unwilling to take you as her apprentice. You need someone who knows more of magic. Serrose is that sensitive, but it's taken centuries to develop. And that's the answer to your question. *You* might be able to track by magic, and almost certainly you *could* do so with the centuries of practice and refinement that elves have, but most people can not do it at all. There may be a few dark mages in the Empire of Eltaes who could. The Wizard-King himself might be able to. But not many others."

She nodded reflectively. There was something in the wind. She was not sure if it was magic, but it definitely felt strange – cold and clammy, in a weird sort of way she could not put to words. At the same time, something in her rebelled hotly against the idea that she was an exceptionally strong mage. It could not be! It could not! The world just was not like that! It was *destiny*. It flew in the face of everything she believed about freedom. These thoughts vied for supreme claim to her attention.

But, in everything, there's somebody – *or a few people – who are exceptional. There has to be someone with extremely powerful and sensitive magical abilities. Why* shouldn't *it be you?*

If I am to be able to protect my freedom, if I am to set others free, then isn't it right I have this magic? What if it does not control me, does not force me onto a predestined path, but is given me that I may do this thing I choose? Perhaps, because I have chosen to be and do what I have? If the dragonmages could be made, then couldn't I be given this after *and because I* had *chosen?*

But I don't want that! I don't want that kind of attention. It's almost as bad as destiny! I want to do and be what I choose on my own terms, with my own resources, because I want to!

She tried to wrestle her thoughts into a coherent whole and master them. What exactly did she feel? Why exactly did she feel it?

I guess I want no one to have power over me. Want was too weak a word; she did not merely want; she believed and insisted, she determined. *I don't want anyone to have the power to* give *me power or to* make *me anything, and I don't want anyone to have the power to take away power or abilities from me, or to make me not something! And I don't think anyone, including myself, should have these powers over others. I think the world* cannot *be such that anyone has these powers over anyone else. But I suppose I didn't make the world, and I don't control it.*

That thought did nothing at all to moderate her feelings. It was not that she thought *she* should control the world. She found that as repellent as the thought that others did. *No* one should be controlled by the decisions of anyone else. No one should be destined to anything.

What Serrose had asked her earlier came back to her then. What *would* such a world look like? How would it be possible for everyone to be able to make *whatever* choices they wanted, however good or evil, however much they impinged on the choices and desires of others? Would it really work even if everyone were exactly equal in power? *Was* such equality in power even possible, or would the different choices cause differences in power? Was she even okay with people having less power for choosing to do ill with it – that is, to try to control others? Would they be uncontrolled themselves, would anyone be really free to choose exactly what he or she wanted, if some 'choices' brought less power – were not fully choices at all? She was sure there had to be a way for what she wanted to be real – it seemed so *right!*

There should be no such thing as arbitrary power. There shouldn't be life-magic. There shouldn't be death-magic. Nothing should exist with the kind of power I look to have or that the Wizard-King definitely does have! That's what I think.

But what kind of world would that be? Would she complain about the fact that dragons were, in many ways, stronger than humans, next? What choices should people have? How would it work? If people were deprived of power for mis-using it, that would mean there was some*one* or some*thing* that was interfering with people's choices – and even if that interference was solely occasioned by interfering with *others'* choices, was it not still interference and control? Who drew the line?

Love, I suppose, she thought, looking at Radiance. But no one should ever be forced into the kind of bond she shared with Radiance! No one should ever be forced into anything, not even love! And love did not force. She, of all people, with the bond she shared with her dragon, knew that!

Alian interrupted her thoughts, then, and said, "We're going to camp here tonight, while I check out the wind patterns."

"You're going to leave us here?" Something like fear, and like challenge, but that she would never admit even to Radiance, laced her tone.

"No." Alian shook his head. "I will use magic. I have enough for that. Reading and mapping the wind was a skill Yetra, and later on I, cherished and developed, since it is *very* useful when one must fly long distances over uncharted territory or around wild magics."

"It *does* sound useful," she commented, no longer challenging, but thoughtful now, "especially if you want to cross an ocean, and if you could use it to find land…"

"With experience, it can be used to find land. Land alters the flow of the wind. But, no, I'm not going to teach you this right now. I doubt your control is delicate enough yet, and if Serrose is wary of teaching one with as strong and unique magic as yourself, I am, as well."

She nodded her acceptance, but she felt that Alian's opposition to teaching her was nowhere near as strong as Serrose's. She *might* be able to convince him, and she could watch. She might learn from that. But what she said was, "There's something odd about this wind."

"There is," said Alian. "There often is something a little odd about the winds that blow across the Guardian Isles. But I and Serrose have been there before, and found nothing to be afraid of – well, other than some wild beasts and the occasional outlaw who manages to survive the process of getting there, but those aren't really dangers to dragons or… kin of dragons, dragonmages."

"Oh," said Camilla, eyes fixed on the horizon, where the blue-gray of the sea met the gray-white of a cloudy sky. "But oughtn't I to know how to read the wind? If the forces of the Northern Horror have cut us off from the Sea Elves, or chased them away, would it not be best if I can still make my way across the sea?"

Alian chuckled. "Perhaps I should not teach you then! However talented you may be, some things take time to learn. The wind-patterns change from season to season, and even year to year, and in ways far more complex than I can grasp. I would hardly trust my skills to that degree, and there is simply no way to understand the wind well enough to know an island from other things, and to know *where* that island is from far off, with only a few weeks of learning. Even so, I doubt these dragons will have the stamina to cross the ocean, even with wind-reading. There are very far stretches without even an islet."

"Hmm." Camilla pursed her lips. That did not sound anything like Serrose's firm, and sometimes scornful, refusals. It also did not sound like she was going to get her way. But maybe she *was* wrong. She had thought it was a good idea, but was it possible it was not? Yet the sudden attack of the Wizard-King on Ilesh made her very wary of his power, and she suspected something had changed recently, for him to have attacked Ilesh now, and not before. Could he have attacked the Sea Elves too? Was there a reason to think he had not? Or that the way to them was still open? After all, they were closer to Eltaes than Illesh was.

She voiced her concerns to Alian.

"That is a concern," he replied. "More of a concern is that he has made himself enough of a nuisance that the Sea Elves have abandoned Ellenesia altogether and no longer trade on this be-cursed continent. There's also the possibility that they might look for a good harbor site in the south and move there. In case of that, keep your eyes open, for they will probably sail down the eastern side of the Guardian Isles, and you might catch sight of their ships. They might even drop anchor and land. Though few humans can sail between the isles and hope not to dash their ships against the rocks, for the Sea Elves they are probably no great difficulty. If you see their ships come this way, my advice is to try to make contact with them, but be careful – dragons have sometimes burned their ships, and so they are wary of dragons flying towards them over open ocean."

Camilla nodded. Everything was so complicated! She growled to herself, very softly, but she suspected Alian heard it anyways. Still, she liked him better than Serrose. Was it something somehow horribly inbred into the Wood Elf nature, which in some fashion Serrose still possessed, to treat humans as slaves or inferiors to be ordered around, instead of equals to be respected? And why could she not just blast the Wizard-King? If she had to be so exceptionally and uniquely powerful, at least magically speaking, why could she not just destroy the enemy in one fell blow of magic?

Protecting

Serrose settled on the ground, tucking his wings around himself, and watched Alian and the three young dragons soar into the moonrise. He was certain Alian was not convinced of his arguments as to why he was safe, despite his exhaustion, but what mattered was not whether or not Alian was convinced, but that she went. Alian would be in far more danger than he was. Her time period of exposure would be much longer, and she had far less magic and sensitivity. The three dragons and their riders were not much help, either. Oh, Camilla might do things, but with that power she had and her lack of finesse, she would probably blast the entire area. She might succeed in killing her target; she would almost certainly succeed in killing herself; she might kill everything around her. No, Alian was in significantly more danger than he was and, exhausted as he was, Serrose lay there, contemplating the situation and wondering if there was anything he could do about it. It might be as foolhardy as Alian's desire to stay with him until he recovered from his exhaustion, but he could not help it.

Well, first things first, he told himself. *First I will see to the eggs and better securing the sanctuary. Then, I will see what I can do about making Alian and the others safer.* After all, that *was* their primary task: to ensure the freedom and survival of the Dragonriders – the Sha'adhri as they were called in Aneri. It was, Serrose thought, a good word, since Dragonriders specifically referred only to the rider, whereas Sha'adhri meant dragon and rider equally. He wondered whether Sha'adhri was an ancient word for 'Dragonrider' from a lost language, and was used the way it was because its composition was forgotten, or whether it had another origin.

I wonder: should we have taken care not to have eggs? I would not hesitate to give my life for theirs, if we hadn't had eggs. It is not as if, for all intents and purposes, this is not a second life, given me for that very purpose, but the eggs… Were we even intended to become a separate, self-sustaining race? No other eggs have hatched yet, that we know of. I could be fretting about infertile eggs, for all I know.

But on the off-chances that the eggs *were* fertile, with little ones growing within them… Serrose mostly thought they were fertile. For one thing, he and Alian both had a "sense" about how close they were to hatching, which he did not think they would have if there were no living creature in the eggs.

He sent out a probe to verify that there was no new magic he could sense in the area, and then promptly fell asleep.

In the morning, he flew back towards the sanctuary. He did not bother flying at night for two reasons. One of these was that he could fly much faster now that he was unburdened and did not have to keep pace with the young or wounded. The other was that he did not care if he *was* seen and followed.

Though he was concerned about the safety of the sanctuary if it were not guarded, he suspected that, especially if he prepared, he could hold it against almost anything – probably not against the Wizard-King, and possibly not against a team of powerful mages, such as the team Sërien had been instrumental in gathering to challenge the Wizard-King.

But he doubted there was anything that would be a threat to his ability to protect the sanctuary in the area. If the Wizard-King came himself, which was not impossible given that he had so recently been in Ilesh, then nothing anyone did would protect the sanctuary *or* the eggs. All Serrose could hope for if it came to that would be to distract him long enough for the others to get away before he was killed or captured, and he suspected he could not manage even that. His heart constricted at the thought of the Wizard-King capturing the eggs, but he pushed those thoughts from his mind. Fear and worry did no good. He should have learned that long ago. The Lord of the Light was looking out for them personally. He had rescued those from whom the dragonmages had come from the clutches of the Wizard-King, and he would certainly see to the souls of the dragonmages and their off-spring also, if not in one way and at one time, then in another way and at another time. Besides, there was no reason to suspect the Wizard-King *knew* about them, and if he did not know about them, then there was no reason for him to investigate the border of Ilesh. Well, that might not be true, since he probably wanted to understand what made the border of Ilesh the dangerous, unpredictable thing it was.

However, if the Wizard-King decided to explore the border of Ilesh, it might take him a long time. Whatever confidence Serrose had in his ability to hold off the Wizard-King, he had no more confidence in the Wizard-King's ability to probe, or survive, the defenses of Ilesh. Those were ancient magics, and Serrose had the feeling that they were more subtle and powerful than he knew, and that most of them were latent. They also felt more sentient than most magic, though he did not trust their sentience. It was entirely possible that the appearance of a being as evil as the Wizard-King would trigger latent, sleeping magic into doing something entirely unexpected.

Of course, the Wizard-King did get into *Ilesh,* Serrose reminded himself. But the border of Ilesh was not the same in all places, and the dragonmages had chosen an area saturated with the wildest, strongest magics to build their sanctuary.

It is amusing to consider the Wizard-King getting destroyed while trying to figure out the border of Ilesh, but somehow I don't think that is going to happen. He forcefully pulled his mind away from fantasizing about a possibility that was satisfying and amusing to contemplate, but ultimately unlikely and useless to consider. Possibly worse than useless; it was a waste of time, and it might make him more likely to respond poorly to whatever did happen.

Two evenings later, Serrose dipped out of an air current and angled down over his sanctuary. As far as he could tell, nothing had happened, and the defenses certainly had not been breached, but it felt lonely and forlorn without the presence of Alian. He had never before been apart from Alian for more than a day before, and for decades before that Sërien and Yetra had never been apart, so coming "home" without Alian reinforced a loneliness that was already brewing inside of him.

He felt like crying by the time he landed, so strong was the sense of loneliness that being "home" without Alian brought to him, even though he had never even thought of this sanctuary as a permanent home. The draconic instincts in him might not even allow for a permanent home but, other things besides, this sanctuary was a waiting place for the Sha'adhri of Ellenesia, not a true home. He landed clumsily and stood for a moment, his wings unfolded, his head and tail drooping, trying to fight past the sense of desertion, the sadness and depression.

I have things to do. And once I make sure this place is safe, and our eggs are not about to hatch, I shall go and make sure that Alian is safe too, he promised himself. So thinking, he straightened and shifted into the female elf form.

The intermediate state always felt funny to Serrose. No matter how often she did it, the amethyst and violet mist and the shifting of her body felt funny, and funny *was* descriptive. She was not sure whether or not she liked the feeling. It was closer to ticklish in quality and effect than anything else she could think of, but on the superficial level of physical sensations, it was nothing like feeling ticklish. At any rate, the feeling helped her shed a little of that melancholy. She straightened her shoulders and walked towards the house.

A few minutes later, she was in the room with the eggs. When she rested her hand on them and stretched out her mind to the egg, she knew that the creatures within were living – and that they were not about to hatch. She guessed they had another few weeks, and she was almost certain that she had a few days. *Though how do I know? I've never done this before. Neither has Alian. We could be wrong.* She put the thought aside, and spent a few moments resting with the eggs. Before she knew it, she was asleep.

The next morning, she set herself to further ward the sanctuary. Though she did not need focuses for her spells to avoid harming herself, there were things for which she needed them. One of these was amplifying her power, and another was setting ward spells. The dragonmages had realized this rather early in their existence, and they had collected the things they might need to set ward spells which required various anchor points. After getting herself a very small meal, a mere snack, Serrose went into their storage or treasure room, and collected what she needed to set the anchors and channel-points for a layered and complex ward. Common quartz crystals had their places alongside assorted rocks of indeterminate type but of very special sizes and shapes, and expensive gems that she might not be able to replace.

Next, she set them out, laying them out in deliberate patterns around the sanctuary, and specially preparing each one, infusing it with a little of her magic. This ward was intended to weave in and out of the existing border protections in such a way as to support them and be supported by them, but not to rely on them. To do it properly, it would require several days, and she intended to give it those days. She wanted something she could reasonably trust to foil all but the strongest attempts to enter the sanctuary without her will, so that she could then make sure Alian was safe, without any worry that she was abandoning her due duty to their eggs.

When the dark mage had attacked Radiance and Camilla so close to their sanctuary, she and Alian had immediately decided that they needed to provide themselves and their eggs with an extra measure of protection, and there was no way that she was rushing this. It was, possibly, the most complex and intricate piece of magic that either she or Sërien had ever attempted, and the more so because she did not understand most of the spells she was interweaving it with. A few of them were a magic much like Sërien's, and these she understood well. Others she recognized as a magic very ancient, older than most, if not all, the trees in the forest, and possibly as ancient as some rocks, though she could not be certain about that. Yet it was not age that marked these spells apart. They were almost alive in a way she did not understand, more like the songs of the Sea Elves and the enhancements on their ships than anything else she had ever seen, and yet quite unlike the Sea Elf magic – if possible, even more alive, almost sentient, or else interwoven with some other sentience. She could not probe its heart or anchors, and it echoed far beyond her reach.

She was very surprised that Camilla had been able to navigate it, as she must have to have gotten where she was when the dark mage attacked her, and this had made Serrose think hard and long about what she taught the gold-rider. The young woman was altogether too sure of herself, a trait strange in a slave, but perhaps it was what had made her such an attractive prospect for the gold, or perhaps it was an effect of being Attached to the gold – but Serrose thought there was more to it than that. At any rate, magic in the hands of one as powerful and as over-confident as Camilla was could be a dangerous thing, both to herself and to those around her. Moreover, the young woman's magic was both like and unlike Serrose's in a way she was not sure how to deal with. Serrose honestly thought that Camilla would be better trained by the Cave Elves, since according to her source – who Serrose was confident was not misinformed – they were the experts in the discipline of magic that she followed, though to a very real degree, all magic was intertwined and one on some level. *Probably,* Serrose thought, *the best thing for Camilla would be the Cave Elves, and a dragonmage or two, since her magic is draconic in a way no one else's is, and we* might *be able to help with that. But we need a better word than dragonmage.*

She thrust all of that out of her mind. It needed to be considered sometime, but right now it was distracting her from very important work. She would think about Camilla and what she needed later, as well as what *they* should be called.

It took the entirety of the first day just to prepare the spell-work, and even that was exhausting However, several days of dedicated, taxing work later, the wards were complete, and the eggs did not feel any closer to hatching. Serrose transformed into his male dragon form, and took off. He did not intend to be in any danger of getting caught, but he did intend to throw enough magic into the area to thoroughly pull any hunters off Alian's trail. Mostly, he would fly high in the air, where he would be scarcely visible from the ground and only the most powerful mages might be able to reach him, and create starbursts of magic energy. He might also follow Alian and the others some distance to make sure they were not being followed, at least not with any signs he could read. He would have done this earlier, since it might be too late now, but he had to make sure their eggs were safe.

Hopefully, he would be back in a few days. Neither he nor Alian were comfortable leaving the eggs alone, even for a short time, especially now that they were getting close to hatching – they thought another month – and he had told Alian that he was going back to guard the eggs. He had guarded the eggs, but he was not exactly staying with them, and he felt that Alian would not be at all happy about that, especially if he stayed away from them for long.

Dangers

A day and a night after they had landed on the beach, the seven of them flew across the ocean to an island that Alian had described to Camilla as "the nearest, not in terms of the length of a strictly straight path from the beach, but in terms of ease and speed; you can think of the wind as a little like mountain ranges and valleys, only very rapidly changing mountains and valleys, but it is very like mountains and valleys, in that sometimes it is easy to go one direction, but not the other direction, as when it is easy to go down a mountain but not up it, and sometimes two points seem close together, but when it comes to getting from one to the other, they are far apart, just as it is easier to travel across a flat plan than across mountains. Mind, the parallel is not exact, so don't ever rely on it or make conclusions from it."

Camilla had nodded. She could accept *that* readily enough.

Once the islands came into view, she understood why they were so treacherous for ships. They looked much like she imagined mountains might look if the world were flooded under fathoms and fathoms of water. Jagged rocks and little cliffs, rocky slopes and peaks pierced the sea everywhere around the island, and waves constantly crashed against the rocks, some of which showed only when the troughs of the waves passed around them, and were completely submerged under the peaks. In other places, showers of foam told her there was rock near the surface of the water. The islands themselves consisted of rocky slopes and valleys and, here and there, a plateau rising up from the sea, clothed with grasses and ferns and various trees, many of which she recognized as the same kinds she had seen in Ilesh, but a few of them remarkably different.

It's beautiful! she exclaimed to Radiance.

The dragon agreed, and added that it looked like a wonderful place for dragons to make what homes they desired and to nest.

That's just what I was thinking! It was such a beautiful, attractive place that she almost felt a lure to abandon everything else, all her other resolutions and loyalties and cares, and make their abode here, right now. One thing stopped her mind from gliding on that wind. Where would the prospective Dragonriders come from, the candidates for the eggs, and, more urgently, how would they avoid the grasp of the Wizard-King? She doubted he needed ships, or that he could not use his magic to get them across the rocks if he did need ships. *And if I do survive confronting and defeating the Wizard-King – which I fully intend to do – then we will come back here, and live here, and raise the next generation of – human – Dragonriders here. It will be so perfect.*

Alian stayed with them for several weeks, teaching them how to set traps, and how to kindle fires, and how to cook with fire, until he was confident that at least two of them had a good grasp on every task and every part of a task. As often as she could, Camilla took herself and Radiance far away from Sylvara, and Lavilor and Sleet often went with her. She was trying to ignore the fact that Sylvara existed, for every time she thought of the other woman she wanted to make her feel what she was and had done, but she did not have the power to do so. She was fairly certain that Alian did not approve of rage and vengeance and hatred, but even if he had not been around, what could she really do to Sylvara? She was more than certain that if they really fought, she would win. Her magic had returned fully, and she did not think it would be hard to make fire, but she did not truly *want* to kill Sylvara. She almost wanted to kill her, and she was not sure she would have refrained from killing her if she were not Attached to Shimmer, but, as it is, she did not want to kill her. *I just want her to leave. To go away and never come back. I don't want to ever see her again. I don't want to ever think about her again. She isn't half-way sorry for all the things she's made me and others suffer with her snitching – I would never fault her for laziness, but first not working hard and then snitching on others? It makes me feel like throttling her.*

That was something else that was beginning to concern Camilla, and she hated that it made her half-way agree with Serrose about not teaching her too much. She was concerned that if Sylvara irritated her too much she would end up inadvertently killing her. She could almost *taste* the fire in the back of her mouth. In a moment of rage, it might explode out from her, flowing along the lines of her body and along lines of force extended from her mind.

Then, one evening, Alian told them that he was confident that they would be able to take care of themselves and to find the Sea Elves. He flew back over the ocean towards Serrose and their eggs, and the next morning, Camilla and Radiance climbed up to the summit of the mountain isle. It was a bare rock, jagged in places where wind and weather had caused it to crack and pieces had fallen away, and it was worn smooth by centuries and millenia of wind and rain and melting snow. A chill, eerie wind blew about it, raising goosebumps on her face and arms and whistling under Radiance's wings. It made her feel alive and free in an exultant, eerie way. The sky and the wind now called to her just as strongly as fire called to her, and she could not even begin to name the resonance it struck in her soul.

As she had once before, she raised her arms to the sky and sang.

Call away, call me away
The broad, ever broad spaces beyond
The winds that make their way
In dizzying ascent all around
The earth and the sky, night and the day

Where sun shines 'mid icy chill
Where freedom is bright, without a name
Higher than this high hill
Even low, where restraint never came
There birds fly, and not I, till I will

She lapsed into silence, but it seemed as if her song was carried on by the wind, whistling around the mountain peak. She knelt on the bare rock, placing one hand on the earth, and holding one hand out to the sky, while Radiance wrapped her tail around her rider.

"There is something in the wind. Something eerie and strange," they said together and to one another. They felt it clearly, and wondered how Alian had dismissed it – unless her senses really *were* that much stronger than the dragonmages'. She felt it now, stronger and surer than ever, a low, eerie call, mixed with desperation and sorrow and longing. It rode the wind, and it sighed and moaned within the wind.

Sudden fear struck her. The last time she and Radiance had been captured, it had been after she sang. Would her song now call some dark, evil thing to them, and would it take them? Without Serrose and Alian around, this time they could not be rescued, and with them Lavilor and Sleet would probably also be taken! *Have I really done this?* she wondered. *Have I really doomed it all? Am I this horrible? No! It cannot be. I cannot. I must. I do not have this power. But no! Have I brought evil on us all? Am I even the one who brought the Northern Horror down on Ilesh? What am I even thinking?*

Radiance's mind caressed her own, and Camilla knew the dragon was as deep in trouble as she was herself. Vainly, as if fighting through sludge, her mind tried to process what was going on. Had evil in fact come? Was it her song that had called it, or her fears? Did the evil come from within her?

A dark rough gray-green hand grasped her chin with bruising force and made her look up into a monstrous, ill-formed face with yellow eyes and fangs. Her heart froze. *Radiance,* she called feebly, in the deepest place of her soul, guarded from the fear and panic by the bond of love they shared. *I am here.*

Laughter like ice grating on ice in the depths of hell grated on Camilla's ears with sickening pain, driving daggers of incoherent fear through her over and over again. Maybe all her worst fears were true. Maybe her hopes were mis-placed. Maybe love was not freedom. Maybe freedom was not stronger than slavery and love was not stronger than hate. Maybe they were all doomed to be the tormented slaves of the Wizard-King of Eltaes forever, their minds and souls forever trapped in an agony of hopelessness, despair and unlove. Maybe she and Radiance would be separated and condemned to an unending hell of undeath where they themselves became evil.

"*Camilla,*" came the whisper of her dragon's mind, as faint and besieged as her own. "*Radiance,*" Camilla responded. Their thoughts froze, half-formed.

An arrow whistled through the air, like the light of a tinkling star. Camilla did not at first recognize it as the sound of an arrow, but it freed her mind from the clogging fear and despair, and at the same time she noticed that the creature no longer gripped her chin in its bruising grasp. Blinking, startled, reaching out to Radiance in a kind of repentant grasp for re-union, she noticed that the creature, which she now recognized as an orc, lay limp with the wound of an arrow in its back – but of the arrow there was no trace.

Did you see that? she asked Radiance.

"*Neither of us did. But we both felt it,*" replied the dragon.

She nodded, shaken. *But how? How did that happen to us? I could hardly feel you. I...* Her mind-voice lapsed into a withered silence, as she considered what had happened. It reminded her starkly of her experience in the prison cell, but it was far, far worse.

She rose, stumbled over a few paces, slipped on the sheer rock, and collapsed into Radiance's shoulder. "*Radiance,*" she sobbed out, crying. She could not bring herself to face it, to face either her fears or what had happened. Part of her cried out in withering despair. Was the fear true? No. She could save herself. No one could do that to another. But why should she be exempt, when others were not? Another part of her insisted it must be only some nightmare. What had that arrow even been and where had it come from? How had it broken the spell of terror? But she – or Radiance – could see the dead, sprawled form of the orc, and was not the evil called the *Nightmare* as well as the Northern Horror? Wasn't the Nightmare the older, more encompassing name, whereas the Northern Horror described a particular manifestation of the Nightmare? That was certainly the idea she had gotten from Serrose and Alian, not that anything had to be true because they said or thought it, but it kind of made sense.

Deep and ancient, buried under layer after layer of elven-wrought change, Camilla could feel, too, the sense within Radiance that the gist of the experience was the same whether it occurred in what people called dreams or in what people called the real world, and she found herself heartily agreeing with that thought. It made perfect, eminent sense, so deep and ringing that she could not say how it made sense, and could no more argue with it than she could explain it.

The wind still whistled around them, chilling her, but it was now as if whatever soul rode or infused it, there was now a wall between her and that soul. It felt empty, deprived of its meaning, however ecstatic or eerie, wild or far it had been. She thought the wind was still the same, and that it was her ability to feel that was different.

It was like this before, she thought. *I lost the magic after I was in the prison, and I lose something of it now, again.*

"*Something comes,*" said Radiance.

She straightened and stepped away from the dragon's side. *Where?* she asked, as she looked out over the peak and across to the mist-shrouded wooded isles further east.

The dragon's reply was cryptic and strange, but now Camilla felt it, too. Something came, something that was of that eastern isle. It stepped out of the shadow of a great rock and stepped towards them.

She gasped and fell backwards, into Radiance's shoulder. It was an elf, but it was like no elf she had seen before! It was tall, and it had smoky black hair, under which or in which ran flickers of red light that resembled flames. Its eyes, too, were red and flickered slightly, around the dark pupils. Its skin was gray, with a brown-red tinge, and was rough and uneven, like tree-bark. Its lips were dark gray-purple. As she stared at it, shocked and confused, she realized that its form wavered slightly; it mostly looked solid and opaque, but sometimes it faded a little and she could see through it.

The creature advanced, slowly and cautiously, and held up a hand. "Greetings," it said, and strangely Camilla understood it with perfect ease, though the word was strange and unfamiliar. Its strange, red eyes moved over them and then she saw it start slightly, but the start seemed to contain recognition, as it assessed the body of the slain orc.

It spoke again, still in the language Camilla did not know, and yet she understood it. "What and who are you, and why have you come to the Isles of Exile?"

"The Isles of Exile?" asked Camilla in astonishment.

"Do not question me. Instead answer for your presence in the lands I guard," said the strange elf.

"I did not know of your presence. We flee from the Wizard-King." She did not speak of the Wood Elves of Ilesh.

The elf canted his head in a strange way. "I know not of the Wizard-King, and you should know that these isles bear little friendship either to your kind, human, or to the elven people who exiled us to these isles, if they still persist in the Forlorn Lands."

"The Wood Elves exiled you?" Camilla asked, taken aback.

"In ancient days, which humans have long forgotten, and which perhaps even they have long forgotten," he answered. "It was so long ago even we scarcely remember, but it seems that we, or some of us, offended some queen of theirs or other in the distant past, and then that later others of their people joined us. Long has our past been, and in it many things have occurred.

There was an ancient time when a nation of men and Dragonriders dwelt in these isles, but that was long ago, and it has been many millenia that these isles have been ours alone, and no friendship have we had with others."

Camilla spoke for both herself and Radiance. "Then why do you come here now, for even if you consider this island your dominion, clearly you do not keep it, and you do not seem to come in hostility to us?"

The elf canted his head again, and as he considered his form faded until it looked like a stain of smoke upon the air. When he spoke again, his voice was distantly resonant. "I am Aglaretë, one of the Grove-born of the Dark Woods. Long and long has my life been, for I am one of those who are joined to the Fire Trees to provide our people with the sustenance which they lost in that long-ago age in which the olden Wood Spirits abandoned and scorned the ancestors of my people. As such, it is difficult for me to travel this far from my grove, and farther I cannot go, though others of my people could, if they desired. But few among them would bear you any friendship. Either they or our trees would be liable to turn against you and slay you before you knew it, and I do not want that fate to befall you."

Camilla nodded, and she did not protest that she could protect herself. She doubted that she could. The magic that she sensed about this odd elf was deeply tied to this place, and might be far stronger than what she could grasp. "Why did the dragonmages not know you dwelt here? Why did you never move to discourage or warn them?"

"Dragonmages?" Aglaretë asked, pondering her words for a moment. Just as she was about to explain, he said, "Oh yes. Those things. They are very strange creatures, and they never tarried too long near our lands. But they are such that I do not think any zealous wanderers of my people could have found and then slain them. Instead we hid from them."

Camilla's quick mind had already considered something else. "And what of the occasional outlaw they said they had found here?"

"This chain of islands is large. There are parts of it that are far from the Dark Woods and the Fire Groves. It may be that it was in those parts they found them. Or it may be that we miss some. If a human has little magic and does not disturb the natural magic and rhythm of a place, they might long go unnoticed by my people, or by myself. Or it may be that those outlaws they found had only recently made their way here, and were soon slain. I do not know."

"What I can do? Radiance – my dragon – is wounded and cannot fly far. The continent is a place of great peril, ruled by a Wizard-King who has brought the Northern Darkness and makes his captives into undead slaves. The Wood Elves of Ilesh have been overcome by his power, but even so they would be no refuge to us. They keep dragons as slaves, having twisted their natures by foul magic, and I too, with my family and a father who died while I was still young slaving under them, have been kept as slaves. Even when I Recognized

Radiance, they kept me as a slave and found ways to torture me for having Recognized their prized gold queen-mother."

Aglaretë canted his head in that weird way again. "Gold queen-mother?" he asked. "Last my people knew the dragons, some of them were gold, to be sure, but what you say implies something other than that."

"It is so," said Camilla. She felt fiery anger rise in her breast, and in Radiance, as she spoke, recalling these things. "The elves – the Wood Elves – used their magic to change the dragons, since dragons are not meant to be ridden by elves and were not thriving. Among other changes, they made gold females and silver males who feel the need to mate more strongly and lay larger clutches of eggs. They have changed their natures, too, so that they are more able to be Attached to the elves and more subservient to them. It is cruel, and I and Radiance have found out a little of what dragons ought to be like from the dragonmages, who have been across the sea and mingled with the dragons and Dragonriders there – either that, or they have a friend from across the sea. I'm not sure if it was never clear, or if I do not remember."

Aglaretë listened intently. Finally, he raised his hand and said, "Enough. I get the picture. But you should know – my people, too, are Wood Elves, perhaps even more so than the Ileshians, for we are one with our woods, some of us like myself profoundly so. And I sense, too, that a very deep magic runs in your own blood, Camilla, and in that of your dragon – a very deep fire, akin to our own fire, but yet awesomely different. I believe you about the crime of the Ileshians against the dragons – I see it, now that I think to look for it, in Radiance. I am sorry, but I do not think we of the Groves of Fire have the magic to undo this horrible thing." He paused and looked straight at her, and Camilla had the feeling that he was learning things she had not said, but was thinking – and was thinking of saying. "Nor, Dragonrider, can I train you. Our lives may both be fire, but my life and nature and my magic and thought are far too different from your own for me to even begin to teach you. Perhaps I could show you a few things that would be of use to you, if you knew your own magic well, but as things are now, I doubt I can share anything with you."

Absent-mindedly stroking Radiance's scales, she replied, "But most of the magic I know I learned, in one way or another, from elves and elven magic. Everyone tells me they cannot teach me, but I'm sure it's not true."

"I don't know who else has told you they cannot teach you, and I do not know what the magic of Ilesh is like, but I do know that I cannot teach you magic. *Look*. Can you not see that the magic that sustains my being, that is my life, is other than your own? That if, by some wonder, you could learn it – or rather become it, for it is not a learning, but a being – you would not want to do so."

"I certainly would not want to be tied to an island or even a chain of islands," she answered. "I am going to defeat the Wizard-King, and I doubt I could do it from an isolated island. But... but I had hoped to come here again, when I have slain the Wizard-King, and raise the next generation of dragons and human Dragonriders, Radiance's eggs and the eggs of whoever I can rescue from the Wizard-King, in these islands."

"Where were you intending to go when Radiance heals?"

"To the Sea Elves. We were hoping to take passage across the ocean to the other land, where there are untainted dragons, and other elves whom I have been told are masters of magic and will be able to teach me."

"Ah. Their songs sometimes drift to us on the wind and the waves. Beautiful they are, and sometimes I wonder if we Fire Elves would have been better to choose their path after the Wood Spirits forsook us, rather than making this one of our own." There was a deep sadness in Aglaretë's voice, mixed with a questioning uncertainty. "But I know little of them other than the snatches of their song, which float through my dreams, and though those are hauntingly beautiful and awaken old, strange desires in me, I have no love for the sea. I do not even know where to look for them."

"The dragonmages said that they have a northern harbor, but that if the Wizard-King harasses them too much, they might sail down along the eastern side of these isles to make themselves a harbor in the south."

"I will watch for that, and I will try to contact you if I learn anything. I regret that I can do nothing for Radiance, but I fear my powers are not for healing dragons. I will do what I can to keep you safe from the others of my people, and, again, if I fear that you are in immediate danger, I will do my best to warn you."

"Why?" asked Camilla, looking into a face in which the fiery eyes no longer seemed so strange.

"I do not know, daughter of humans and rider of dragons. I did not know until I felt you, and your struggle with the Nightmare. Perhaps that is another reason why I never warned the dragonmages – that I care for you as I never did for them. But I must go now. This is hard for me."

Even as he spoke, his voice grew softer, like an echo, and his form wavered, turning smokier and smokier, as if it were being drawn back and back and back towards wherever his grove stood. *"He goes,"* said Radiance.

Camilla collapsed into her shoulder, crying again. *And there are more dangers than I ever dreamed possible.* While the Fire Elf had spoken to them, she had had no space or time to think about the encounter with the orc and the fear and despair that had overcome her. Now, she could not believe that her own mind and heart had been manipulated so. It was impossible. Her whole being rose in protest against it.

"We should probably go back," she said. *But I wonder if we should visit here often. If it is so hard for Aglaretë to reach this far, he might be unable to contact us with anything he learns if he has to reach any farther. And I understand that other Fire Elves are not so constrained.*

It was strange. He was so different from the elves she knew, that her instinctive reaction against elves had not applied to him – and she wondered if she would find the Sea Elves the same way – and yet it appeared that his people might not be any better than the Ileshian Wood Elves. *Or maybe than all people,* she wondered. What did she really know of humans, other than that the Wizard-King ruled many of them, and that the sight of Radiance, wounded and chained, had aroused very little, if any, pity, and none of it ready to act? Of the humans she personally knew, Sylvara was not the only snitch – she was simply the one who had been the greatest problem to Camilla.

Waking

Do you really have no idea what we're going to do?

They had left the land behind a day earlier, laden with food and water for Kario, brought to them by another Dragonrider at Nelexi's request. Flameheart had gotten the distinct impression that the rider really did not like her at all, and that she had cooperated only because neither she nor her dragon could imagine spurning the Obsidian Guardian.

"Yes, I don't know what we're going to do," replied Nelexi. *"This is the fourth time I've told you this. The Ellenari often know different things than we do, their experience with time being so different that in this I am far more like you than I am like any of them, but they do not know everything, and they, like us, have limited knowledge. An important difference in many situations is that, their relationship to time being what it is, getting where and when they need to be is rather a different process."*

"Uh-huh," said Flameheart. She leaned out from the saddle. It was really strange flying this far above the ocean. All she saw from her vantage point were long lines of alternating shades of blue-green, and here and there a few starbursts of white foam, presumably where the waves crashed on a reef or small island. Wisps of cloud drifted through the sky above and around them, and her whole heart ached to be running across the plains, catching lizards, chasing spring butterflies, and whatever else caught her fancy. She wriggled in the saddle, itching to be able to move freely.

Nelexi tried to share with her, her own experience of flying, of the freedom and width, the glory of the skies and the wind, but though this sharing alleviated her yearning, it was not really enough.

"This might be part of why obsidian dragons almost always choose those who already ride a dragon," Nelexi had said to her once. *"Though I am bonded with you more tightly than with any of my previous riders, it is still not the bond other dragons and riders have, and so I cannot share with you what I have and am in the same way. Also,"* and this she said with a slight sigh, *"though I am a creature of the wind, as well as of fire, as are all dragons, I am less a creature of wind than are many other dragons, though I am a bearer of the earthfire as only the Obsidian Guardian can be."*

But though the black dragon tried to explain things, Kario did not understand. She loved Nelexi with all her heart and would not be parted from her for anything, yet she was heartsick for the plains of her home and her family. She worried, too, despite her best efforts, about what she would do in the War of the Gods. No matter that Nelexi loved her and that she loved Nelexi, what use was she really, where the Old Gods and the Great Powers were concerned? She was glad to be loved by the dragon, but she could not stop feeling nervous, unworthy, useless.

Nelexi directed her attention to the lines of the waves undulating in the sea below them. *"Perhaps I should not have told you that I was a god,"* said the dragon, *"and I think it is time for me to remind you of other things. Usefulness and worthiness are lies of the Nightmare. Even power is a lie of the Nightmare. There is only being, and all being is beloved and sacred in the eyes of Shallim-Araldor, who has many names among many peoples, and is called also the Lord of Light and the Lord of Love. Even thinking in terms of war is misleading, though I have often spoken to you in those words, for it makes you think of loss and fear and usefulness, and all those are lies. None of us are useful, little rider, and none of us are useless. To think of usefulness and uselessness violates what you know of love, of being and nature, and our relationship. The Nightmare is that which does not know love: it is utterly alien to what ties us and makes us one. And don't your own people's legends and stories teach you that not even the strongest, most skilled warrior can fight even an orc, if fear and hate, instead of love, control his heart?"*

Yes, but the spear or arrow is still necessary to kill the orc. And even if I have love, I have none of that.

"There are other nightmare creatures which no spear or arrow can hurt," said Nelexi.

Yes. There are the medusar, and other things that are very horrible. But don't those require the weapons of the gods to slay them?

"There are things against which the power of the Ellenari avails not. But you think still of usefulness. What is the real victory against the Nightmare, Flameheart? What is the real victory? What is life? What is your desire? To love and to be beloved, to be happy. Right?"

Yes. She nodded slightly, even though Nelexi could not see and did not need the gesture.

"Then," began the voice of solid fire, when Flameheart felt her pause, considering something. After several minutes of steady flying, she spoke again. *"I don't think these worries are your nature, and I think I am addressing them in the wrong way. You are lonely. You feel very alone and very far from home, and very small and needy. Perhaps I should not have chosen you. Perhaps I should have waited longer for you. But I needed you. I love you so much, and I have waited so long. I wish I could give you everything you need, but now I wonder if I have chosen rightly, though something in my heart tells me that I have, that I need you, that we were made for one another and to love one another."*

For a long time they flew in silence. Finally, Nelexi continued, *"But I really don't think these fears are yours. I think they're mostly the way that you're expressing and experiencing your discomfort at the upheaval in your life and your loneliness."*

Flameheart did not know what to say. *"I love you. I'm glad for your friendship."*

Nelexi did not respond in words, but Flameheart felt from her a strong sense of love and of friendship, and of value; a sense of belonging of such terrific intensity that for a moment it frightened her, but that she felt that it was her own belonging. It could no more be terrifying to her than Nelexi's own fire could threaten the obsidian dragon.

The sun was warm and beat down mercilessly on them, while the air felt moist, when she suddenly noticed that Nelexi was dropping altitude smoothly but quickly. *What is it?* she asked. *I don't see an island.*

"*There's an island all right. We're pretty high – I can fly higher than most dragons – and you might miss it, though. It's not big, but it has nice fish.*"

For you. Not for me, replied Flameheart. *Do you know where every island in this vast sea is?*

Nelexi shook her long neck, and Flameheart suspected that she was doing it to tease her. It certainly shook *her* around a bit. "*I don't know where every island is in this sea, but I have been this way before. Some of the islands I discovered myself, but most I learned either from other dragons who had been across the sea or from birds. Some of the birds never land in their long flight, but many of them have keen eyes and birds have memories that are, in some ways, very like dragon memories. But this island is fairly close to the shore. It isn't big, but it is rather well-known, and has been for many generations of humans. As for those fish – some of them are of a kind that humans in some lands will eat raw. They're considered quite a delicacy. I wouldn't mention them for myself. Remember, I eat rocks mostly, and I don't even eat rocks often unless I have to fight.*"

I remember, but it's hard to imagine how little you have to eat or how a creature like you isn't a meat-eater! Didn't you once hunt meat, before you became the Obsidian Guardian when you were just another obsidian dragon, so many years ago maybe you don't remember it, and maybe you liked fish like those back then. I'm fairly certain I don't want to eat raw fish.

Nelexi laughed, and the deep rumble in her chest vibrated up her rider's body. "*Oh, I remember those days well enough. But how did you learn about how the Obsidian Guardian is made? I'm fairly certain I never told you.*"

The question surprised her for a moment. How did she know? But she was not wrong; there was no touch of such a tone in Nelexi's voice. *It fits, I think,* she mused, trying to figure it out. *Also, I think another of the riders who was willing to talk to me civilly – maybe Zhaizen – or one of the Light Elves might have told me.*

"*Or maybe you just knew. Even now that I have been with you for some time, I still forget how different this bonding is from all the others I have known, little rider. And if you want to try the fish, but not raw, we can find a way to cook them for you.*"

Maybe, she replied noncommittally. They were low enough now that it was easy for her to see the little island below them, a little ahead and to the right. It was close enough she could even see why it had been hard to for her to see: the foliage was of a very curious color, darker and bluer than any grass, and most trees, that she had seen.

Is it an island of those blue pine or – what was the other kind called? – trees? Do they grow outside the mountains?

"*Some of them do, but, no, those aren't conifer trees of any sort. I suppose we're still not low enough for you to see. This island does not have real trees at all, though it may have things your people would consider a tree. Those blue colors are a species of grass and shrub-like plants. You will see for yourself soon.*"

A few minutes later, Nelexi landed a little heavily. *I'm tired,* she told her rider. *I can fly straight for many days at a time, but it can still be exhausting, and now I have been in the sky for almost two days without rest.*

"It's fine," she said out loud, half-laughing, as she climbed out of the saddle. "I suspect you jarred yourself much harder than you jolted me. It's not half as bad as a ship."

"*I'm sorry you hated that so much. During the time when I was waiting for you to grow up, I tried to explore the sea and find if there were any islands we could stop by for our journey, but that part of the sea is very desolate – well, when it comes to land. It's very hard for most dragons to cross.*" She turned her head to look at her rider, who was climbing rather slowly down her shoulder. "*I didn't tell you, did I? I'm not the only large creature that doesn't eat meat. There are some very large whales in the ocean that eat very, very tiny plants.*"

Oh. Kario sat down in the grass. *I didn't know.* A smile curved her lips, and she looked up at the dragon. She enjoyed the things Nelexi shared with her.

"*A lot of people don't. A lot of dragons don't. I wouldn't have expected you to know. But I was thinking. Your people speak of the Old Gods, and I think that's a misleading way to talk and think about the Nightmare. There really isn't a better word I know of than that, and it might help you to understand if you think of the 'Nightmare' instead of 'we're going to fight the Old Gods'. I don't know why your people call them the Old Gods, and there might be an appropriateness to it that I don't understand, but I don't think you understand it, either. But think of our enemy for a moment as the Nightmare. All the nightmares of human and dragon kind, and of many other peoples and races as well – loneliness and despair, hatred, anguish and loss, uselessness, guilt, and above all fear. These are the Nightmare that haunts this world; they are not the Waking World, of which we know little, for few of us are yet half-awake. And how do you defeat or fight a Nightmare?*"

Flameheart sat quietly, meticulously tearing apart blades of grass. *Well, a nightmare isn't real, right? So I suppose you don't really* fight *it. You don't* believe *it. You recognize that it's not real, that it's just a nightmare you're having, and that you're going to wake up soon.* She paused in her thoughts for a while, and when she resumed she was speaking softly, almost without noticing it. "It's really weird to think about. I suppose you tell the nightmare to go away, maybe? You think about all the good things you know are real, or that you would like to dream about, I suppose. That is, if you *know* you're dreaming. But oftentimes you don't know you're dreaming. And we – if what you're saying is right, then none of us have ever really been Awake."

"Something like that, but analogies are never perfect. We have glimpses of the Waking World; in a way, we live in the Waking World, but in a dream infested with the Nightmare, if that makes any sense. But I'm trying to give you a feel for things. This is a story, a parable. But do you understand a little?"

I think so. A little. And I think it makes sense of how the most important thing isn't whether or not you can fight with a sword or a spear, or something like that, dragonfire I guess, but yet some of the nightmare creatures, like orcs, almost always have to be killed that way. But is death then waking up?

"It can be. It is a step on the journey to being Awake."

That makes sense. It is a little like certain stories of my people. But I suppose the Nightmare only exists, then, because people are afraid – of whatever it is, loneliness, not belonging, not being loved. Whatever. So, if I were to somehow completely overcome fear, and not be afraid of anything, but be absolutely certain in the victory of your love for me and mine for you, to not be afraid or fear or hate at all – would that mean I wouldn't see or feel the Nightmare at all? Would it mean wherever I went, any nightmare creatures would just die or whatever? Would they not be able to kill me? What would happen?

"I don't know precisely. I don't think anyone does. The Ellenari do not live as we live; they are not born, and they do not age in any sense like that in which even I age, but they do not fear or hate at all. They are completely invulnerable to the Nightmare, though it requires something of them to fight it, and there are some nightmare creatures or manifestations which they cannot defeat, and some which they cannot even do anything against at times. I am as near to immortal as any creature born of the worlds is so far. While Areaer lives, I also will live. Do you know about the Dragon-sword and the Bearers of the Dragon-sword?"

Flameheart shook her head. "I've only barely heard of that. I think you mentioned it to me once or twice."

"So I have. All those who have borne the Dragon-sword have died fighting the Nightmare, in the very hour and moment of their triumph. That is not merely coincidence, and the strange ideas a few people have gotten into their heads about destinies and curses is quite wrong. Their deaths are an integral part of their triumph."

"But when everyone is no longer afraid, is certain of love and the victory of love, then the Nightmare will be no more?"

"Yes, and that is the victory we seek."

"I know that," she whispered, leaning back against Nelexi's side, under the shade of her wing. The dragon's body was hot, but so was everything else, and at least she had some shade under the dragon's wing. She was fairly certain that it was not really hotter than it often was in the plains of her home, but it was a lot wetter, and that made her hotter. "You told me that a long time ago. Maybe the day we first met." She closed her eyes, and then wiggled away from the dragon's side and lay down in the grass, trying to get more comfortable.

Isn't the Nightmare real? she continued. *I was under the impression that some creatures can become nightmare creatures if they go bad enough.*

"That's true enough, in a way," said Nelexi.

Are all nightmare creatures that way?

"I don't know."

Can those nightmare creatures ever become un-nightmared?

"I – don't know. The Ellenari seem to think that those creatures which were once of more or less the same kind as they – if I may put it thus; the Ellenari would not find my explanation suitable – are corrupted for all time. But then again, though they know that it is so, they do not understand how any creature can once do evil and then be purified. But I'm pretty sure that not all nightmare creatures are nightmare creatures in quite the same way – that, of those nightmare creatures which definitely come from real creatures, they may not all be those creatures from which they come to the same extent. I don't think any of us can understand these things yet, if we will ever – remember, this is the Nightmare. You know how nightmares are, and I think there is a similarity of sorts there, too. We shouldn't try to understand the Nightmare too much."

Does that mean that some *nightmare creatures can become un-nightmared? That, maybe, some of them we shouldn't try to kill, but instead to rescue?*

"If you feel that way, I won't argue with you. It may be possible for some. There is always a first, and each of us is a first – and only. But it is not something I have heard of before. Remember, in most cases, I don't think the nightmare creatures are real creatures. There are plenty of real creatures going down the nightmare path, all over the place, but I don't really know what nightmare creatures are. They are, if it makes sense, nightmares. They're not often alive. And I think once something becomes a 'nightmare creature' carrying the presence of the Nightmare in the way nightmare creatures do – well, I'm not even sure that, in all but a few rare cases, that's even a good way of putting it. I think you shouldn't be thinking about this too much. It's not like you're going to be killing anything bigger than an ant or a lizard anytime soon, is it? And – I do not know if it matters, but many nightmare creatures are what is considered undead and – I wouldn't tell this to anyone else, since I'm unsure, and people sometimes hear in what others say far more than they meant, or

else interpret it in their own way – but I'm unsure whether even orcs might be a kind of half-undead."

At that moment, that distinction did not interest Flameheart. *You're thinking about something very specific when you talk about a few rare cases of creatures becoming nightmare creatures, aren't you?*

Nelexi shook her head, in a way that reminded Flameheart of an animal shaking its head to clear it of flies – an issue she doubted the dragon had. *"I am. There are obsidian dragons who cling to life in this world when they should not. All obsidian dragons are not usual mortals – they grow in size and strength, and in some degree in intelligence and magic, but they do not grow old, and they are less vulnerable to attack than most mortal creatures. They must choose to fly into the volcano when the time comes for them to pass on from this phase of life. Perhaps it is as if some creatures had the choice to refuse to be born. There are almost always things that happen in the life and choices of an obsidian dragon that foreshadow this refusal to return to the Fire of Areaer, but that choice can be thought of as the defining one that makes an obsidian dragon into a nightmare dragon, though sometimes it takes a long time to make as humans and most dragons count years."*

I see. She wound a piece of grass through her fingers, deep in what Nelexi was saying, and her attempts to understand. *Perhaps they are stuck in their nightmare, and are unable to wake until they are thrown out of the place they have stuck themselves. But isn't there a danger of killing creatures one really shouldn't kill?*

"For which reason these things are not widely taught, though bits and pieces of them end up in many tales and myths, and I am afraid that may be the work of the Nightmare, for the bits and pieces are often corrupt. That is the danger – of thinking of everything one does not like, or even simply everything that wants to kill one, that is fighting, in one way or another, on the side of the Nightmare, as a nightmare creature. But neither the Sea Elves nor the Sha'adhri are nightmare creatures. Though I doubt that anyone who is honest and good-willed, who knows or seeks love in whatever way is suited to her nature and that point in her life, will make such a terrible mistake – but I do not know. Usually, unless the Nightmare is very strong within one's own soul, one knows a nightmare creature apart from other things, for it is a force of fear and hate; it is not simply something acting in a nightmare, but the incarnation of Nightmare, a manifestation of it. It is not a tainted thing; it is the taint itself, taking the form of a thing, while not truly being. It is Nightmare." Nelexi took a deep breath, and paused for a moment. Then she asked, *"Do you understand, now? That it is not a weakness or a liability that you are Kario Flameheart, my beloved rider, and not the Dragon-Warrior? For I have always loved your heart."*

Flameheart nodded, as well as she could while lying down. *I do. Remember, I asked if we should not be killing them at all?*

"You did, and you are right. It is not your place to kill the nightmare creatures as others do. It is your place to be something else, something just as beautiful and lovely. I think you show us the Waking World as... not more than others do, for something I have learned in my long life is that more often means nothing – this is an easy concept for dragons, even obsidian dragons, but I have had many riders who did not find it so. And it is often easy to perceive, and there is truth in the perception, that something shows 'more' truth when it shows us a truth that we have not yet seen. And you show what it means to be Awake as I have not seen before, though I might feel it so clearly with you because I am bonded to you as I have been to no one else, and so I see what you are as I saw none of my previous riders." She reached her neck even further along her body, and blew gently under her wing and into Kario's face.

Freedom

They turned a corner around a rock, and found themselves standing at the top of a ridge. Climbing towards them were both the silver dragons and their riders.

She cast a welcoming smile towards her brother and quickly turned her fiercest glare on Sylvara. "Stay out of my life, you snitch and would-be slave," she growled, ignoring the ache throbbing in her jaw.

Sylvara took a slow, hesitant step forward. "Camilla," she said, in a soft, subdued tone that angered the other almost beyond thought. She had always been like that, talking like that, even while she plotted the pain and abuse of others! "Camilla, I'm really very sorry." She cast a strange glance, half furtive, half full of longing and appreciation, at Shimmer, who had settled on his haunches and tucked his tail around himself. "I felt with Shimmer that something had gone wrong. I want to come... to help. I'm really sorry for the way I used to act. I never noticed that there was anyone except myself, and Shimmer has made me see that's wrong."

Camilla took a step forward herself, walking as lithely as a stalking cat. "Really, Sylvara? I am tired of your piteous-sounding lies. You are a shanxthar," she said, referring to a mythical creature in one of the stories her mother had told her, "that wails and whines as if injured and in deadly pain, and then strikes with its deadly venom the man or woman who comes to rescue you. But I know this, and I will have naught to do with you."

Sylvara cast her eyes down. Then she said, "Have you really not noticed that I've changed? Have I done so poorly as that? I've been trying to be helpful, wherever I could."

"Of course you have," Camilla half-purred, half-growled, as she took another cat-like step forward. "Of course you would. You know that I would never tolerate anything less. You would be afraid to drive me to too much anger with you. Do you think I would dream of letting you eat and live off my and my brother's and our dragons' hard work?"

For a few long moments Sylvara did not speak, but continued to stare at the ground, while Shimmer took on an intent attitude. Then she raised her eyes and met Camilla's. "I know I've done so much that it's hard for you to believe me now," she said, "but I promise. Shimmer has changed me. I want to help. I want to make up for everything I've done wrong to you. I'm really sorry, and I'm here to help."

Camilla stepped forward again. She was vaguely aware of Radiance following her. "Shimmer changed you?" she asked, mockingly. "Really. I distinctly recall you tormenting me after we both Recognized, when the elves had taken us away from the others."

"Shimmer," said Sylvara, and Camilla could not tell if she was pleading with the dragon, or if she was about to say something to herself. She straightened her back to stand as tall as she could. "It... took a long time for me to really understand."

"Oh right." She took another step forward, but stopped mid-stride when Shimmer's mind-voice flashed through her mind like a silvery rainbow and the sound of misting rain. *"Camilla, Dragonrider, Dragonspeaker, Dragonkeeper, my rider tells you the truth. She is changing. We are both growing."*

She stayed frozen, unable to deny what she heard, and unable to deal with it. Radiance – was it Radiance, or was it her own mind? – had suggested something similar to her earlier, but everything about Sylvara, especially her contrition, reminded her of the girl who had tormented her, of the sly, deceitful double-face, the constant spying and snitching. She did not think she could *ever* trust Sylvara, even though a dragon, who could not lie, told her that Sylvara had changed and grown trustworthy; even if Sylvara proved her trustworthiness, it could never be proved *to* her. Even though what Shimmer had told her even made a sort of sense. As he grew older, as his mind grew more mature and his influence grew more solid, as his rider grew closer to him – something Camilla and Radiance had experienced only infinitesimally, being already so close from the beginning – there was no doubt that that his part in who she was would grow, and that she might be slowly and gradually, but inexorably, changed by the bond. Yet Camilla could not accept it. Sylvara's mannerisms would always provoke her rage and anger at the girl's deceitful, insane betrayal, almost as if she desired slavery and took the side of those who enslaved – and there was almost nothing Camilla hated more than that, though she could not quite say why, only that she hated Sylvara more than almost any elf, with the exception only of the life-mages who had changed the dragons.

Finally, she said, "I think it is best for us... to leave each other alone."

"But what if you are injured? What if you need my help?" asked Sylvara.

"I will never need your help," said Camilla, locking stares with her. "I will stop condemning you, but only if you stay away from me."

Sylvara bowed her head, turned away, then climbed onto Shimmer's back. He spread his wings, lifted them, and was in the air with surprising grace. Camilla's heart ached with inconceivable pain. That grace ought to be Radiance's, but she was still stiff and sore almost over her entire body!

The thought was interrupted by a deep sense of approval and satisfaction. Her dragon was truly one with her in her solution to the problem with Sylvara.

As Shimmer glided away, Lavilor and Sleet approached her. Almost crying, her brother flung his arms around her, and she kissed him through sore lips. "What's wrong?" she asked.

"Aren't you hurt?" he said.

"Not very badly. I will get better."

"What happened up there?"

"We were attacked by some of those nightmare creatures."

"Servants of the Wizard-King?" asked Lavilor.

"I don't know. Maybe. They were orcs."

"So does the Wizard-King know where we are?"

"I don't think so. Someone or something killed the orc. It was probably just wandering around, looking for something bad to do." Not that Camilla really knew anything about it, but she doubted the Wizard-King knew where they were or that, if he did, he would send one orc to capture her and Radiance.

"Do you know anything about who rescued you?"

"Not really. It might have been a Fire Elf called Aglaretë."

"A Fire Elf?" asked Lavilor.

"Yes. I think they used to be the same kind of thing as the elves of Ilesh, but a long, long time ago, so long ago most elves don't even remember it, the elves of Ilesh exiled them and cast them out, and they became Fire Elves. It sounds like some tree spirits or something forsook them, and they needed some magical bond to live, and so they found a way to make themselves Fire Trees and become Fire Elves, and that some of them live in the Fire Trees in a way I don't understand. They're very unlike the elves we know, but most of them don't like strangers and will kill them to keep them away from their lands and trees, so it would be a bad idea for us to go to their islands."

Her brother released her and sat down on a bit of grass. "Fire Trees?" he asked, incredulously. "But trees... trees don't like fire."

"Perhaps. And I've not seen them, I've just heard about them. I don't understand it, but it's some kind of magic. And this elf... he looked really strange. He had eyes that looked like flames, and he had skin and hair that looked like it had burnt, like charcoal or ash, but it looked like there was still a little fire in his hair."

Lavilor nodded. He did not say anything for a few moments. Then he said, "Do you think I will ever see Mom again? It seems most likely that she *has* to be dead by now."

"I don't know," said Camilla. "Some people might have escaped somehow. And I am *going* to defeat the Wizard-King and free all his captives, one way or the other!"

Lavilor looked up at her. "Camilla?" he said.

"Yes?" she asked, surprised at his sudden change of mood and tone.

"You," he began, and then stopped again. Camilla was tempted to reach out into his mind, reasoning that he clearly intended to communicate something to her and was only struggling with words, and then thought better of it. Humans were not dragons. Even she was not quite a dragon. If she had to, she could do that, but she probably gathered enough simply by being open in the ways she was, without reaching out deliberately and unnecessarily. "You...

You seem... I... You seem very angry and afraid. Do you really believe that?"

"Of course I believe that. It *will* be. As sure as I exist." Underneath it all, though, she knew that she was afraid – just a little, very little afraid, and yet terribly, horribly so, afraid that she would not be able to defeat the Wizard-King, or that it might be possible for her and Radiance to be enslaved, and that fear had been brought nearer her consciousness and into her thought by the events earlier that day. Now, she cursed the fact that Lavilor brought it to her attention again.

A few minutes passed, while Camilla ached, and then Lavilor asked, so softly the wind almost carried his words away and she would not have been able to hear them had she not been one who spoke as dragons speak, "Don't you believe that the Lord of Light will take care of things, whether or not you can defeat the king?"

An anger Camilla *never* felt towards her brother flared up in her, even as she remembered that she and Radiance had thought before that her focus on anger was not helpful. "What?" she asked. "Why would I ever believe in the Lord of Light at all? What has he ever done to show me he exists? Or cares? Someone as powerful as that!"

Lavilor spoke with quiet earnestness. "But he *does* exist. I know it."

She crossed her arms over her chest and stared at him. "*How?!* I certainly don't!"

Infuriatingly, his quiet look contested her statement. Then he said, "I just do. He speaks to me."

"Oh, and what does he say?"

"That he loves me and Sleet. That he loves everyone. That he will rescue us all and bring us back together in his perfect land."

"Harumph," said Camilla.

"Are you mad at me?" asked Lavilor.

"No. I'm just mad."

"Because I believe in the Lord of Light?"

"I don't know. I'm mad. Things *shouldn't* be the way they are. People *are* free. And if the Lord of Light exists, why doesn't he make sure of that? And..." Her voice trailed away. How could she explain to Lavilor all her thoughts about freedom and destiny? She was not even sure what she thought. She only knew there was something *very* wrong with the world, but she still did not know what freedom was or what it meant, or if it was even inherently possible, and what had Serrose said about perfect love being freedom and freedom never being complete until everyone loved and no one hated, but each one being freer the more he loved?

Against Camilla's expectations, Sylvara proved to be helpful, working hard and diligently to take care of their needs. Camilla and Radiance went every day to the mountain peak, in case Aglaretë needed to speak to her about further developments or information. She spent hours every day massaging Radiance as well as she could through the dragon's scale armor, trying to loosen and soothe her muscles. They spent many of these hours on the mountain peak, and gradually she began to feel that this might be, in some ways, the nicest time she had yet had in her life. The work of preparing wood for fires and cooking food, of finding the herbs and roots and berries Alian had shown them was not the mind-draining all-encompassing thing that work for the elves had been. She was driven to it by the need to eat and live, not by slave-masters who might punish her if they caught her slacking, or doing something they considered disrespectful. She could do it in whatever attitude she felt like, and express herself in any way she desired, without threat of punishment. And she could take breaks whenever she wanted to, as well.

As for Radiance, she was still far too troubled by her wounds to hunt, but she was getting better every day, and often she soared lazily in the skies. Sleet and Shimmer were becoming quite proficient hunters, and so no one lacked for meat. Thus, her enjoyment was marred only by the loss of her mother and the worry she might not even be alive, as well as Radiance's inability to fully enjoy the skies. If not for these, it would have been a time of unshadowed freedom and delight. The winds that blew from the east were still strange and eerie, but they did not have the horrible feel of the Wizard-King's magic which, somehow, now seemed so far away that her belief in and outrage at it were placed at one remove. Once it had been a few days, even her confrontation with the orc and what it had done to her seemed like less than a memory, something that seemed strange to her when she thought about it. Sometimes she sat on a hump of ground and wondered why. It had been so frightening and horrifying at first, and she had been so shaken, but now, as her face was just beginning to get less stiff, she hardly even believed it had happened. She wondered if she felt the way she did, both about the elves, and about the Wizard-King, and even the orc because she was tired and there was no immediate crisis to demand her attention. The previous weeks had been demanding, and Radiance was exhausted from healing her wounds. She shared in that exhaustion.

As that exhaustion faded a little, she started to realized how much she had never had time and space to appreciate the true beauty and wonder of the world before. She could stare at the bright blue summer sky for minutes on end, unwearying of its perfect, exact color, pure and bright, blinding in the intensity of its blueness. Almost every morning and evening the rising or setting sun turned the clouds that blew off the sea or hung about other islands into a glorious panoply of shifting, melding color that not only rivaled but outdid the fanciest tapestries and cloaks of the elves. The forests clothed the mountains in variegated shades of green and green-blues, but here and there the rocky bones of the land showed through, often largely clothed with green or yellow moss, fringed with orange lichen. Sometimes, the scenes made her heart almost writhe in anger at the cruelty and injustice of the elves, that they would hoard to themselves all the good in the world and make both dragons and humans their slaves! Yet, as often and almost as quickly as her heart turned to these angry, bitter thoughts, the purity and beauty of her surroundings drew her back out of anger into admiration and enjoyment, into pleasure. Her weariness, or the weariness she shared with Radiance, contributed also, for it was hard to sustain an emotion of such intense energy as anger when weary, yet her pleasure at the beauty and purity of the world around her, while sometimes ecstatically, almost painfully, intense, required almost no energy on her own part. She could simply bask in it, whether in the warm sunshine or in the flamboyant or mellow shades of sunrise or sunset.

In some ways, the work she had to do now was also more pleasant than that which she had often been made to do by the elves. Not only was there no one telling her not to slack, or treating her as an inferior, which meant a great deal in itself, but a good deal of the work was just *nicer* than many of the things the elves wanted. Part of that was because she was doing it for herself, like preparing meat which was not particularly nice, but there was a kind of pleasure in digging up roots, or gathering berries and herbs, even if her back was a little sore afterwards. The wind blew around her, the leaves of the trees sang around her, and scents, some aromatic and some very soft and some tangy presented themselves to her nostrils – or to Radiance's; it was much the same, though smells were different for the human or for the dragon – in a way which she could only think of as melodic. She could even eat the berries and some of the leaves while collecting them, and that, too, was a delight.

Sometimes, she would stretch out her arms and walk through a glade singing, sometimes exuberantly and often more calmly. It was a pleasure beyond measuring. The elves had never liked her or any of the slaves singing, and she had certainly never dared to sing freely around them, not that she had wanted to sing much before. Perhaps as a child, but if so it had been so thoroughly discouraged that she had forgotten it, and even the tendency had slumbered as if in a coma. Since she had fled Ilesh, she had sung only twice, and twice it had been a wild and exultant experience, rich with magic to a greater or lesser degree, and twice it had been followed, even interrupted, by disaster of a greater or lesser degree. Now, she was discovering her song again, her own and no other's, and it seemed to her beautiful with undeveloped beauties and possibilities, the song of a very young child. Her delight in it was tainted by sorrow, and even more by anger that this side of human growth and experience had been denied to her and to so many others, but between the weariness and her relationship with Radiance and between the beauty around her and the delight of her own song, that anger often passed, and the wonder of her own song often left her soul throbbing with pleasure. It was as if, in singing, the distinction between the form of her own thought and the form of the world around her faded, and the two were merged into one enchanting expression of beauty, full often of thoughts and beauties that were mostly undeveloped and yet developed so that they seemed to her to be strange and new, unique, lovely, and sometimes hauntingly familiar. She was surprised, too, by how often her song was a quiet and calm thing, more like a soft evening breeze or a light summer wind than like a storm or a tempest. Then she realized that dragon flight was not a tempestuous thing, or not only. Mostly it was the slow, calm, beat of wings upon the air, steady and unwavering, or a gliding upon a draft of wind, sometimes more demanding than it was easy, but still gentle. This gentleness, almost leisure, even if it was one that consisted largely of steady and dedicated labor, was very much an attribute of her new life.

That this was freedom was no disappointment at all. She had never been able to truly imagine freedom before. The farthest she had ever gotten was the fight for it, and she found the quiet and the plainness of this to be a wonder almost as ecstatic as any drama. Nothing could be less like the servitude and drudgery of slavery. The reality had turned out to be something better than she had ever dreamed, if only because she had never dreamed of it at all.

One day, she sat alone on a rock after singing for a while, her fingers and chin stained with berry juice, and remarked on how she and Radiance had felt when they had first seen these mountains, and their dream of staying here and raising future generations of dragons and Dragonriders here. Was it some quality of these islands – perhaps influenced by the Fire Elves' magic – that lent this contentment and satisfaction, or was it a quality of any land where one had a moment to rest and make a life outside the dominance of one's oppressors? Even then, there had been the temptation to forget what she had determined to do, and now she found herself almost forgetting it indeed, hardly thinking about it at all, except now and then to wish that everyone else could enjoy this freedom, but not with the determination, the certainty and the dedication with which she had always fought before. Why? What was happening to her? Was it not something good or natural, but the touch of the Nightmare that materialized itself in the attack of the orc? Yet it felt so good…

I'm not a slave. I'm free. I'm doing what I want, and it wouldn't do any good for me to be put lots of energy into something I can, at the moment, do nothing about. Perhaps it is better to accept that now is a time for growth, for healing and resting, that must come if I and Radiance are ever to grow into our strength and defeat the Wizard-King. Perhaps I have spent too much time being angry, and perhaps more anger won't help my magic. I am fairly certain it won't help Radiance heal. So I am content.

But she fought the inclination to think, *I wish it could just stay this way, and I didn't have to fight the Northern Horror.* She *had* to defeat the Darkness and free the slaves. She *would* do so. She had chosen it. It *would* be.

Others

They remained on that island for a long time, waiting for the dragons to grow stronger, and life continued. Camilla and Lavilor often played together, inventing a variety of games from running around to trying to build tree forts. Often, Camilla felt too angry and sad to play, since it reminded her of all that she and so many human mothers and fathers and children had lost through uncounted generations because of their enslavement by the elves, but Lavilor once told her, "Just because we couldn't have it then, and others couldn't have it either, is that any reason to not enjoy things now?" She agreed with him and the dragons, and the draconic part of her own mind made her instantly see the sense of it, so it was not as if she could even think about arguing.

And, why would we let the elves continue to steal from us just because they did so in the past? We would be continuing to perpetrate their crime upon ourselves, she thought, trying to feel less guilty. Gradually, the moments of anger and sorrow that crushed all playfulness grew less common, but they never ceased altogether, and sometimes they leapt upon her with undiminished strength. Still, all in all, she enjoyed playing with Lavilor and exploring the world around them, and since it made Lavilor happier, she tried to play with him as often as she could. Even so, she knew he missed her mother and thought of what they were losing even now at least as much as she did. Sometimes, it made *him* so sad he did not want to play, and that made her the saddest of all, for he was usually the most interested in playing, whether that was catch-me-if-you-can, hide-and-seek, build-our-fort, who-can-catch-more-tree-frogs or who-can-look-more-like-a-mud-monster, among many others.

Sometimes Sylvara tried to join them, but Camilla never allowed that.

Sometimes the dragons watched the seabirds hunt, and soon they decided to try hunting in the sea themselves. As Radiance healed, she grew more interested in hunting. Often she brought her rider to the top of the cliff, or flew her to a cave that opened in a cliff, and left her there, to watch as she hunted. Sunlight flashed from her scales and wings as she soared and circled, and Camilla held her breath in awe when she tucked her wings and dove, a streak of flashing sunlight, towards the sea. She disappeared into the water, head first, and submerged completely, before coming up again. At first she missed her prey far more often than not, but it was a thrilling, satisfying experience for both of them. When she did catch a fish and the thrill of accomplishment and satisfaction rushed through them together, Camilla thought that dragons and Dragonriders were the most privileged beings in all existence, or at least that she and Radiance were such privileged beings, for theirs was not only all the enjoyment of one life, but all the enjoyment of two lives. More even than that, for she not only enjoyed the world for herself and shared Radiance's enjoyment of the world, but she enjoyed Radiance's only delight in her, and so their mutual delight was multiplied.

Summer ran its course, and finally autumn took hold of the isles and there were very few berries to be found anymore. They had to live off the dragons' kills, and the occasional roots which only Sylvara knew how to recognize. This made Camilla very uncomfortable, since she did not want to trust her safety, and even less her little brother's safety, to someone she could not trust not to poison them. Even her draconic sense that told her Sylvara's conscientious behavior was more or less genuine and honest could not make her at ease with it. It only made her able to tolerate it, even though Sylvara ate from the same preparations that she shared with Camilla and her brother, and Camilla did not think Sylvara would be willing to poison herself in order to poison them. The coward had always seemed to her far too self-serving to ever do something that she expected to bring harm to herself.

Yet, somehow, Sylvara seems less entirely self-serving now, as she shared the greater portion of what she found with Camilla and Lavilor, than she ever had before. Camilla was around her too constantly on the small island not to notice it, not to take note of the fact that even though her very presence made her furious, Sylvara seemed genuine in a way she never had before. Her expressions of care were more often muted than over-done, and they did not *feel* counterfeited in the way they always had before.

Camilla had to admit to herself that, as much as she still did not like Sylvara, Recognition had not failed to change her, and it made *sense*. From where she had been entirely self-seeking before, she now *had* to care, at least a little, about Shimmer. As contrary to Sylvara as it seemed to care about another, there could be no doubt that she would risk and suffer herself for her dragon, at the very least; though it had taken her a long time to be able to acknowledge it, she had seen that tenderness and care in Sylvara's interactions with Shimmer and knew that it was not – could not be – faked.

Not that she's really any less self-seeking in loving Shimmer, she thought to herself. *She feels what Shimmer feels, even if not as strongly as I and Radiance do; but at least, there is something other than her own*

selfishness in that relationship. She cares about wants and thoughts of another, instead of only about her own, even though Shimmer is so close to her that his needs are hers. But she must need him, and I suppose it's the greatest difference in the world for her to need someone.

But since anything having to do with Sylvara was upsetting, so she tried not to think about it too much, and now was not the time to dwell on such uncomfortable thoughts, as she watched Radiance hunt. Afternoon was turning into evening, and what looked like a storm was rising out of the western sea. Great billowing, fluffy shapes of clouds and their tattered robes were glowing with pink and orange and ruby highlights and streaks, while underneath and away from the glancing light of the lowering sun they were dark misty gray-purple.

We've so much more leisure here than I ever thought we could have, she thought, looking up at the sky and realizing how little chance she had gotten to do that in the previous sixteen years of her life. It was so beautiful and so magical, and it touched her soul in so many ways she could not even begin to describe it. It was as if water and fire and air were all merged in one soul as perfectly as she and Radiance were one. It made her feel like there really *was* a Lord of All Light who ruled the world and gave his bounty and love to all. Her soul soared on bright wings with a hope that was almost entirely new to her and yet felt like the most natural outgrowth of the love she and Radiance shared, a hope that was somehow softer and yet no less sure than her own resolute determination that she *would* defeat the Wizard-King and free all his captives.

And that reminded her.

It's time to go north and look for the Sea Elves. We can't enjoy this leisure forever. Radiance is fully healed, and the dragons are now big enough to carry us comfortably, and, if need to be, to fly for a long time without rest. With every day we wait, the chances that the Sea Elves have moved on grows.

If only she had the magic to know! But as the hope of that bright afternoon saturated her soul, she wondered if Serrose's unwillingness to teach her magic might have been motivated by something far different from the desire to keep her dependent and vulnerable, and therefore – presumably – easier to control that she had assumed. The bell-like notes Serrose had taught her to use for concentrating on magic had never come naturally to her, and she struggled to find them. Now that she had had some experience exploring her own song, it was clear to her how different and alien they were, how out of tune with her nature, her magic, and her song. Perhaps Serrose was right in hesitating to teach her, and the reasons she had given were truth, not excuses. Her magic was unique and strong, and someone like Serrose was not qualified to help her learn it.

But how does she know the Light Elves know enough or have enough breadth in their knowledge and magic to teach me, if no one has ever been like me before? Perhaps I will have to find my own way, to train myself. And, if that is so, isn't it better if I start sooner rather than later? The thought appealed to her. She had always wanted to play with magic, and she *had* learned much on her own. Now that she kept the elf-sword with her at all time, though there was a ropy scar on her palm, it had long since healed and it no longer pained her. It only bothered her because it was a reminder of the cruelty and evil of the elves of Ilesh, which in turn made her think of the Wizard-King and the Northern Horror and all the helpless dragons – and humans – who might be his captives and slaves.

No. It will not be. I will *change it, even if no one else can or will.* Her determination and resolve, so long slumbering in the peace of their life here, rose in her like an unstoppable tide of fire.

Strangely, she found herself looking into the bright-tinged storm, and saying, "And You will help me, Lord of Light and Love?" She did not know if it was a question or plea, or a statement of confidence, and, even as she said it, she drew back in shock. It was such a strange thing for her to say and feel, something she would have never thought and that felt contrary to what she believed, yet it also felt deeply right, as familiar as her own soul, or Radiance, as much a part of her as her bond with the dragon.

What is happening to me? she thought. First, months earlier, there had been the incident with the orc and, now, this. No, it went further back, to her struggle in the cell after she and Radiance had been brought down from the sky by dark magic. Thoughts and feelings that were not hers, or never had been hers, had been forced upon her, and she had thought and felt them – if whatever thought and felt them could be called her. Yet many of those thoughts and feelings had been all wrong, through and through, horrible to think, horrible to feel, utterly painful. This was not; this felt beautiful and, though pleasure was not the right word, it was far nearer it than pain. Yet, she rebelled against it, also. *She* was master of her soul. What was happening to her?

Then her memories took her even further back, to her Recognition with Radiance. Since that moment, thoughts and feelings that had not been hers and did not come from her had become inextricably part of her life, nay, of her very self. But that had been different, had it not? She had sought that, and even if she had not known what it would be like, she had a feeling that, deep down inside, deeper even than the place where she had always known the elves were lying to her, she *had* known what it was to bond to a dragon. If what the dragons told her was right – and she felt that it was – then from her birth she had a connection to dragons, and though it had to wait, until she met the right dragon, to awake, yet it had been asleep, not dead. Behind all conscious thought and awareness, she had always been influenced by dragons.

A gust of wind almost rocked the cliff ledge on which she sat. It smelled heavy with rain and more wind to come. She reached towards Radiance, and felt her dragon's instant acknowledgement. She could come. It was better to get her rider down from the cliff before the storm grew into its full fury and became difficult to fly through. It would certainly not be an easy matter for Camilla to ride her if she was slick with rain and swerving wildly with every gust. She shook the water off her scales as well as she could and flew towards the ledge where her rider waited.

That night, Camilla told Sylvara and Lavilor that it was time for them to continue north, keeping to the isles closest to the continent. "We're already behind where we should be by now," she explained. "The dragonmages thought we could slowly move north at whatever pace Radiance could handle, but we haven't been able to do that because we can't stay in Fire Elf territory for long and it's best if we can not land there at all. I'm going to see if I can reach Aglaretë and ask him if he can tell us which islands it might be okay to rest on, and which are claimed by the Fire Elves and it would be better if we didn't even land there. Then we'll leave."

In the morning, she went up to the peak with Radiance, to see if she could attract Aglaretë's attention. The last time she had sung her magic on the mountain, he had felt it, and that had been a good part of why he came. She hoped that it would not be like last time in attracting an orc, as well. As she climbed, she considered the fact that she had not told them the other cause for her sudden decision that it was time: the winter was coming on, and it was probably not the best time to be traveling if they could help it. The winter storms would be much harder to fly through, and it would be cold and wet, a combination that none of them would enjoy and that would be doubly hard on Radiance with her still-healing injuries. She wanted to get as far as possible before the winter struck in earnest, since it was most definitely not a good idea to wait for spring or summer to come again. And she had not thought them because – because she felt no need to tell Sylvara anything, and because she did not want to worry Lavilor with thoughts of the future and the hardships and dangers before them more than necessary.

When she neared the peak, she found a rather smooth rock that slanted only slightly, and there she began to dance, weaving a pattern that was sometimes as stately as a flame burning in a still room at times and at other times as exuberant as a fire catching new tinder alight. Radiance swayed in time to the beat of her dance, and in time Camilla added song. As often happened when she danced, she felt as if her being and the dance became one and, as they became one, met with something else, something vast, surreal, and *alive*, though not as she and Radiance were alive. She wondered if this was what magic felt like. There was certainly no other word to describe it, but that was not very descriptive. But what really mattered was that it made her feel *herself*. She lost all sense of time in the flow of the dance and in the deep, veiled power that flowed through the dance and through the song.

Then she felt, through the dance or the wind she did not know, the kiss of another fire and of an eerie, half-chilly wind; the strange mark she now knew to associate with the Fire Elves, but which she had first sensed from the shore of the continent. She stopped her dance and mounted Radiance, who stood with wings half-spread on the edge of the rock. If any hostile Dark Elf or other entity appeared, they would be able to fly away as quickly as possible

But it was only Aglaretë who appeared, and he materialized before them in much the same way as before, so that they never quite saw it it happen. "Camilla! Radiance!" he called, while she was still trying to adjust to his strange appearance, which reminded her in some ways far more of a burnt log than of any living being, let alone of a Wood Elf such as he claimed he and his kind were.

For a moment, she felt awkward, not knowing how to greet him. Then, she realized it was probably unnecessary. Given how much of her mind he seemed to read, and the fact that they understood each other even though they did not speak the same language, he would know her intent. "We would like to know if there is anything you can or would want to tell us," she said, leaning towards him over Radiance's neck. "We must go north, the sooner the better, but we would like to know if there are any areas it would be better to avoid."

There was an odd look in his fiery eyes, one which Camilla thought was wistful. "I have found an elf who I trust and who is willing to act as a guide for you. This will be better than any directions I can give, as she may also be able to diffuse hostilities if you are found by or attract the attention of other Fire Elves, though I would not trust to that."

Camilla nodded, and wondered why she trusted him at all. Radiance had nothing to say, for it was nearly impossible for her to touch his mind and intentions. Whatever his fire was, it was not dragonfire. Maybe it would be better not to trust him, not to wait for his guide. Maybe it would have been better not to come at all. Maybe they should flee this island tonight, and hope that his magic could not follow them.

Why do I suddenly distrust him? she asked, with a motion like shaking water off her shoulders. *I didn't, last time we met. But last time I was shaken by the orc, and it seemed that, if anything, he had something to do with killing it.* Then she remembered more clearly. He had awesome power, here. Even if this was near the edge of his ability to manifest himself, he drew a great deal of power from whatever the source of his life and magic was – probably the Fire Groves he had mentioned. He knew much of her thoughts – anything she considered trying to say, it seemed. If he had wanted to destroy or harm them, he would and could have done it. So why did she distrust him now?

"How did you know I would ask for this?" she asked.

"I knew you did not intend to stay here forever, but to go to the Sea Elves and across the sea. You told me as much. Since that time, I have been looking for a way to make the way safer and easier for you, even as I told you I would try to tell you if I learned anything that might be of benefit to you, or if there was any danger to you. I am glad you thought to come here and dance today. Otherwise, I have trouble telling when you are here and when you are too far away; we have missed each other several times."

Perhaps she *could* escape from him after all, she thought, emboldened. But there was no new reason to distrust him, and she might benefit from the help he offered. She believed the hostility of the Fire Elves in general, and while she was certain that if she were a trained mage, even a self-trained mage, she could protect herself and her friends, she did not think she could do so now without great cost to herself. It might be a foolish fear of all elves that was making her distrust Aglaretë's offer, despite the fact that he was so unlike the Wood Elves she knew that he did not provoke her in the same way. And whoever he sent with her would not be a Wood Elf either, even if she would not be Grove-born like he was.

"Thank you, Aglaretë," she said, bowing her head ever so slightly. She wanted to make her gratitude plain, yet at the same time any gesture that even suggested a possibility of subservience made her blood want to boil. "I am somewhat forgetful of what passed between us, and I wondered how you foresaw so perfectly plans I had not thought that I had conveyed to you in such detail. Your perception is strange to me, since I have encountered it in no other." Somehow, for some reason, her speech patterns matched those in which she perceived his speech to her.

"It is no surprise that you have not encountered it," said Aglaretë, apparently sensing her discomfort at any gesture that might seem to suggest subservience, and bowing deeply from the waist. "Few among even the Grove-born display as much of it as I experience, and the Dark Elves in general exhibit more of it the closer they are to our Fire Trees or some other tree of their choice. Since the Ileshians are not one with their forests as we are with ours, I doubt you would have ever encountered it."

"No. I have not seen it among the Ileshians, and though I don't understand it well, they don't have anything that corresponds to the Grove-born such as yourself."

"I thought not," said Aglaretë. "I do not know how they have survived in the Forlorn Lands, but I sense that this is a conversation which is greatly uncomfortable for both of us. Is there anything else you would desire?"

"I do not think so."

"Then, let us part. But first: if you have need to speak with me again, come to this peak and call my name. I think you will know how, and I will recognize the summons easily. If by mishap or chance you ever find yourself near a Fire Grove, or are taken by the Dark Elves and survive long enough to be brought to one, call my name in the same manner. If you can touch one of the Fire Trees, I will receive the summons with greater clarity and force. Almost any tree in the Dark Woods may serve to convey the summons also, but there is danger others who are closer would know as well. If ever you find yourself in the Dark Woods, and the trees themselves seem to be attacking you, call my name! I may be able to help, but do not trust to this, for I may not arrive in time, and you or one of your friends could die before you know it, so try not to wander into our domains."

"Thank you," said Camilla. "I will."

"Then farewell. I know no blessing to give you, but may the wind be sure under your wings and may the flame always burn bright within you."

With all the courtesy of a queen addressing an equal, and feeling all the better for it, Camilla bowed her body over Radiance's neck and answered, "And may the fire give you its strength, and the earth and wind support you and grant you life together."

Aglaretë smiled. "Watch for the elf I send you to arrive today or tomorrow. Her name will be Aishaena," he said, then turned away. As he walked east towards his land, his form first wavered like smoke in the wind, and then grew more solid.

As soon as he was well out of reach of the swing of her tail, Radiance opened her wings fully, spun round, and took off. Together, she and Camilla spoke to the dragons and Lavilor, telling them what had happened. She still could not bring herself to speak mind-to-mind with Sylvara short of an emergency. She did not like speaking to Sylvara, or hearing her voice, or even seeing her, if it could be helped, no matter what she *thought* about how the woman was changing.

As they flew, it suddenly occurred to her to wonder how the elf Aglaretë sent would be able to speak to them. Briefly, she considered flying back, summoning him, and asking him, but then she decided she did not want to. She was not sure if she wanted to talk to him anymore, she did not wish to appear rude by summoning him in such a way, and he seemed aware of the problem, so he might have simply forgotten to tell her his solution.

Learning

Flameheart picked daintily and hesitantly at the half-charred fish. They had run out of food for her long ago, since Nelexi had brought mostly water-skins which they re-filled whenever they found an island with drinkable water. Even so, they sometimes ran low on water for the human, so Flameheart understood it was a good thing Nelexi had prioritized water, even though she was very hungry. The dragon herself needed to drink only at rare intervals, and not nearly as much as Flameheart thought a creature of her size should, but, then again, what other creature ate rocks or breathed out lava? But it was not the lava-fire that she used to cook Kario's fish. She also had regular dragonfire, but even using the dragonfire she burned the fish to cinders more often than she roasted it in any way Flameheart found remotely edible. Even then Flameheart struggled to eat the stuff even when she was very hungry, and she simply *could not* eat some of the sea weeds Nelexi found for her, so she had gotten rather skinny.

Sometimes they landed on the large islands where they got most of their water, and found many trees, some of which bore fruit which she found reasonably edible, and even liked, but it helped little. She could not eat much fruit without having the runs, and it spoiled too quickly for her to take with her. There were usually animals on the islands as well, but most of those were not any more edible than the fish and certainly nothing like the plains-animals her people hunted. She asked Nelexi to catch snakes for her, and sometimes she tried to cook them herself, using piles of wood she collected and asked Nelexi to light, but while the results were better than Nelexi's attempts, she was not very good at cooking either. Nor did she enjoy getting all the tiny bones out of the meat, something Nelexi could not help her with at all.

But her issues with edible food were not the only reason that she was not finding this a relaxing flight. Nelexi was teaching her languages, even though the dragon still had no idea what they had been called for. She was mostly teaching her Sea Elven, since while the Sea Elf ambassador, Edreen, had spoken the common trade tongue of Aneri, many Sea Elves did not. She was also teaching her a little Eltaen, the common language of the humans in northern Ellenesia, and learning the languages was not boring, but sometimes it made her head feel way too full, or tight, or whatever it was. Nelexi was also telling her some of what had been happening in Ellenesia, about the various nations and peoples and the rise of the Wizard-King of Eltaes.

So, while Flameheart picked at her fish and in part to provide a distraction from its inedible taste and texture, Nelexi told her about how, when the Wizard-King started declaring wars against the nations with most Dragonriders, the other nations began to hunt and outlaw Dragonriders.

"Nelexi," said Kario out loud, staring at her fish and working up the courage to put another piece in her mouth, "why didn't the Sha'adhri help them? Why didn't you help them?"

"I didn't know. Not until later. It was when I was searching for you, little rider, that I was flying through Ellenesia, and I saw the damage done to the land and the people. Seeing it, I decided to keep my search secretive, since I did not want my presence to become known to the enemy if I could help it. One evening I was looking for a cave large enough to hide me, when I stumbled into one that I instantly realized held traces of very powerful and unique magic – though I think few would have recognized the magic or even noticed it, and even I could not discern what it did, or had done. There I found creatures of a kind that had never been before. Another of their 'friends' – someone I have never met – took to calling them dragonmages, for they have the bodies of dragons as well as those of humans or elves. They can shift between forms at will, and they are all mages, but it is hardly an adequate word. They were made by Shallim-Araldor at the end of a battle waged by some Dragonrider-mages against the Wizard-King, and it appears that I woke them by stumbling into that cave. It was they who told me most of what I know about the current state of that continent and the Wizard-King, though the hostility between some of the peoples is so ancient and, apparently, stable that it had not changed much from the last time I had been on Ellenesia, thousands of years ago."

"I thought you're the Guardian of the Dragons, though," said Flameheart, looking with distaste at what was left of her fish. "So, I don't understand. Why weren't you guarding the dragons of Ellenesia? Why didn't you even *know* what was happening?"

"What I do and cannot do is complicated." There was no defensiveness in her tone, for she was not being accused. Her rider was asking only out of curiosity and confusion. *"For another, the situation with the dragons of Ellenesia is complicated. The majority of them are kept as slaves by wood elves. I could not guard them. The quest of freeing them from their captivity is not something the Obsidian Guardian can do alone, or even with a handful of her riders and their dragons, for their captors are also their riders. My place as Guardian of the Dragons and Wings of the Flame of the Earth is different than that."*

I think I understand. But how are the dragons kept as slaves by elven riders?

"It is not something I can explain to you well, or would wish to. Suffice it to say that they have been changed by corrupted elven magic and are in many ways quite unlike most other dragons. More than that, I don't want to try to explain. I – or whoever follows me as Obsidian Guardian – may have some part in healing them, but I cannot free or guard them myself."

Flameheart continued to pick at her fish. *I suppose there are more things to do than anyone could ever do. So far, we've gotten the Sha'adhri and the Sea Elves to make peace.* She sighed. "Do you think the call to come over here could have anything to do with those dragons – or those part-dragon creatures?"

Nelexi laughed, a deep, throaty rumble, that flickered in her mind with flashes of fire. *"Part-dragon is not exactly how anyone would put it. Besides, what is a part-dragon? As far as I know, no dragon has ever mated, or been able to mate, with anything other than a dragon. But it could have something to do with that. We won't know until the time comes."*

Flameheart flicked her tongue across her teeth, trying to rid it of the taste and smell of fish. She restrained herself from asking more about the position of the captive dragons, knowing that Nelexi had shared all that she was going to, at least for the moment, but it was hard not to ask. How was such a thing even possible? It did not make sense. It sounded like nonsense. It was a contradiction in terms for a dragon to be the slave or captive of the rider. Was it that the dragons' riders were kept as captives by the Wood Elves? But, no, that was too simple a situation, and not one which would put them outside the business of the Obsidian Guardian, at least according to everything she understood and some things Nelexi had pretty clear implied. Also, it would not have anything to do with the dragons being changed by elven magic, something she did not understand. How was it possible? Should not the Obsidian Guardian have kept it from happening? But maybe the Obsidian Guardian could not have prevented it. It might have happened before Nelexi even hatched, and the Obsidian Guardian of that time might have been too busy or otherwise prevented from getting involved.

"I think," she said throwing the remains of her fish as far out over the sea as she could, and curling on her side next to Nelexi's huge fore-paw, "that magic belongs to the gods and the god-chosen, and that nobody else should be able to use it, especially if it can change the natures of things or make dragons into the slaves of their riders. Really, I think it should be that way, the way it is among my people."

Nelexi did not reply, but gave her a gentle mental kiss. *"I will wake you when the tide approaches, so you won't have to get wet if you wake up quickly,"* the dragon said.

She moaned softly, trying to shift into a position she would find really comfortable. She did not get a lot of real sleep, even though she often got to doze or half-doze while riding, in between her conversations with Nelexi. She wondered how the dragon managed on such little sleep, though she always remembered that Nelexi was the Obsidian Guardian – a creature of magic and something like a lesser god, ancient beyond all her thought. Her stomach ached, too, and she felt nauseous. She longed for her home, the Plains of Zharda. She longed for a place where she could sleep comfortably, for the bright, hot rays of the sun, for the open, blue sky and the endless slightly rolling plains, and, right now, above all, for nourishing food she could eat without upsetting her stomach.

While Flameheart settled herself in the saddle, Nelexi said, *"This is part of why ancient ones such as myself rarely bond as I have to you. There's so much that you ask and wonder, and that I would like to tell you, for I am ancient and there is much that I know, but you are young and there is much that one must discover oneself, and so I cannot tell you. If I were to try I would do more harm than good, yet it is hard not to tell you, or try to tell you, and impossible to keep glimpses from you. I think this is much of why the Obsidian Guardian only rarely bonds as I have to you, for even in infancy, the Obsidian Guardian is not like other mortals and knows what cannot be truly shared, what an attempt to share would cause more harm than good, for it could not be shared, but only misunderstood and mistaken – a situation which only grows more pronounced the longer the Obsidian Guardian lives."*

"I'm sorry," she murmured, trying to silence her grumbling stomach. She had not eaten, and would not eat the kind of food currently available to her before flying. She had learned the hard way what happened if she did: she vomited it all up, and it was very annoying when she got vomit all over her clothes, something she could not help unless she figured out how to sit backwards so the wind would carry it away from her instead of into her.

"There's no need to say sorry, little Kario, Flameheart. You have not done anything, and you have hurt me in no way. I only wanted you to understand, so you do not get hurt, and so you understand some of my frustration. I am so happy to know you and to have you in this way. I would not have it any other way, nor did you force me to choose you. That was my own free choice, a choice more my own than much that I have done, or have not done. I have shared with you what I have shared with no other, but I want you to understand that I cannot share everything with you. The time will perhaps come when we can, but the difference in what I have known and experienced means that while you are young we cannot be close in the way that so-called 'ordinary' dragons and riders are, for there is a gap between us that cannot be bridged and is far wider than that between young dragons and young riders. Moreover, I think there can be a closeness between those who are unlike in certain ways, and while I am a true dragon and think as a dragon, and am unlike you in ways most other dragons are not, there is also a way in which I am perhaps less unlike... or perhaps more unlike. Both are true... I just want you to understand that there is much I wish I could explain to you, and that perhaps I have even tried to explain to you, but that I cannot."

She did not know how to respond. It did not help that she really did not feel well. Right now, she felt both ravenously hungry and nauseous. *You're thinking of something in particular,* she thought weakly.

That provoked another of those laughs from Nelexi, laughs that Kario felt made her world, but that she could almost never predict, though she knew there was a very real pattern to them. *"Yes. Usually I am thinking of something in particular, and often of many somethings in particular. But I never meant to conceal the most recent one from you, the one which has moved me to respond thusly to you. Doubtless, you remember the last thing you said to me before falling asleep in the crook of my fore-limb, about magic and who should get it."*

"And you were going to say something to me, and then you thought better of it," Flameheart whispered.

"No. I was going to say something to you, and I realized I can't fully explain the situation to you. But I will tell you what I can. Magic is a part of nature. There is no true distinction between magic and nature. And, as you know, the gods are not all true guardians; the name 'Old Gods' has some truth in it, if only that all those who are corrupted by the Nightmare are better represented by the decrepit state of some specimens of certain species as they near death than by youth – to be ancient and young are not opposed, and all the truly ancient are forever young."

At this, Flameheart seamlessly interrupted her. *Didn't you say earlier that you did not know why my people call them the 'Old Gods'? Something about how you did not see the right of it?*

"I did, and I'm not at all certain that this is why your people call them the 'Old Gods'. They might have another reason for it, and one which is no less accurate. But I have also spent time thinking about it since I said that. Age as mortals experience it is not a concept which comes easily to me, but I have seen it often enough, and lived through the failing of enough riders, that when I sorted through things for long enough, I could see it. Also, there is the thought among some peoples that what is old is passing away, so they could be called the 'Old Gods' because their time is over and they will be past forever, though I think that thought might be related?"

I suppose that makes sense, and it does make them sound less frightening, though I don't know if that's how my people think of old age. At any rate, among my people, magic is given only to the Storm Chosen, who is chosen by Zharda and the Sun to bear the Gifts of the Storm against the Old Gods. Magic is never misused. That's how all magic should be.

"In your tales," said Nelexi. *"Zharda, and definitely the Sun, are not quite as you imagine them, though I don't know much about the situation in the Plains of Zharda, but have you ever wondered about the place of the Storm Chosen? About why he or she is called? Magic can be pure and living, or it can be corrupted, as can anything. And it is not the place of the immortals to govern the lives of mortals in all ways."*

But hasn't Zharda done a fair job with our plains?

"*I don't know the full history of the Plains of Zharda. There is much magic in them, as in most places of the world, other than that which is directly Zharda's, depending on how you count magic. And I do know that it would not be good for all places to be governed as the Plains of Zharda are, if in fact what your stories tell is the truth of the matter. It is good for the Plains of Zharda to be, but not all people should be your people. What you ask is for those who desire Love to rule, and for those who are of the Nightmare to have no power or even existence. This shall be the state of the world forever, but it is, as you well know, not the present appearance.*"

I suppose so. Her head drooped with something like resignation. *I still think that about magic though. Some things... well, they're just not the same.*

She felt something like approval, tinged with something like sadness, and flickering with something like laughter, from Nelexi, and leaned down on the dragon's neck, spreading arms wide affectionately.

Then the dragon said, "*Nothing is the same as another thing, as is common knowledge among dragons. And there is much I cannot explain to you so that you will know as I know, and it is better that way. And there is even more that I do not know.*"

But you think I misunderstand magic.

"*You most certainly do misunderstand magic. I probably misunderstand magic, and I certainly do not know all magic and all about magic, and just as certainly I have not and cannot share with you what I do understand about what magic is and what magic is not, just as you have not lived all my experiences. But I can tell you that precisely human magic is not the same as the magic of other races, and that it is impossible to separate some races from the exercise of what you would term magic, as opposed to non-magic. We were discussing once what it means for something to be a nightmare creature, and that we don't know what all nightmare creatures are, or how all nightmare creatures come to be, and so I tell you that there are creatures who wield nightmarish magic, but whose magic is not fully nightmare, though it is nightmare-tinged, and who are themselves beings, not nightmares. If you accept the existence of the Nightmare, and that it often seems to wield cruel and terrible power – for that is what it means that it is the Nightmare – you should be able to accept this also.*"

"It should not be."

"*On that, we are agreed.*"

Darkness

Aishaena was there the following morning. She did not look much like Algaretë. Her eyes, like his, were fiery, but her skin was fairly near in both color and shade to Camilla's, and her black hair shimmered green in the sunlight. She greeted them in slightly accented Ileshian, the only language they knew. Seeing her, Camilla suddenly realized another issue: how would she come with them, since they would be flying on dragonback? *How can I be so stupid?* she asked herself in frustration.

"How will you come with us? We're going to be flying."

Aishaena brushed her hair behind one pointed ear. "I thought I would be able to ride with one of you. I am very light, you know. Elves are. Otherwise, I can move fairly quickly over land and over these seas. I have a little coracle."

Instinctively and immediately, she preferred the second option. She did not care if Aishaena rode with Sylvara, but there was no way she was tolerating Aishaena riding with her little brother, and she was not taking Aishaena with her on Radiance either. *Why do I distrust Aishaena so?* she wondered. *Is it because I will trust no one I do not know to be trustworthy, human or elf or anything else? Is it because she looks more Ileshian than Algaretë, even though no Ileshian Wood Elf could ever have those fiery eyes? Or is it because I should not trust her?* All these thoughts took only a few moments, and Camilla settled on a response she rather liked, since if Aishaena was not trustworthy, she preferred for her to know as little as possible about what they could do. "I'm not sure it's a good idea for you to ride with any of us," she said. "The dragons are barely grown enough to comfortably carry their riders very far, and even if you are very light, I wouldn't want to add to that burden."

Aishaena nodded demurely.

"I really think Shimmer could carry you, if you're that light," said Sylvara. "We could at least make a short flight together to see if it will work."

Camilla cursed to herself. Was Sylvara really that stupid? Maybe the girl was still a traitor. "No," she said firmly, decisively. "If Shimmer misestimates his strength, he might find that he can't really carry two for long enough, and then the coracle would be left behind *and* needed. We wouldn't want that."

"That makes sense," said the Dark Elf. "I'm not sure if it would even be a good idea for me to ride a dragon. I might not do well far above the earth."

"If that's settled," said Camilla, "do we just fly north to the next main island?"

"Yes. That should be safe territory. I will go to the shore and get my coracle. Shall we meet on the southern shore, and decide where to go next from there?"

"I think that will work." She and Lavilor went together to saddle their dragons. Sylvara could do whatever she must separately.

Over the following weeks, they flew north from isle to isle. It was not in all ways harder, since the animals on the new islands had not yet been hunted by the dragons and so were more numerous and less cautious towards them. Yet the hardships of the coming seasons grew greater, also. Cold winds came out of the north, bringing with them sleet and sometimes snow, often forcing the dragons to stay near or on the ground, when otherwise they would have traveled. To make matters worse, it was nearly impossible to hunt in such weather, and once they had to press very hard in order to reach an island outside Dark Elf territory before a storm hit.

To make matters worse, the increasing cold hurt Radiance. She grew stiff whenever she lay down or stopped moving, and injuries that had seemed healed for weeks pained her greatly whenever a cold front swept over them. She moaned and could never get comfortable whenever there was a snow- or hail-storm, and it was sometimes even worse when it was clear. Flying in the cold or the rain was usually agony for her; whenever it was cold enough to cause Camilla to shiver, her dragon was in pain, even though her scales still felt warm. The only thing that offered Radiance any real reprieve was when they could find a good cave for her to sleep in, but those were not available on every island.

A cold fury built in Camilla, sometimes reaching such a pitch that she felt nauseous, though often it lay in the back of her thoughts like ice. Radiance was young. She was not even half-grown yet, and she suffered as the oldest dragons did. It was cruel that this was the price of their freedom, and that so few even had the chance for freedom. Her thoughts often turned dark when she lay at night beside the drowsing dragon, sharing her pain. That she did not grudge, but she hated the elves of Ilesh, and she hated the Wizard-King of Eltaes, and she hated the hostile Dark Elves who nurtured some prejudice against all other races because of some wrong done them in their ancient past, so long ago that no one else remembered it. Above all, she hated the wrong that dominated the world. *Why* did it seem that wrong was stronger than right? That things were more often bad, or more easily went bad, than right? Why did the Darkness have such power? She could not decide whether or not she believed that Love was the Power above all. Sometimes she thought she did, or else she believed in herself, for she determined that she would defeat the Northern Darkness and free the slaves, and change the world. Other times, though she felt no doubt in her determination to succeed, it seemed that Love could not be the Power when slavery and cruelty claimed so many lives and corrupted so much. All she really knew was that she loved Radiance, and Lavilor, and her mother, that she *hated* to the ends of time and the farthest borders of the world all that would harm or enslave them, and that she *would* destroy those things, by the strength of her determination, and her love, and her hate.

She also found herself avoiding Aishaena as much as she avoided Sylvara. She did not like the Dark Elf, and being with Aishaena did not soften her attitude or increase her trust, even when Aishaena shared her past and how she knew their language. Apparently, the Dark Elf had always been interested in languages and was more given to curiosity and exploration than most of her kind, making her something of an outcast among her people. When Aglaretë had shared with her the dilemma of the humans, she had taken her little coracle to the mainland, and then filched scrolls written in the Ileshian tongue and in the Sea Elf one. "I had found, quite early in my research, that all the elven languages are still rather similar, and *far* more similar to each other than to the human languages, so I knew it would be much easier for me to learn Sea Elven than another language the Sea Elves might speak for trading purposes," she explained. She had been looking into the development of the elven languages for a long time, and it was not too difficult for her to learn the basics of other elven tongues than her own. She explained that while her grasp of Ileshian was relatively accurate but crude – which it was; the longer she had been with them, the more Camilla had noticed that her grammar was very basic and often wrong, and that her vocabulary, while usually adequate, was small and unrefined – she expected her Sea Elven to be barely adequate. "I can probably convey basic needs to them, but my accent is probably even worse in Sea Elven than in Ileshian, and I know that my grammar is very poor. Hopefully, it will be good enough, and the Sea Elves are not as hostile to others as my own people are. Being a trading nation, I doubt they could be."

Somehow, none of it made Camilla trust or like Aishaena any more, even though her story made sense. Whenever she was around the Dark Elf, she watched her like a panther watching his opponent in a mating contest or stalking his prey, and she would not practice her magic, her dance, or her song around Aishaena either. Instead she practiced in secret; on the warmest nights, and despite the pain it cost them, she and Radiance would rise in the middle of the night and seek a place as far from the others as they could find, to be alone together and practice. Lavilor and Sleet often came with them. She always reached out to her little brother and woke him with a gentle mental touch to let him know where and when they were going.

When he and Sleet came with her, she always enjoyed the time with him, away from the presence of people she did not trust, and she thought he felt similarly, though he never spoke about it. Though far less hostile and angry, he, too, seemed to distrust Aishaena, though he appeared to be far more comfortable with Sylvara than she was, and before Aishaena appeared and made friends with Sylvara, Camilla had tried not to discourage Lavilor from interacting with Sylvara. Now she did, since she doubted he thought, as she did, about who was really a threat and what people's connections might mean, but she realized that she did not know how he thought.

She was only now realizing how little she really knew him, how much he thought that she did not know. That, too, aroused her anger at the elves. They were brother and sister and should have been able to know each other. Even now, though sometimes she tried to talk to him, to get to know his thoughts and feelings, one or the other of them was often too tired to be talkative, and he and Sleet were sometimes too tired to come. When they did not come, and sometimes when they did, Camilla would lay against Radiance's side and watch the stars, and the large moon, when it was up. It seemed to her that the stars sang, and even that they sang to her. She did not know what feeling it was that they roused within her, but it was something like the feeling of her quieter, more stately song. It was freedom, but not excited or wild – no, it was wild in the sense that no hand tamed it, but its energy was restrained and directed, or rather purposeful – knowing its purpose, directed towards it. More than that, she could not understand, but she felt certain that there was more, and something in her heart responded to this more that she could not comprehend.

Being with Lavilor often brought something out in her that Camilla was not sure what to think or feel about. One night, under a nearly-full moon, she was telling him about her experience when she was watching Radiance fish and the storm had rolled in, gilded with brilliant colors by the setting sun, and she had felt that it was dancing, and that the Lord of Light of which he had spoken must be real. She even told him how she had asked the Lord of Light to help her, or perhaps expressed confidence that he would, surprising herself. "Most of the time I don't feel like such a person exists at all," she finished. "But I did then. I don't understand it, and it surprised me even then, but I felt like I knew him, and like the storm knew him or was his hand – and not like we think of a storm at all, but more like how Mom held me and kissed me when I was a baby."

"He is like that," her brother had said, in a thoughtful and subdued tone. "Almost like the mother of all of us." Then he had added, even more quietly, "You seem very angry and confused."

"I am," she admitted. "I don't understand. I want to believe it. I feel like I do. Like believing that isn't different from who I am, one with Radiance and utterly in love with her, yet it seems strange, even contrary, to other ... parts of who I am, who *we* are."

"Like what?"

"It's hard to explain. My freedom. The freedom of everything else. Love is freedom, but being forced or conquered can never be love or freedom."

Lavilor had said nothing for a while, but had snuggled up against Sleet's neck, putting his arm over the dragon's shining silver scales. There were times when Sleet seemed the most beautiful creature in the world to Camilla, though she was more in love with Radiance's golden glory. Then he said, "I think you think things too far, sister. You worry and hate too much. You ought to just enjoy things more."

"Aren't you sad a lot?" she asked.

He rubbed his cheek gently against the scales of Sleet's neck. "Sometimes. But that doesn't mean we should coat ourselves in worry and hate like we do in the mud when it's warm enough."

"Why not? Don't you hate? I *must* hate what's wrong. I *will* undo it."

Lavilor shook his head. "I'm sad. I want Mom. I hope she's alive. I want us all to be happy together. I miss her so much." He looked at Sleet, who had turned his head to face him, and the boy's eyes and the dragon's rainbow-eyes locked on each other. Then Lavilor and Sleet spoke to Camilla together. Their voices, one vocal and one mental, even harmonized in a way that she found entrancingly beautiful. *"We miss and grieve for the loss of others because we love."*

"And I hate because I love."

"That is true," said Sleet alone now, though Lavilor looked on with an expression that told Camilla that his mind and input were not absent from the conversation, *"but your hate also distracts you from your love."*

She growled softly. She never forgot her love for Radiance, not even for a moment – how could she, when their thoughts were hardly separate and often were *not* separate? It was in their nature to hate and burn their enemies, and if it was so that hate distracted from love, then sorrow distracted from enjoyment just as much. She recalled something Serrose had said about love and freedom in an imperfect world. While the world was corrupt and shadowed by the wings of the Northern Darkness, one could not help but be imperfect, and that did not mean one was doing anything wrong or that there was something one could do better. *Though there probably are things we could do better, still we don't see why we should think Lavilor knows what they are for us.*

"I'm really cold," she said, "and it's only getting colder. Let's talk more about this later. I want to get back to our den."

About half an hour later, she lay curled against Radiance's side, wincing herself with the dragon's pain. *I was happier,* she thought, *when we were on the first island, and I could just think about the here and now, and I felt no urgency, and... there were times when I was unhappy, when I remembered what has happened, and what I am going to do, but mostly I didn't think about it, and I wasn't thinking about the things I hate, and I was happy. I want to be happy, but I must not forget what I am, what I am doing, and how can I forget the things I hate around Aishaena?* Suddenly, her half-sleepy mind recognized her thought with a jolt, like surprise, like discovery, like realization. *She* does *make me think of the other elves, the slave-masters, and, yes, Sylvara... the old Sylvara, though I never really stopped seeing the old Sylvara, so I can't tell if Sylvara has changed or gotten worse since being friends with her. There has to be a way to be... happy. Isn't the Nightmare's power supposed to be fear and bitterness – unhappiness?*

But her mind was sluggish with weariness, and with that thought in their minds, she and Radiance fell asleep.

The next morning, when the three humans met to warm their breakfast, they realized that Aishaena was gone. A quick survey by the dragons showed her coracle to be absent. She had told them the previous night that only one major island, which was outside the territory claimed by any of the Dark Elf clans, lay between them and a long, strenuous flight to the shore of the continent. From there, if they kept to the shore, they would soon see the Sea Elf harbor and city of Ansaifar.

Camilla did not know how she felt about Aishaena's disappearance. Part of her was distrustful of the Dark Elf and any action she took, and she feared that Aishaena had left without telling them in order to betray them to enemies of some sort. And why had she given them the impression that she meant to guide them, not only out of the Dark Elf lands, but all the way to the Sea Elves, for which reason she had learned some Sea Elven in addition to learning enough to get by in Ileshian? Another part of Camilla was purely glad, relieved to be free of Aishaena's presence and feeling that while Aishaena had definitely merited no trust, she had not done anything to earn particular distrust. What if Camilla's worries had nothing to do with reality – or, rather, had only to do with *her* past and her fears, and not with Aishaena at all, though part of her said, *Has Sylvara gotten any nicer over the last weeks? No. Being with Aishaena only made her more irritating, made her seem more at odds. Perhaps, there is hope for her, but that Dark Elf was certainly a bad influence.* The thought surprised her, for Camilla was never taken to thinking kindly of Sylvara. Was she scrambling for any excuse to hate Aishaena, and if so for what reason – that Aishaena *was* an elf? Aglaretë had hardly seemed an elf, and Serrose, even though she looked like one, was really not, but Aishaena was just an odd-looking elf with perhaps some different abilities than the elves with which Camilla was most familiar.

Feeling a need to be cautious and to get as far away as she could from this place as quickly as possible, Camilla convinced Sylvara and Lavilor that they must fly to the continent, and then find Ansaifar, as quickly as possible. She would not even have trusted Aishaena's directions, except that they were virtually the same as Serrose's and Alian's directions.

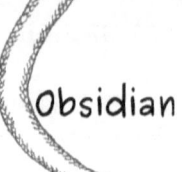

Obsidian

Flameheart woke from a troubled, hungry doze in a flash. Startlement, and then fear, rushed over her as she came instantly and fully awake.

Leaning over Nelexi's shoulder, she saw the cause for her waking, and why Nelexi was bracing for battle. Far below them circled several obsidian dragons; they were black like Nelexi, but only slightly larger than the colored dragons, and the wings and stripe that on Nelexi were a glorious golden red were on them shades of tan and brown. Below them Sea Elf ships rode the sea, though these she could not see with her own eyes, but knew about through her bond with Nelexi.

"Don't fear, little rider," said Nelexi, her voice calm as the summer breeze, strong as earth itself, and bright as fire. *"Do not fear. Love me. I love you."*

Panic cut like an arrow through the armor of Nelexi's voice. *But I can't do anything! I don't know how.*

"Love me," said Nelexi again, and already the wind was racing past them, whistling in her ears, as the huge black dragon tucked her wings and dove out of the air-stream she had been riding.

Almost instinctively, Flameheart pulled the cloak the Cave Elves had given her tighter around her head. Her stomach turned and felt like it had been left behind. She clung to the saddle, feeling as if *she* would be left behind. She had not known Nelexi could dive so fast. *Really,* she protested, her mind feeling like the melting snow Nelexi had once shown her on the slopes of the Aravin Mountains. *I don't know anything. I don't have a weapon. I don't know how to fight. I'm just a liability. Just a rider you have to worry about keeping alive, when you can scarcely be hurt.*

"Love me, Flameheart, Kario," insisted Nelexi. *"Remember. Awake. You are being silly. Remember when you first saw me and you thought I was an enemy. Did you fear death then? So do not fear death now. That fear, not death, is the Nightmare. Love me. I love you."*

With what felt to her like a sudden jolt, Nelexi's wings opened and they leveled out. The dragon drew herself together, and Kario knew she was about to breathe out her lava-fire. Kario curled as close into the saddle as she could, trying to be as small as possible. *What does it mean to love you?* she asked in a very small mental voice.

"You know. You know you love me and you are glad to be my rider, even though your people have rejected you because of me. You know you want to be with me. Love me, Flameheart."

Even as Nelexi spoke, one of the obsidian dragons who circled riderless below her lifted his head and spoke also. *"What are you doing here, Obsidian Guardian? We heard you were on the other side of the world, teaching a new, helpless rider."*

I am helpless, thought Flameheart.

"Helplessness is a lie, Flameheart," said Nelexi. *"You are loved. You love. Do not believe the Nightmare. Do not live in it."* Even as she spoke, Flameheart felt her propel herself through the air, beating her wings to push herself forward – and down. Her mouth opened and a stream or blast of molten red flame poured from her maw. The heat of it made Kario break out into a sudden sweat. At the same time, it drove from her mind all the panic and fear and feeling of helplessness. She did not understand why she suddenly felt different, or what she felt, but as she clung to Nelexi, the terror faded. *I am glad to be with you,* she said, *but I feel like I ought to be helping in some way.*

"You do," said Nelexi shortly, and next moment Flameheart understood why. Nelexi was not as nimble as the smaller dragons, and it took all her attention to make sure none of the others flanked her in order to attack her rider.

I'm sorry, she thought, trying to tuck her thought in lest it distract Nelexi.

"Don't be," said the dragon as she swung her black tail and sent one of the other dragons spinning through the air, one wing crushed. *"I'll never leave you."*

Flameheart knew what that meant. She was Nelexi's last rider. If she died here, it would not be long before Nelexi flew into the Volcano for the second time and joined her. Somehow, though, death had no meaning to her in that moment. All she saw was the heat and the brightness of Nelexi's fire. Perhaps, then, it meant more than just that.

The scream of the falling dragon tore at her ears, but it felt strangely hollowed, empty of meaning. There was no life or desire in it, only pain and mindless terror. *What do they fear if they neither live nor love?* she wondered.

"Everything," replied Nelexi. She swung around, and Flameheart crouched still lower, as she passed under the swinging tail of a smaller black dragon, who turned that very moment, as if to breathe fire over Nelexi's back and her rider. Nelexi brought herself and her head around in time, and instead of catching Kario in his flames, the other black dragon was caught in her fire. He, too, gave a horrible screech that was all fear and terror, and no failing grasp for life. Flameheart felt that she would never forget it, and for a brief moment she felt it was the truth, if truth is not too positive a word for it: as if the world were simply an abyss of terror, a bottomless gap of fear and loneliness with no bounds to anywhere. Then Nelexi roared, and the terror passed so quickly that she felt as if it had never happened; she hardly remembered it at all, recalling only a vague terror from another world that had never been.

Again, Nelexi dove, and Kario was vaguely aware of another black dragon passing over them. How many of the things were there? She had not thought there were very many obsidian dragons in the world. A couple seconds later, she had something else to think about. They were nearing the sea at a frightful speed. Sea Elf ships scattered this way and that, and arrows arced through the air at a black dragon who dove just a little ahead of Nelexi towards the tightest concentration of the ships. She felt so dizzy she hardly even knew what was happening. Then there was a jolt, a short flash of fire, and she felt Nelexi's neck and head before her move in sudden motion. A second later, a great wave flung itself against her dragon's chest, and sea-spray splattered over her. Then she felt them rise again, but only for a moment. Even as she felt Nelexi descending, she looked up into the face of another black dragon diving at them. Then she saw nothing at all. She shut her eyes and held her breath as they descended into the ocean. It felt cold.

"Patience, Flameheart. Don't panic. This is just for a moment, but my size is no disadvantage in the water, and their fire is nearly harmless here," whispered Nelexi's calm, steadying voice. Even so, it was all she could do not to panic. She had never been under water before, and she could not swim – not that she could have swum anyways, or needed to, bound into the saddle as she was.

Then, Nelexi's head broke the water. Her tail lashed under her, and she took off again, skimming low over the waves, grazing her tail through their peaks.

The two remaining black dragons who circled down towards the elven ships looked at them for one brief moment, then turned and fled.

You spoke to them, didn't you? asked Kario.

"Yes. It was the only way I could do anything before they burned that ship. Otherwise, I might have killed another one, but they would have burned the ship before I could get to them."

I could see that. She was shivering now, in the aftermath of fear and sweat, and being dunked in the ocean. *How many of them were there? I didn't think there were very many obsidian dragons, let alone very many nightmare ones.*

"There aren't. There's probably one or two more out there, but I don't get them very often. They stay far away from me, and they usually flee in all different directions if I do manage to get remotely close, which means I can maybe get one of them. This time they chose differently."

Because of me, right?

"Yes," said Nelexi, chuckling a little. *"Because they, too, saw you as a liability – which you are not. Or at least as someone they might be able to kill – and even to hurt me by killing. But instead I killed three of them."*

How can anything so... so dead-like... I mean, they seem able to think and all that, but they... don't sound alive?

"Because they are nightmare creatures," answered Nelexi. She might have been going to say more, but at that moment the sound of cheering and

singing Sea Elves reached their ears. As soon as the obsidian dragons had fled and Nelexi was seen again, the ships congregated around her, and the elves cheered. Even before the nightmare dragons fled, the elves had started trying to bring their ships closer together, under Nelexi's wings, only scattering when a dragon actually dove at them.

Is this what we were called about? asked Flameheart, realizing that this might have been a very real danger to the peace they had brought about. The Sea Elves might not know about the situation with obsidian dragons, and that they had nothing to do with the Sha'adhri and were entirely outside the domain of the Sha'adhri to punish. They might feel betrayed, and even if a few of their spokesmen knew better and tried to talk them out of it, it might be the end of the peace treaty, and a return to open war with the Sea Elves attacking any dragon they saw, especially if they were out at sea.

"It could have something to do with it," said Nelexi very noncommittally. Kario could tell that she was concentrating hard on the Sea Elves, who had now brought their ships very close about the dragon.

Then Flmaeheart leaned forward and vomited. The stress had been too much, and now that she was relaxing and the tension was over, she felt quite sick.

Several of the elves jumped back. She was pretty sure some of them had called something that sounded like, "Is she okay?" but she did not know their language very well, so she could not understand anything they said over all the other sounds.

"No, that's what they said," confirmed Nelexi. The dragon projected herself in a way that felt slightly odd to Flameheart, but also familiar. Then she realized that Nelexi was speaking in the way she used when she was teaching Flameheart languages, not the way she used when she was sharing with her. "We are glad we came in time. Those dragons were none of ours, and have not been for a very long time. They are our mortal enemies. My rider is sick. She has not been able to eat well since we left Aneri." To Kario, she said, "I judge the continental shore is only a few weeks from here with the winds I expect."

Good, said Flameheart wearily.

"Is there anything we can offer you?" one of the elves on a ship almost directly under Nelexi's nose asked.

"For myself, nothing," answered the dragon. "For my rider: what kind of food might you have?"

Also, is there any way to get me warm?

It took some time and effort, and before it was over she was shivering violently, but Nelexi and the Sea Elves worked out a plan to get her warm, though there was little that they could do about food for her, since the Sea Elves had mostly dried fish and a few biscuits. Still, it would be better than what they had before. When everything had been arranged, Nelexi dropped into the sea again and gently tucked one of the ships into a curve she made with her tail. She then extended her wing out, so that the tip of it rested gently against the ship's railing. Along this, Flameheart carefully crawled, feeling all the time that one wrong move would send her slipping and tumbling into the ocean.

"Don't worry," Nelexi kept telling her. *"If you fall, I could catch you anyways, but one of the Sea Elves will have no trouble diving in and getting you. It will be no worse than another dunking, and you will be warmed up soon."*

I'd better not fall, she insisted. *If I can't make it this way, I'll never be able to get back on you without a dunking, and then I'll be frozen flying.*

She had been wet before when flying, but not drenched like she was now. Nelexi had almost always been able to fly either around or above the storm, so they were never in the middle of pouring rain. Additionally, the cloak the Cave Elves had given her, while it did nothing to keep her from getting soaked when she was immersed in water all around, was water-resistant and even now was only damp, unlike the rest of her clothes which were thoroughly soaked.

Finally, she made it onto the ship without another dunking, though there had been a few close moments. Strong Sea Elves pulled her the last few feet off of Nelexi's warm wing and onto the ship deck. "Oohs" and "aahs" greeted her, as they saw her cloak and then the lightstone she wore around her neck, but they brought her a gown that was much too big for her, and led her into a little sort of room on the deck where she would be able to change in some privacy. There, she stripped off her soaking clothes and changed in the shift provided by the elves. As she slipped it over her head and it felt about her shoulders, she noted with some irritation that she would hardly be able to walk in it, as it was longer than she was from head to heel. She wrapped her cloak around her again and burrowed, still shivering, into the pillows the Sea Elves apparently used for a bed.

"Sleep well darling, fire of my heart," said Nelexi softly.

Flameheart had not thought she was really tired – just very cold, and very hungry, but even colder than she was hungry – yet she was fast asleep within a few minutes.

When she woke, it was completely dark, and she was still cold, though not as cold. She could not remember being in such complete darkness for a long time – if ever. Even when she slept tucked under Nelexi's wing, there was more light than this, and the tents of her people had certainly not been as dark as this, except for maybe on a fully-clouded moonless night, and the caves of the Light Elves had never been completely dark because of the lightstones. Where was her own lightstone?

"*Peace, child,*" came Nelexi's comforting voice, though the dragon flew above and a little ahead of where she floated in a ship on the sea. Kario turned over, and the chain that held the lightstone came out from under the pillow. It shone only very softly through the fabric of her cloak, but it was enough light to dispel her dread of the dark. She got to her feet, knowing that there were Sea Elves awake on the ship at all times, and wondering if one of them could help her to a little food and water, when she suddenly tripped and fell, encumbered by her shift.

A moment later, she found herself laughing with Nelexi at her mishap. She got up and gathered the cloth up in her hands, then more cautiously stepped forward again. She gently pushed open the door of the cabin, then stopped. *Nelexi?* she asked. *Why... is the elven fleet going the same direction we were?*

"*No, but they will go with us for as long as we want it. We saved their fleet, and I think you need to be on solid land again, soon, and to eat the things we can find there. I wouldn't mind being on solid land again myself. Besides, we may be supposed to be somewhere in Ellenesia soon, though we have done at least something for which we were called.*"

But... I don't want to impose on them too much.

"*These are your needs, and we have more than paid for it. Besides, if any of those dragons circle back and see me still with the fleet, they are likely to leave it alone for a long time.*"

Won't they leave it alone anyways? I thought they are quite scared of you, since you can kill them, and they cannot kill you.

"*Exactly, but it depends on their determination to destroy this fleet. Even if I save the fleet once, if a whole fleet disappears and nothing but burning hulks are ever found, the Sea Elves may blame the Sha'adhri, whatever we say about the matter.*"

Even as Nelexi spoke, Flameheart heard the soft sound of approaching footsteps. A soft voice asked, "That's you, Dragonrider, isn't it? Is there anything you need?"

"Some of those biscuits, please. I am hungry," she answered, stumbling over the Sea Elf words.

"Very well. I will be back in a moment. That is a beautiful lamp you have."

She sat down against the wall, feeling weak. Overhead, the breeze whispered against the sail. She thought she could almost feel the magic in the ship, in its very timbers and sails, helping it to ride the ocean and taming the wind to *its* riders' purposes. She recalled the songs the Sea Elves often sang as they sailed their ships, or as they sat upon the prow watching the open sea, songs full of a haunting magic that she felt certain continually renewed the magic of their ships, and continually tamed sea and wind to their desires.

Her eyelids were drooping when the Sea Elf returned, though it had only been a couple of minutes. "Here are two of those biscuits," she said. "That's all I have right now. When dawn comes, I'll call one of the other ships over, and get whatever they have for you."

"Thank you," said Flameheart, gingerly taking the biscuits. "I... I don't want to be trouble."

"Don't worry," said the elf in a soft voice. "You aren't. You and the dragon saved all our lives. I shudder to think what those dragons might have done to our fleet, if you had not been there to protect us."

"They can be killed," said Flameheart.

"I know, but not easily. Not as easily as they can burn even our ships. Many of us would have died first, and possibly all of us." The Sea Elf knelt down across from her. "No, we thank you, but if I may ask for anything, magic of other sorts interests me, and I perceive that your cloak, as well as your lamp, is a kind of magic unknown to us."

"The cloak is a gift from some elves who lives in caves that are full of lightstones of many colors. That is also where I found my 'lamp'," said Flameheart, holding out a little of the fabric for the elf to feel.

"So it is. Marvelous. I've heard tales that there are other elven-kin in other parts of the world, though most of them are little more than rumors. Though Wood Elves come out from them now and again, the Ancient Forests are closed to us, and only powerful mages can go in or out of them. The elves of whom other tales tell are even harder to find, if indeed they be. We are the only elven kindred that mingles freely with other peoples. Do you know what the magic in this cloak does?"

"A little of it. For one thing, I can see through it fairly well, but it keeps me from being wind-burned," she explained after a few moments of chewing, her mouth still full of the hard biscuit.

"Forgive me," said the elf. "I see that you are hungry. I do not want to keep you that way. If I may speak with you again when you are less hungry, my name is Areenka."

"Thank you. I'll talk with you more, Areenka." The elf rose gracefully, a pale shadow in the moonlight, and Flameheart turned her full attention to nibbling the biscuits. Her stomach churned with anticipation.

When she had finished both the biscuits, she was still cold and very hungry, but she felt better than she had in days, or even weeks. The sea was very gentle at the moment, which meant that she really was not seasick. She carefully walked back into the cabin, after tripping another time on her shift, and burrowed back into the pillows, hoping that no one felt too irritated at sharing his or her bed.

True to her word, Areenka woke Flameheart – who was only dozing lightly – at dawn, with several more of the tough, chewy biscuits. While Flameheart startled to nibble at the biscuits, Areenka offered profuse, if rather proud, thanks and congratulations on being one of the prime movers in seeing the long war between the Sha'adhri and the Nations of the Sea finally ended, "a most profitable situation for both peoples, especially as neither of us enjoy being killed or seeing our friends killed, or even killing others, very much," she said. She then plied Flameheart with questions about the Cave or Light Elves and their magic, their lifestyle, and their beliefs, as well as how their language differed from the Sea Elven tongue.

To this last, Flameheart said quite simply, "I don't know. We always spoke in the Anerian trade tongue, so I know no more of their language than a few names."

"Ah. Do you speak Anerian more fluently and easily?" Areenka asked, then, and instantly switched to Anerian, in which she henceforth asked all her questions and made all her comments.

Before long, Flameheart was sick of the strange interrogation. She felt half like a guest of honor, half like an exotic pet, and she enjoyed neither feeling. To make matters worse – or to exacerbate both feelings – several other Sea Elves had come over from other ships, and the sea was rising, which meant she would soon be seasick.

"Then tell them it was time you joined me in the sky," suggested Nelexi. *"I'd rather capture the ship in the nook of my tail and have you climb on board* me *while the sea is quiet anyways."*

So would I. I'm less likely to fall in the water that way, replied Kario gratefully, and told the Sea Elves what she desired.

They hastened to make things ready as quickly and graciously as they could manage while still sounding full of themselves, at least to Flameheart, and in a minute Nelexi's huge black and glowing red bulk came floating or draping out of the sky and into the sea. With a soft jolt, she wrapped her tail securely but gently around the ship, and a few moments later, with another soft jolt that gently rocked the vessel, her wing connected with the deck.

Flameheart smiled at the watching elves. "Thanks for your help, and the biscuits," she said shyly, then clambered onto the dragon wing.

Several minutes later, she was pain-stakingly securing herself back into the saddle, the state of which had not improved at all from being drenched in salt-water. *"That's all right,"* said Nelexi. *"We've only a couple more weeks ahead of us before we reach the continent, and I'll get the Sea Elves who are still there to make us a new one. It'll be no trouble."*

Flameheart laughed at the sound of her dragon's mind-voice. "Somehow, it's good to be riding you, touching you, again, even if you never left mental touch with me," she said aloud, as she finished securing herself.

"That's perfect then. Let's see how well I can get myself out of here without getting things any wetter than necessary. Speaking of which, I'm rather itchy to get out of this saddle myself, but I'll wait until we can get a new one. I'm not sure how easy it would be to get it back on, given its current state." Gentle amusement colored her voice pink and lemon-green.

Flameheart smiled in response.

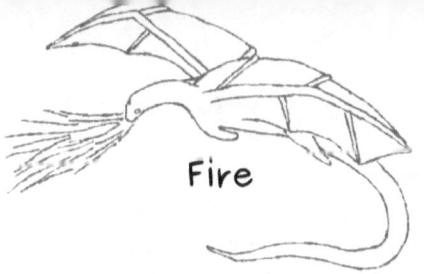

Fire

A sense of danger drove Camilla onward, and she could not forget that Aishaena had implied, if not outright said, that she would stay with them all the way to the Sea Elves. Despite the fact that she wondered if she would hate them, even more than she hated Aishaena or if, not being elves of the forest at all, she would not mind them much, she was almost desperate to get there. Unfortunately she had no real idea how far they still had to go, and therefore could not know whether pushing hard would get them there faster, or whether they would be exhausted long before they got there and it would actually slow them down. Nonetheless, she had a burning urge to get away, so she convinced the others that they needed to get to the continent as quickly as possible.

It was a grueling flight that, despite the fact that she was urging it in obedience to her own instincts, galled her, making her feel like prey, when she would have turned on whatever threatened her and incinerated it. However, they were all so utterly exhausted that, when the dragons glided rather clumsily in over the shore under a just-waning moon, they lay down in the sand about a dragon-length past the point where the waves reached, and were asleep almost as quickly as their riders unsaddled them. The humans were all asleep barely a minute later, under their wings.

Later in the night, she woke, feeling as if an icy hand had been placed on her side. Even as she woke, she thought she could still feel the chill.

"*I feel it, too.*" Radiance's voice was groggy and still flat with extreme exhaustion.

Camilla placed her hand on Radiance's scales, which were comfortingly warm, and inched forward along her side, out from beneath her wing. Gently, she touched the minds of Lavilor and Sleet and found them fast asleep, if slightly troubled in their dreams. She even dared to do what she had never done before and touched the mind of Sylvara, but she was deep in a dreamless sleep, and Camilla could not tell if she was restless or not.

"*Someone tries to tear us apart,*" said Radiance, her voice still weary and her thoughts hardly making sense. Her hand still on the dragon's scales, Camilla knelt, looking up at the stars and the moon descending the western sky, it's disk already cut in half by the mountains which rose somewhere far inland.

We're near, if not within, the lands held by Eltaes and the Northern Horror, she thought, considering the mountains. Then a shadow spread across the stars, and formed into the shapes of diving dragons. There was a cacophony of noise, yells and cries of torment and mindless hate that threatened to drive her mad. Briefly, she determined she would not fall again under the nightmare spell, as she had when attacked by the orc, yet the terror and the fear were stronger now. The horror clutched her in icy talons, and she finally understood what Radiance had half-seen.

If we're separated, we die. We cannot exist apart, she thought, clinging to the dragon, clinging to the fire, trying to take comfort and to find somewhere she could stand within herself – or within the love she shared with Radiance – somewhere where the horror could not grasp her to draw her forth. *If there is something of the Lord of Light in our bond, and he alone can fight and conquer the Nightmare, then, surely, in our bond there is refuge,* she told herself, though it was hard to hear her own thoughts through the cacophony of cries, through the hatred and the pain and the overwhelming fear. It was an icy current that pulled her thoughts away faster than they could take shape.

Then, somehow, she and Radiance considered what they saw, diving at them, ever clearer now against the stars. Almost one they were, now, and, deep within the cacophony of torment, Camilla felt something else.

Neither dragon nor rider thought. Camilla threw her hands up, as if to ward off the horror that rushed in to steal her soul, as the dragons, very close now, tilted into a dive – dark shadowy creatures, not dragons at all now, but forms of shadow in the shape of dragons, though some of them gleamed white and gray in the last flash of moonlight. Behind, the sea frothed and the gentle rolling waves turned into a clamor of surf, as a wind rose off the sea. Down from the back of one of the shadow-creatures shot an arrow. Beside Camilla, Radiance, weary as she was, shifted, raised her wings, and lifted her tail, preparing to fight. Not far from them, Sleet and Shimmer stirred. Camilla felt Lavilor as if he stood beside her, in her arms, and she communed with him, mind-to-mind.

Fire rushed up through her body, and with it came a music, a song, that was deeply familiar to her, and yet stronger and stranger than ever, burning like fire, and also like tempered steel. With the fire came first ecstasy and then torment that drove out the cacophony of horror with its intensity. Along her arms the fire coalesced into leaping tongues of burning, flickering heat. Around her hands it formed yet brighter and thicker, and rushed forth in a stream like a jet of dragon fire, where it caught the nearest of the shadow-dragons from where it stooped in the sky, less than a dragon-length above her head.

The red-yellow-orange flames lit the shore-line and reflected off the dragon's scales like red stars, even as the first bolt of lightning flashed from a still clear sky overhead. The shadow-dragon screamed, and the sound tore at Camilla's soul, even as her fire licked across its body, and where her fire surrounded it in an aura of flickering, dancing tongues of burning light, it appeared no longer a form of gaunt shadow, but a red-scaled dragon, held for the moment in a vice of fire.

"Bend. My name is Bend."

The dragon's voice was mingled despair and pain and fear, and a bright dawn-colored fire of Recognition.

"Ben. Your name is Ben. Our name is Radiance-and-Camilla," she replied, her own voice a flame, as she changed his name. But even as she

spoke, her consciousness faded in a flood of agony, and a dozen more bolts of white-blue lightning struck out of the starry sky. Several struck the sand not far from the Dragonriders, and others struck the fleeing shadow forms, before they vanished suddenly in a flash of darkness.

Meanwhile, Ben landed heavily on the sand. He wobbled as he stepped forward, then collapsed to the sand. Radiance stood guard over her rider, wings half-raised, and he hardly remembered what it felt like to be a dragon. He remembered only darkness, slavery, and mindless torment, and the vague memory of an elf, a memory so formless and vague even his dragon's mind could not grasp it – and, written across it all, in runes of blazing fire, the voice of the dragon-mage, the dragonkeeper, like an afterimage of the sun still glowing in the darkness of his mind. All he wanted was to touch again that soul of fire, but she was deep in an unconsciousness of weariness, shock, and pain. The dragon seemed almost as shocked as the dragonkeeper, hardly able to speak.

By now, Shimmer, Sleet and their riders were wide awake, but the two humans only stared dumbly at the large red dragon lying in a disorganized heap on the sand – large compared to their own dragons, though he was not big for a grown dragon. Even the dragons barely understood what they saw, but, after a few moments, Sylvara stepped out from under Shimmer's wing. She curtsied briefly to the red dragon, unable to speak with him or to know what had passed between him and Camilla, and stepped around him, heading for where Camilla lay in the sand. Strange images rippled in her mind, showing her something of what had happened. Cold fears which she had no spare attention for clung to her, but she knew one thing she could do: Camilla might refuse any help or aid from her when awake, but she was unconscious right now and could neither know nor protest if Sylvara looked to see if she was in any way hurt and did anything she could to help if she was. Sylvara was determined that she would no longer be the thing she had once been. Instead of callous and cruel, she meant now to be kind and compassionate, and she hoped to start here with Camilla, since the woman always rejected her kindness and compassion whenever she was aware of it.

She knelt over Camilla's slumped form, self-conscious under the measuring eye of Radiance who did not seem all the way there, and struggled to see anything in the darkness, though she was fairly certain Camilla's hands – both of them, this time – were badly burned. She remembered having heard – or perhaps Shimmer had heard – Serrose or Alian say that a mage could burn more easily if she were badly scarred, and she wondered if she might have been able to help Camilla and get the elves to treat her better if she had tried in the past, but it was too late for that now. Regret would not help Camilla now,

even if Sylvara was, partially, to blame. She wondered what she could do. Would soaking her cloak in the ocean-water, which was cool, help? Or should she unsheathe the magesword and lay Camilla's hands over its hilt? She hesitated to do the later, thinking of the torture that would ordinarily be, but the magesword seemed to help Camilla with the burning that came from her magic. It would probably not do any more damage, Sylvara thought – though she realized she knew almost nothing – and Camilla was unconscious and, presumably, unable to feel pain, at least of the physical sort.

I'll do that. It won't be worse than the sand, at any rate. But what else should I do? She decided, still shaking under Radiance's watchful eye, as she lifted Camilla's cloak out of the way and cautiously drew the magesword, which did not come to life and provide any helpful golden glow when in her hands.

The sound of another dragon's wings beating the air startled her, but Shimmer assured her, *"It is Alian."*

Thank goodness. She will know what to do here!

She spread her cloak over the sand and laid the magesword on it, not wanting to damage the blade. Then she gently laid one of Camilla's hands on the hilt, and then straightened and stepped away from Radiance.

She found herself face to face with Alian in his human form. "Shimmer has told me as much as he could," he said, "and that you don't know what to do. I will take over from here. My magic can do what you cannot, anyways."

She nodded, dumb, and stepped away. She was half-disappointed that she could not do more. She wanted to prove, if only to herself, that she had changed, that she had others' interests at heart now. Going back to Shimmer and laying down against his side, trying to ignore the protests of her stomach, did not seem likely to do that, but she reminded herself, she *had* done what she could, and Alian had rather clearly indicated that he no longer desired her presence. It was not as if she could do anything about getting a meal at this hour of the night, however hungry everyone would be in the morning – or was, already, she thought, as her own stomach growled and clenched around itself. She was not a dragonspeaker and could do nothing for the red dragon. She doubted she could watch for an attack: a storm was blowing off the sea, and it would be too foggy for her to see anything in the dark soon, if not outright pouring.

There really was not anything more she could do to be of help.

In the morning, she woke to find Alian roasting venison over a smokeless fire that somehow burned even in the rain. There was another freshly-slain deer laying nearby in the sand.

"That's for Radiance and the red dragon," he said, pointing to the carcass as she approached, picking her way through the soaking sand. "Your Shimmer apparently ate without waking you, and Sleet has eaten, too. This is for you humans." He indicated his fire.

She sat down close to the fire. "I..."

"Did what you knew. I'm glad I got here, though I wonder if it might have been more helpful if I'd been a few minutes earlier."

She nodded slightly, staring into the flames. She could not think of anything to say. Finally, she asked, "Do you have any more idea what happened than I do?"

"It seems that Camilla used a great deal of magic – dragonmagic by the feel of it – to free a dragon enslaved by the witch-craft of a servant of the Nightmare, though I couldn't with certainty say which one or even if I ever met the witch. If anyone deserves the name dragon-mage, it's her. My and Serrose's magic isn't nearly as draconic as that was."

Sylvara nodded again. "There were more of them... I think. But do you think Camilla and Radiance, and the red dragon, will be all right?"

"Yes. At least, in a manner of speaking. I don't know if my magic will prevent scarring as much as I would hope it does, and I don't know how long-lasting or what exactly the direct effect of the magic will be on Camilla and Radiance. We'll have to know more about the red dragon and his past to know how he will do, but I think they will all live."

Sylvara nodded again. A lingering shock that turned her whole mind slushy silenced any words she might have had, and the flames entranced her, slowly flickering a new thought into her mind. After a while, she realized she had forgotten Alian was there. "Do you think I have any magic at all?" she asked, without turning from the fire.

Alian turned his gaze from the fire to look at her closely. "Why? Unless something very strange happens or the Lord of Light intervenes almost as directly as he did to make me and those like me, I'm almost certain you will not have the kind of magic Camilla does."

She turned from the flames to return his gaze. "No. I mean more like what you have. Could I learn magic that can be used to heal simple wounds? Or... maybe," she glanced sideways at the fire, "to cook in a storm?"

"Given what we've seen in dragonriders before, I think it very likely you have some magic and can learn to use it a little, but it might not be very impressive."

"That's okay. I just want to be able to help in whatever way I can," said Sylvara.

"Then I will teach you as well as I can," he said, returning his gaze to the cooking, "but it might be good for you also to learn from the Light Elf mages. The dragon-ness, even though it is not true dragonhood, in my nature makes magic very different for me, so it might be hard for me to teach you well."

"That's okay. But, if I may ask?"

Alian indicated that she could ask whatever she wanted.

"How did the hatching go? How are your babies?"

"They are doing well. Serrose is with them, since she is the stronger mage. In a few months, or whenever she judges it is a good time, she will probably be bringing them along."

"Is that safe?"

"It's safer with Serrose than it would be with me. Also, they will wait until the newborns are ready to fly, so they will make fairly good speed. Hopefully, no one but us even knows of their existence." He took a thin piece of the meat, which was making Sylvara's mouth water, and laid it aside to cool.

"Would you like me to take that to Camilla as soon as it's cool?"

"You may as well. Even if she is not ready to eat, I'm sure Lavilor is quite hungry, and he's waiting with her."

"I will, then," said Sylvara, determining to eat only after there was enough for the others. "By the way, how far away are we from the Sea Elves?"

"Practically, it depends on how well Radiance, Camilla, and the red can travel, and how contrary the winds are, which I can't read well right now. Under good conditions, we're maybe three days from the harbor, but with contrary winds and a weak dragon or two, it could easily take more than like five times that long."

A sea of fire danced around her, bathing her wounds and binding them in a stately dance of heat and light. It was like nothing Camilla, or any of her friends, had ever experienced before, and yet it seemed that it had always been part of them, had always been calling their names, had always been reaching out to them through their names. It was song and it was light; it was stately dance and roaring flame; it was pressure and heat and escaping fire. It burned away the darkness and the cold, the horror and the chains of terror.

Ben was there. She felt his presence, his flame in the fire, as well as the flame that was the joining of her soul and Radiance's, unfathomably bright and dear. She laid her hand on his scales and looked into his eyes, as he remembered, and his memories were burned in the fire as the three of them met, and from the burning a song arose, a song of which she could never after remember more than a few words, but the few that she could remember were as follows, though they have scarcely anything of their true glory and feel without the dancing of the fire and the music of the burning.

Depth of fire, heart of earth
Brightest, heaviest stone, crushing
All around, place of birth
Never ending, deeper burning

Purging fire, depth deepest
Under the weight of rising fire
Breathing skies, from our rest
Molten burning, seas swimming e'er

Then, in the midst of the song that would forevermore haunt Camilla's dreams and her every half-distracted thought, whispering to her suddenly out of the breath of wind, the warmth of the sun, the flicker of a flame, or from within a song or a dance, *always* seeming to hover barely out of reach whenever she touched the deep, ancient dragonmagic, but never becoming clear enough for her to hear its words or recall its magic tune, the dream abruptly ended.

She opened her eyes, to the feel of Radiance in her soul and Ben's touch in her mind. At first, she did not notice the tantalizing smell of roast venison. Her eyes alighted first on the golden glory of Radiance's scales, and then sought the burnished crimson of Ben's. Lavilor's soft voice fell soothingly on her ears. *"Radiance!"* she cried, and then, *"Ben!"* Joy at his freedom and his bond with her rushed over her in a greeting from Ben, and an embrace as of fire joined them all. Then she shifted, trying to move, and agony in her hands and arms thrust full memory of what had happened in the night upon her. She gasped softly.

Lavilor, sitting beside her and leaning against Radiance's shoulder, leaned over her. "Hi!" he said, in a soft, joyous voice, even as both Shimmer and Sleet greeted her as well. "It's good to see you awake. Are you hungry?"

"And thirsty," she said, "but I can't..."

"Take care of it yourself. I know. But getting water will be no difficulty. It's pouring outside. Also, Alian is here. I'll help you."

"Thanks." *Alian is here?* she considered, her mind moving a bit slowly after everything. *So he arrived just after* that *happened. And I knew it was pouring. I know almost everything Radiance knows, if not everything, and, now, a great deal that Ben knows. I hadn't known it was possible to bond to a second and full-grown dragon who has even bonded before, though I think his first rider was an elf who wasn't very close to him. I wonder, is what I have with Ben what most dragons and riders have together, or is it weaker... I doubt it's stronger. At least this seems to be a warmer rain that most have been recently.*

Already, Ben had turned from where he lay near to Radiance and was tearing ravenously into the deer left for them, with all the ecstasy of pleasure and need long-denied, long unfelt, and now fulfilled. He could not remember the last time he had been able to eat. While he was, in many ways, not as weak as a truly starving dragon, having been scarcely alive and maintained in his captivity by dark magic, he was still as hungry as any dragon near death from starvation. Even the sensation of raindrops thundering against his scales was a long-lost pleasure of immeasurable extent.

A few minutes later, Lavilor returned with a skin of water for her and hot meat. Camilla reached out her hands, and pain twanged and burned across her fingers and arms, as if fire again leapt and raced along them. She gasped.

"Relax," chided her brother lovingly. "I'll do this for you. It won't be a problem." He held out the water skin to her mouth.

She only got a little of the water. A great deal more of it ran down her shirt, soaking her.

She moved again, moving her hands by accident, and gasped again. "It's not so easy," she said, trying to be cheerful, but instead wishing she could rip the bandages off and do it for herself. She was certain she *could*. She had done things that could not have been much less painful when the elves were using the magic burning her palm to torture her, but she did not really *want* to, and there was also the warning that the more she scarred, the more easily she might burn in the future. *Unfortunately, I'm going to be cold*, she thought, while she and Lavilor worked on improving their method.

Finally, she halted the attempt. "I'm not very thirsty now, so let's try more later."

"Are you sure?" he said. "You're wet right now. If we work on this later, you'll have started to dry, and you'll just get wet again."

"Yes, I'm sure," said Camilla, nodding emphatically and concentrating on keeping her hands completely relaxed and not even twitching her arms. "Right now, I'm dreadfully hungry. It's been far longer since any of us ate well than since we drank well, and if I'm seeing correctly, you've probably already eaten, so you've forgotten how hungry I am." She smiled up at him as she said this. "We can work more on drinking after I eat something. Also, that warm steak will make me less cold."

"Very well," he said in an amused tone. He broke off a piece of the venison, which had cooled while they worked on drinking and was already only slightly warm. Trying to fight her unease at being unable to do anything for herself, Camilla opened her mouth to receive the morsel, and burst into laughter even she would not have anticipated. Even worse, it was hard to keep still and not hurt herself while laughing, though that might have helped her stop laughing sooner, but Lavilor was giggling too, and that most certainly did not help her stop laughing.

When they were finally able to stop, he held out the morsel out to her again. "Hi, little ducky," Lavilor said, as he moved to place it on her tongue.

This time, Camilla bit her tongue when she broke out laughing at her brother's comment. "D-don't!" she gasped through the laughter. "P-p-please don't! I d-d-don't n-need th-th-this!"

"But you need to laugh more than anything else I and Sleet think," he forced through his own giggles.

"No! I need to eat!" she said, anger giving her the force to stop laughing long enough to speak clearly.

"Very well. I won't. This time," said Lavilor, suppressing his own giggles which still managed to bubble up and burst through his voice.

"Th-thank you," said Camilla wearily. "By the way, really, you shouldn't. It's *so* easy for me to hurt myself unless I'm really thinking about not moving certain parts, and that's hard to do while I'm laughing."

"Very well, then," he said, offering her the morsel for the third time. "I'll wait a few days then, for your wounds to heal a little and for you to get less hungry. But, really, you need to laugh more, sister. And it is *so* funny. I'm even your *younger* brother, feeding you like a mother duck feeds her ducklings!"

"Do not!" yelled Camilla loud enough that Lavilor flinched.

"Really," said Lavilor, shaking his head in a most disappointed fashion. "Anyway, why don't I get another piece, still warm and hot, for you? I'm sure you'll like that better, and Alian is still cooking them."

"Yes, thank you, though how he cooks in this rain I don't know."

"Easy. You ought to be able to figure it out. Magic," he called over his shoulder as he rose and stepped out from the shelter of Radiance's wing and into the rain.

Suddenly, she realized that Radiance had her part in making her laugh. *"We haven't laughed enough, Rider, heart of my heart,* Radiance," said the dragon. *"We are Radiance. We are not shadow or darkness. We are the brightness, the radiance, the flashing gold of the sun, the brilliance of the day. How can we not laugh?"*

You're right, Camilla agreed heartily, *but can we please wait for me to either heal a little or get used to not moving my hands? It would be a shame for me to be putting up with doing nothing in order to not scar more than absolutely necessary, only to ruin it by laughing.*

"I am content for now. You have laughed, and the laughter in us is living, not dying. But I don't think laughing will interfere with your healing nearly as much as all the other things you want to do. Nor do I think the

scarring is making you burn more easily when you use magic. But I and all others who love you would like to spare you unnecessary pain – and to make you laugh." All through her words sparked flashes of fire, not a fierce and raging burning, but a dance of flickering flames – exactly like laughter. With a mental snuggle and embrace, and a corresponding tightening of her wing around her rider, the dragon said, *"I want to laugh and soar and fly with you so much."*

    I love you, too, Radiance, said Camilla, feeling strangely happier than she had in a long time. *And you, Ben. You, too, will laugh and soar with us.*

Continue Camilla's story in *Scars of Fire*

"The Nightmare Lord, the Dark Prince, sat on his throne in Eltaes and ground his teeth – not that he usually had teeth, exactly, but he had to put up with it since if he abandoned this body it could fall to pieces and he might not be able to re-possess it. He could not believe what he felt. It sheered through the magic that was an extension of his being like agony, and he could not believe any but another Otherborn could conduct or direct that much power without being burned to a crisped, smoking corpse by it, yet this power was distinctly mortal. For a moment he wondered if it was that Obsidian Guardian ..."

Or get Serrose's story in *Promise of Fire*

Sign up to be notified about new releases:
https://books2read.com/r/B-A-OUYQ-HMXXB

Follow me on Goodreads:
https://www.goodreads.com/author/show/20243136.Raina_Nightingale

Follow me on BookBub:
https://www.bookbub.com/authors/raina-nightingale

Weekly reviews, ramblings of all sorts, and occasional art posts, on my blog:
https://enthralledbylove.com

And if you liked Heart of Fire, please leave an honest review on your favorite book platforms. It really helps readers and independent authors to find each other.

www.ingramcontent.com/pod-product-compliance
Lightning Source LLC
Chambersburg PA
CBHW052137170626
46812CB00004B/1472